PRAISE FOR W. L. RIPLEY AND *SPRINGER'S GAMBIT*!

"Ripley's latest is undoubtedly his greatest! *Springer's Gambit* is a high-octane thriller with a refreshingly unusual plot, a wonderful book that's easy to get into and impossible to put down."

—Tim Green, Author of *Outlaws*

"Boston has Spenser. South Florida has Travis McGee. Now the New West has Cole Springer—a two-fisted piano player with a sharp wit and brooding soul. This is the best-written crime novel I've read since the debut of James Lee Burke's Dave Robicheaux."

—Ace Atkins, Author of *Leavin' Trunk Blues*

"*Springer's Gambit* is both fluent and riveting. Cole Springer is a comer…and so is W. L. Ripley"

—Robert B. Parker

"This one's going to be fun. The plot keeps you guessing, the banter keeps you laughing, and the sexual chemistry keeps you hoping. Don't these guys know they're supposed to be in an Elmore Leonard novel?"

—*Booklist*

READY TO PUSH BACK

Springer looked at Janzen and raised his eyebrows. There was a dueling mannequin, a padded dummy with a heart-shaped target on its chest that Janzen probably used to practice thrusting his sword. Springer stood, reached into his pocket and brought out the .32 Tomcat, sighted in on the mannequin, and squeezed the trigger. The crack of the small weapon was sharp in the large room, echoing and fading.

"Dammit, Springer," said Janzen. "Are you deranged?"

"You're crazy, man," said Vince, his nostrils wide, the whites of his eyes showing.

"See, I will shoot." Springer said, "And, I'm always ready for guys like you, Vince. Think you can remember that?"

"I'll see you again."

"You're not careful, you'll see me one time too many."

Other *Leisure* books by W. L. Ripley:

SPRINGER'S GAMBIT

W. L. RIPLEY

PRESSING THE BET

LEISURE BOOKS NEW YORK CITY

*For my father and the other heroes of the
388th bomber group (WWII).*

*Also for Reece Lauren, Andrew James,
Olivia Grace, and a player to be named later.*

A LEISURE BOOK®

March 2008

Published by

Dorchester Publishing Co., Inc.
200 Madison Avenue
New York, NY 10016

ISBN-10: 0-8439-5994-0
ISBN-13: 978-0-8439-5994-9

Printed in the United States of America.

Visit us on the web at www.dorchesterpub.com.

AUTHOR'S NOTE

I hereby deny that I surreptitiously rip off snippets of comic conversation from my sons and daughters and am mystified whenever these snippets seep into the manuscript. I have no idea how that happens.

However, as I often tell them, you can't copyright conversation anyway, so quit whining and hand me the remote.

True heroism is a private thing.
      —W. B. Yeats

A man's gotta be honest to live outside the law.
      —Bob Dylan

PROLOGUE

Jesse Robinson was sitting in a Vegas hotel bar when he said, "I'm going to tell you something nobody knows but me and only one other person"—he hesitated a moment—"maybe two other people know about."

Telling that person turned out to be a mistake.

Because Jesse Robinson didn't matter all that much.

He didn't matter to the Vegas pit boss who dialed 911 and said, "Found some colored guy just outside of town in a ditch," or to the dispatcher who passed it on. The first cop on the scene, a young trooper from Oregon, with chafing armpits because he hadn't adjusted to the desert heat, called it back in to Nevada Highway Patrol, saying, "Black male, age indeterminate, no ID, looks like he's been dead for several hours. Pretty chewed. Coyotes and buzzards have been working on him."

The ME who examined the corpse decided "the subject" had been dead for eighteen hours as the result of "head trauma and multiple contusions." They filed him in the morgue under a John Doe, fingerprinted him, sent the prints to the National Crime Information Center, and nothing came back. He was wearing a necklace with the initials J.R. on the back that was identified as belonging to Jesse Robinson. They sent two uniforms to Jesse Robinson's address. No answer. Nothing to suggest a struggle at his apartment.

Jesse Robinson, age thirty-seven, two priors. Possession with intent and assault, the second charge dropped. The corpse was the right height and approximate weight according to the department of Taxation Computers. After a couple of preliminary investigations that quickly fizzled, Vegas PD dismissed the death as a mugging gone wrong. They pushed the morgue drawer shut and forgot about him. Just another indifferent casualty of the Vegas nightlife.

Nobody was very concerned about Jesse Robinson. Nobody but his father, Nathaniel Hawthorne Robinson.

There was a problem. Vegas Metro needed someone to ID the body, and Nate Robinson was flat on his back in a Denver hospital, in traction.

Somebody had to go to Vegas, and Cole Springer had been Jesse's best friend back in the day when mostly they were thinking about cheerleaders and days at the beach.

Which is why Springer was on a flight to Vegas, five grand in cash in his carry-on, with Tobi Ryder's angry reaction to the whole affair bouncing like a Ping-Pong ball in his head. He'd misjudged her capacity for his lifestyle. Hadn't imagined it would end like that.

There was another problem, though.

Springer wasn't supposed to go to Vegas. Not now. Not ever.

ONE

"Community service," that's what they told Springer when he pleaded guilty to disturbing the peace. They gave him twenty hours, and he did it at the local Salvation Army loading these huge bales of clothing that would be shipped to SA posts that would distribute them to the needy. The really good stuff went to the SA stores to be sold.

He'd disturbed the peace. Okay. He'd done more than that. He'd stolen a car. A car belonging to one Lonnie "Red" Cavanaugh. He hadn't really stolen it; he had kept it as collateral when Cavanaugh reneged on a bet. Cavanaugh bet Springer ten thousand—that's right, calling it ten dimes when he did it—bet Springer ten grand on a minor-league baseball game.

The bet, at first, was that "Snake" McNally, Red's nephew and a pitcher for the Vegas Triple-A team, would hold their opponent to less than four runs. Springer telling Cavanaugh he would go him one better and bet Red that McNally wouldn't get a single out in the game. "That's how bad the kid is," he'd said, trying to get Cavanaugh to jump at the bet.

Cavanaugh did jump at the bet—ten grand—laughing at Springer and telling him how he was going to regret this sucker bet and he could make a side bet on which batter would be the first out. But Springer told him how it didn't matter who made the first out because McNally wasn't going to get anybody out and was going to be replaced "sooner than you can imagine," then watched Cavanaugh get red in the face.

What Cavanaugh didn't know was that Springer had inside information on the game. It wasn't that Springer was a gambler or fixed the bet. It was a fluke, a coincidence.

He'd run into an old friend who played on the team. This guy told him that Snake was being sent down to A ball and was being bumped on the rotation by this "fee-nom" the friend told him the big club was wanting to bring up to the show for a pennant run in August.

"You see, the organ-I-zation be tired of Snake drinking and gambling and showing up at the park looking like the inside a flat tire. They also be tired of his ERA looking like a speed limit sign."

So Springer baited Red, who he didn't like, and the kid never started the game and Springer won the bet.

However, here's where the rub was.

See, Cavanaugh, being a poor sport, was of the opinion that his nephew not even getting to *start* the game somehow negated the wager. Springer pointing out to Cavanaugh that the bet was never that the kid was going to start the game and get somebody out; no, the bet was that McNally would not get *anyone* out and that he would be *replaced sooner than you can imagine*.

However, Cavanaugh being Cavanaugh, and a thug besides, told Springer he was not going to pay him.

Springer protested, but with a couple of Cavanaugh's "employees" buttressing Cavanaugh's argument, Springer backed off.

But only for the moment.

Because Springer never backed off. Not then, not ever.

Instead, Springer hot-wired Cavanaugh's brand-new Cadillac El Dorado convertible and drove it around Vegas for a couple of days before parking it in the fountains at Caesar's, which made Cavanaugh madder than a Mormon at a Baptist tent revival and sent him to the doctor to be treated for "hypertension."

Cavanaugh had been on medication since that time in order to regulate his blood pressure.

"Wasn't for me, you'd never known," said Springer. "And you still owe me ten thousand dollars."

And it wasn't that Cavanaugh pressed charges on the Caddy. No, Red Cavanaugh wouldn't involve the police. He was allergic to law enforcement. It was Caesar's that pressed charges for putting the car in their fountain, Springer telling the manager, "You don't think it attracted a crowd?"

So he did his 20 hours and left town.

But not before Red Cavanaugh had a couple of his employees tell him that Red didn't want to see him back in town. Not ever.

But Springer slipped back into town once in a while.

Aspen, Colorado, Present

How it went for Springer was on Monday, Nate Robinson called Springer from his hospital room about the killing and how the Vegas police weren't doing anything about it. Las Vegas PD called Nate Robinson asking if they knew the whereabouts of his son. Nate

told them he hadn't heard from Jesse in two months.
When he asked them why they wanted to know, they
asked if Nate could come to Vegas and help them clear
up the identity of the body.

"They saying my boy was mugged," Nate told
Springer. "Why beat him that bad they can't tell who
he is, you tell me that?" This was one hour before
Springer was supposed to go to the West Coast with
Tobi Ryder. For weeks they'd been planning a trip to
Carmel, do the Monterey coastline road trip, and
Tobi had planned her vacation around it. Springer
decided he had to look into this thing with Jesse
Robinson. Jesse was a high school buddy got himself,
apparently, crossways with some badasses who were
tight with the Vegas establishment. The word was going out that Jesse was a two-time loser sliding down
the ladder of the Vegas underworld, but his father
wasn't buying it.

"My boy didn't run no drugs and he ain't no criminal," Nate told Springer. Springer wasn't so sure. Last
time Springer talked to him, Jesse Robinson was wearing five-hundred-dollar suits and driving a Porsche
Boxster, rattling $100 chips in his hand. Pit bosses and
parking valets called him "Mr. Robinson." "You got
to look at things different, Springs. It's a changing
world, man, y'know. Look around. Take what you
need, but don't empty out the store."

Springer figured Jesse had been up to something, but
Nate Robinson made things different. Nate Robinson
worked for Springer. Springer relied on the old man.
They drank coffee together most mornings, played
cards down at the barbershop Wednesday night after
Nate got back from church. "Lord forgive me for gambling and for taking this poor fool's money." That's
what he'd say after winning a hand while Springer
would be reaching for another beer.

It was Nate Robinson brought him home-cooked meals from his church in an untidy time after Kristen died, about the time Springer started opening the Jack Daniel's on the way home from the liquor stores and it was Nate told him, "Straighten up, boy, you're acting like a damned fool. You know Kristen wouldn't like this. Why make her life of no account?"

And now it was Springer's turn to be there for Nate.

"Somebody's got to go, Cole," Nate said, his voice lacking the confident ring Springer was used to. "I hate to ask, but I can't think of no one else to go. He's my only child, and his mother, God rest her soul, been gone these many years."

So he was going. For Nate's sake. Then Springer didn't know what to tell Tobi that would make her happy. She seemed to be mad at him a lot lately. What could you do about it? The situation was what it was and she knew what he'd do, and that upset her.

She told him she understood why he should help Nate. And why she knew, just *knew,* he would go. What she didn't like is he wouldn't stop there. That he, being how he was, wouldn't stop at just asking around. Then she gave him a look, watching him. He nodded at her, which annoyed her, he could tell, her telling him, don't sit there looking at me trying to wait me out. Him saying he didn't know what she was talking about, even though he did. Her saying, I'm familiar with all your little tricks. I've seen your crap before.

He tried to tell her that Nate was upset and he was only going to try to get information to ease Nate's mind, but she wasn't having it.

"I know you, Cole. There's nothing you can do to help the situation. You'll involve yourself, start poking around, and the police will resent it. It'll make things worse. Also, both of us know you can't go there. There are people there that don't like you and want you dead. You can see that, can't you?"

"How about wishing me luck?"

She shook her head slowly, exasperated. She was giving him her cop look now. Pretty good at it, too. He reached up to touch her face and she leaned away from it.

"Cole, dammit, I'm not kidding. I know you think you can avoid them, but they see you and tell Cavanaugh and it'll start all over again."

"Maybe it's time that got settled."

She closed her eyes. "God."

"Well, I'd better get going. I'll call when I get there, tell you how it's going." That seemed to set her off, which was happening a lot more. It just worked out that he picked the wrong things to say and do, and he never knew what they were until he'd already said them.

"Don't bother calling, Cole. Just forget it."

"That's it?" He was thinking of things to say, believing anything he said wouldn't help. He started to shrug, realizing what a mistake that would be, so he didn't say anything and walked out. Closed the door.

John Prine would say, "If heartaches were commercials, we'd all be on TV."

When Springer got off the plane at Vegas the desert heat hit him like a hammer. Different than Aspen. Aspen was low-humidity, medium-cool days. Vegas was windy-hot and even the nights, in a town where the clock set no agendas, were scintillating. Waiting for him at the airport was Sanborn Meeks.

Sanborn Meeks was a professional gambler who ran a business called Sunrise Investigations—Let Us Shine Some Light on the Problem. The business had only one employee, Sanborn Meeks. Meeks was more like a sixties hippie in his Hawaiian shirts and his beard and sunglasses than a private investigator. More con man than detective. Once he was supposed to be looking into a case of infidelity for a Vegas man. Sure enough, the wife was stepping out. Meeks cut himself into the action, telling her, "C'mon, baby, share the wealth; otherwise I gotta pass on this information to your old man. I've seen your pre-nup and you don't want that. So why not see if we can help each other out."

Meeks greeted him. "Hey, Springs, man, what's going on? Wow, I can't believe you're here. Hey, let me get that bag for you." Springer handed Meeks the bag, told him not to open it, Meeks placing a hand to his heart, acting hurt. Springer asked, "You have the weapon, Sandy?"

Sanborn Meeks lowered his Oakley sunglasses with a finger, looked over the rim with raised eyes, saying, "Who takes care of you, babe? I got it. Sweet gun. Thirty-two Beretta. Clean, no history."

"Was hoping for something bigger. Thirty-two's okay for shooting cats."

"Bitch, bitch, bitch. It may not be a heavyweight, but if you got to shoot somebody more than seven times you need lessons. You're in Vegas. You won't be wearing anything you can hide some .40 caliber cannon or a .357 that would rip through an engine block. Lightweight's the way to go in this heat. The gun has to fit the climate, man. When I do a job, I do the job."

"What's it cost?"

"The no-haggle price, for you"—smiling now—"is only nine bills."

"But I really like to haggle, and I can pick up a new one, anywhere, for three."

"But there's the hassle of going around the gun shops, the waiting period, and then it has one of those registered numbers. This one's clean, no numbers, no way to trace it."

"What makes you think I'm going to shoot anybody?"

Meeks shrugged, "You're paying for peace of mind. If you do have to pop a cap, there's the comfort of knowing you can just throw it away and nobody knows it was yours."

"Except you, of course."

Sanborn Meeks nodded. Springer nodded back. Springer said, "Let me see your eyes again."

"Why," said Meeks, chuckling.

"You flying?"

"Man, I don't do that shit when I'm working."

"Then take the sunglasses off. We're inside."

"They're $300 sunglasses. You *wear* them. You pay three bills, you want people to see 'em. Where'd you get that shirt anyway? Sears? Man, you dress like some bozo from Podunk, Missouri. Listen, you want to check out the action? I can get you into a card game at the Bellagio with some banker types who tip every card like they turned it up for you."

"I just want the weapon and the information I asked about."

"Information is expensive."

Springer looked at him. Sanborn Meeks said, "Five bills."

"I'll give you five for the Beretta. I need a car. Did you get me a car?"

"Five for the Beretta? And you think I'm the one doing chemicals. Listen at you. The fucking gun *cost me* five."

"You're the cut-rate king, Sandy. Let's see if I can reconstruct a more probable scenario. You give some crackhead a hundred bucks and a bottle of cheap wine telling him it's Napa Valley, or you got it in exchange for silence in one of your divorce cases. How am I doing so far?" Sanborn moving his head side to side, looking around the air terminal, his mouth pursed, looking disappointed. Sanborn Meeks said, "Man, you try to help somebody out . . ." Springer said, "You're going to act hurt now?" Sanborn saying, "I just can't get behind this lack of faith, man. I'm giving you my best effort here, and it's going, well, unappreciated."

Springer scratched the back of his head and stretched. "I'll give you the grand but that's it. And I need something bigger. A nine but maybe a .380 would work. Think you can take care of that without charging me double what it's worth?"

"Hey, I'm also charging for my silence. Maybe people want to know what you're doing here."

Springer looked at Sanborn, giving him the look, waiting him out.

"Okay, quit looking at me," Sanborn said, holding up a hand like he was deflecting something. "Look, I'm giving you my good-guy rate."

"And I'm offering my not-hold-Sanborn-off-the-balcony-by-his-ears final offer."

Holding his arms out now, plaintive. "Damn, Springs. Why you getting all cold about this? Always like that. Man, we're a team. I can help you out on this thing, you tell me what's going on."

"No. Just the weapon and the information."

Giving him the hurt look now. Springer thinking this is the kind of stuff he put up with for involving Meeks. Knowing Meeks liked to think of himself as an adventure guy rather than some hustler, but a nice guy for a con artist. Meeks said, "I'm licensed. You need my license. Keep you out of shit with the authorities."

Springer, looking around the terminal for the baggage claim, said, "Promise me you won't detect anything."

Meeks spreading his arms and raising his eyes like pleading with God.

Springer looked back at him and said, "Sandy, tell me, how is it you became a private investigator?"

"Man, it's me. I get to carry a gun and look into the dark side of people's lives. It's exciting, and dammit, I like it. Besides, a guy's gotta pay the rent. Sometimes Lady Luck starts shacking up with other guys at the table, you know? See, I applied to drive an armored car, took the driving test, got the license, was balls-out ready to ride shotgun on the green machine. But they wouldn't take me."

"Why's that?"

"You know why."

"Because you couldn't pass the urine test and you have a criminal record?"

He nodded. "It ain't fair, man, that's for sure."

"Give me the name, Sanborn."

"This is gold, man. I give you this, you're going to want to give me a bonus. Or we partner up. Meeks and Springer." Putting his name first. "This is bona fide good shit."

"The name."

"Okay, okay. Guy's name is Chucky Hughes. Calls himself Chewy."

"Tell me about him."

Leaving the airport, Springer checked into the hotel and picked up the car Sanborn had reserved at Alamo, a blue V-6 Mustang convertible which would be great for getaways if he was chased by bicycle cops or racing blue-haired ladies down the strip. He called and made an appointment to view the corpse and they said he could come by the next afternoon.

So he would be looking for Chucky Hughes. Hughes was a street pimp and hustler who worked the conventions. His street name was Chewy. "See, about two weeks before he was killed, Jesse got arrested for assaulting Chewy," said Sanborn Meeks. Springer, thinking how crazy it'd be to pick a fight with Jesse Robinson, asked what the fight was about, but Sanborn said he didn't know.

He'd just have to ask Chewy.

Tuesday, late afternoon, Chewy's standing on the corner, see? His corner. He owned the motherfucker, chasing off the other rip-off bastards. Pimping in Vegas was weird trade, brother, what with the legal brothels and such. But there were still dudes, whiteys with wives and such, who didn't want to be seen going to the Mustang Ranch or some other when Chewy could line them up, no questions asked. Pimping in Vegas was a crime when you didn't get a license, get all those shots. Chewy didn't think of himself as a pimp as much as he considered himself a broker, an honorable-sounding title, worked for a couple of legal cribs paying out his cut to the local power structure so he didn't catch the lead pipe flu going around. Day-trippers from Kansas liked to think it was dirty shit, so he pretended it was illicit. No telling what turned on white folks.

Besides, he didn't dress up in no velvet or drive a tricked-out Cadillac like that television shit. Wasn't his way. He dressed down. Polo shirts and Docker slacks. That's the ticket, baby. Don't call no 'tention to yourself and tip the cabbies and the valets and the bellhops and they'd turn the Johns onto Chewy's enterprise.

So Chewy's standing on his corner, lookin' good, waiting for his cell phone to vibrate when this sizable white boy strolls up, but right away Chewy sees he's no client and the guy's got this look on his face like he was trouble. Not looking mean, you see, but looking . . . well, looking like there was shit going on in his head you didn't want to know about. That kinda look.

Man walks up to Chewy, says, "I want to know about you and Jesse Robinson." Not "Are you Chewy" or introducing himself. Just comes up and says it all coldlike, this composed motherfucker not worried about how Chewy's going to react to this bullshit.

"Man, I don't know any Jesse Robinson." Chewy looking down the street both ways so the man would know he wasn't interested. Looking back at him now, giving him the stare. "You see me working here, right? So why don't you take your vanilla-wafer self on down to the MGM Grand and play the slots?"

"That sounds evasive," the man says. "I'm not sure I like evasive."

"Don't give a shit what you like, baby." Let the man know how he felt about it, but the dude making him nervous anyway. Man's too confident, too sure. Big white boy, too. Not all that tall, but muscular, like a wide receiver or an outfielder. Guy looked like he was made of coiled spring. You didn't notice it right off 'til he got up close and you could see the shoulders working under the shirt. Chewy says, "You the heat? Think you can come up and talk shit at me? That what you do? Go 'round fucking with the niggaz?"

Man smiled at that. What's he so amused about? Wasn't no reason for it. Chewy didn't see one funny thing in it. The man saying, "Why'd Jesse Robinson take the time to slap you around? I know I wouldn't want him coming around looking for me."

See, there he goes again, like Chewy wasn't even talking to him. Not answering no questions, but asking 'em. "Man, I'm gonna tell you again, Chewy don't know no Jesse Robinson."

"He piss you off enough to do something about it?"

"Ain't nobody fuck with me, that got good sense. You got any?" Let him know Chewy was nobody to mess with. "How long you think I last people be thumping around on me? Or I give out information might be classified. There a sign behind me somewhere says White Boy Information Center? You see one like that? This Jesse dude, he come around, I'll bitch-slap his ass so hard his grandkids be born with a headache." He chuckled at it. "Boy. Bitch-slap you, too, you don't get the fuck out my face."

Now the man scratching the side of his face, looking all amused-like still. Under his breath, the man saying, bitch-slap Jesse? That's funny. Like the man was talking to himself. Then to Chewy now, he says, "I'm not a cop. Just a friend of Jesse's. Why'd Jesse hassle you?"

"You ain't listenin'. I keep saying it and you keep playing it. Now it's time for you to say good night." So Chewy pulled out a blade and showed it to the man, telling him, "You see it?"

"Cut it out, okay?" says the man, like Chewy had a candy bar in his hand instead of a blade. The dude's smile was starting to get scary, too. Not that the smile had changed, but his eyes had changed, and there was no good reason for the man to be smiling. Man had a look said, "It don't matter what you do, I'm in charge here." Now, the man was saying, "Put it away. I have to take it away from you it'll draw a crowd."

"Think you can do it, that it?"

"Done it before."

"You some kind of tough guy?"

"Why find out? All I want to know is what I've asked."

"Cost you, then."

"How much?"

"Much you got?"

Man shrugging now. "Maybe I'll just go ahead and take the knife and see if you become more conversant. That work out for you?"

Pissing Chewy off again. "Maybe you can't take Chewy."

"What if I can? Give that some thought. Why get cut up?"

"So, we negotiating now?" Chewy thinking about it. Needed to be more philosophical about things, that was the way. Better things to do than tussle with some crazy guy. Why get in a hassle there was money to be made? He put the knife away.

Man said, "Sure, I'll start the bidding at fifty."

"Man, I don't take a piss for fitty bucks."

"Well, I don't want to see that anyway. A Benjamin and my gratitude. That's the ceiling."

"Let's see it, then."

"You don't trust me?"

"Man, five minutes ago I don't even know you." The guy fucking around, amusing hisself. This was a guy could piss you off quick.

The man pulled out a wad of bills and handed Chewy a C-note. Chewy put it away and said, "Okay, here's the deal. Jesse and I were seeing the same girl."

"Sounds like Jesse."

"Yeah? Well, he didn't like it and we had words that led to a scuffle. Wasn't much, some shoving, name-calling, but the owner of the establishment's a friend of mine and he didn't like that happening at his place. Bad for business, the tourists not into violence, you see. So he called it in. I dropped the charges later.

No big deal. Besides, like you say, who wants trouble with a guy like that?"

"There are smarter things to do."

"Why you talk the way you do?"

Ignoring him, the dude says, "Who would want to kill Jesse? He have any enemies?"

"Jesse?" Chewy was thinking about it. When he started talking again he dropped the street accent. "Yeah, some people didn't care for him. Jesse was his own man. He didn't walk around people and he didn't walk softly. He seemed to have money or access to it. Jesse was getting full of himself. He was a rising star here in town, and some people wanted him to know his place."

"And what was his place?"

"He's black. That's not all of it. It's not quite like it used to be in the old days, but he's still black, this is still Vegas, and he wasn't an owner or a man of means, but he was a good cardplayer, both in and out of the casinos, you catch my drift. Jesse was an okay dude, but he thought he was a tough guy and . . . hell, he was kind of a tough guy and you know him, so you know that. Anyway, there are people in this town who don't react well to that. We just had the one problem and we got over it."

"So, who else should I talk to?"

Chewy shook his head. "No. Can't help you there. I do that and I get a visit."

"From who?"

"It's still a made town, no matter about that Hollywood Funland shit going up."

"Police on the payroll?"

"Some of that, maybe. Yeah. It's a big city with money like any other. I mean, the mafia doesn't run everything anymore, but there's still people I shy away from. I'll tell you this. The buzz was Jesse was fencing stolen property. Diamonds, shit like that. Something else. Word is Jesse was into blackmail."

"Blackmailing who?"

"I don't know and that's the truth. Why are you so interested in Jesse?"

The man nodded, thinking about it, lifting one hand, and said, "He was my best friend once."

"Well, good luck with all that."

The man, turning his head a little bit now, looking at Chewy, saying, "What happened to the pimp accent?"

Chewy shrugged. "Tourists like it."

TWO

But Springer got a name from Chewy. Cost him another hundred and Chewy said, "I didn't give you this name someone asks." The name was Sonny Parker. Sonny "the Shark." One of the old guys used to run things and still kept a hand in. Retired but still a player. According to Sanborn Meeks, "Man, Springs, this dude is all about being a swinging dick. Used to be the kind of guy you crossed and maybe you end up in an urn on somebody's fireplace. Different now, different town, but he's still nobody you want visiting late at night. Supposed to be retired, but if somebody drops a twenty-dollar checker in the men's room he knows about it. Got ears all over town and knows how to process information, you get my meaning. He's in with the politicians, the celebrities, everybody. You want to see him, he plays golf every Wednesday afternoon with a couple of 'business associates,'" Sanborn making quotation marks with his fingers, a habit people had that made Springer tired. Sanborn telling him he'd go with him, Springer saying not this time, Sanborn saying when then? Springer telling him he'd let him know.

The golf course, Sanborn told him, was one of

those places still used caddies, no electric carts buzzing around the place. No shorts allowed, collared shirt only. Very staid, very traditional, very Palm Desert–like. There were fountains and streams and concession booths at strategic locations that served champagne and imported cigars along with the beer and Wild Turkey.

When Springer attempted to gain access to the place, he was informed by a guy in a mauve polo shirt and white slacks that "Greenwood is a private club. You can only play if you're a member or the guest of a member. Sorry about that." Thinking that was something, calling a place in the middle of a desert Greenwood.

So Springer drove the rental Mustang up the road, parked it, jumped the fence, and started off across the course, looking for Parker. Sanborn had told him, "He looks like a Greek but he's a purebred wop. Got this wavy salt-and-pepper hair, big mustache. Like that guy in *Midnight Run*. Not DeNiro or Grodin. The other one. The bad one, Dennis Farina. Yeah, that's the one. Was in *Snatch*, too."

Springer thanked him and told him nobody said "wop" anymore. "Guinea," either.

Sanborn spreading his arms, and in that Southern California accent telling him, "What're you now, the etiquette monitor? Man, talking to you is hard work, you know that?"

Which is why Springer was walking across this green oasis in the desert, golfers in designer clothes with custom golf clubs looking at him, Springer waving sometimes, letting them know it was okay he was here. But he saw cell phones coming out and figured it was a matter of time before somebody complained.

The trick was to walk the holes in reverse; that way the golfers wouldn't be walking away from him. He found Parker on number seven, chipping up. It was a threesome. Parker, an older accountant-lawyer type, and another guy who looked familiar but Springer couldn't place him, everybody dressed very Bing Crosby with light-colored slacks and pastel golf shirts. Then there were the caddies. Two regulation caddies and a third caddy looked like he worked security at gangster conventions.

"Sonny Parker?" said Springer, approaching a green that looked like lime icing on a birthday cake.

Parker looked up, cigar clenched in his teeth, big smile, looking amused, with his white teeth gleaming through the mustache, said, "The fuck're you?"

"I've got five, gets you seven, says I can put the ball from where you're standing within ten feet of the hole."

Parker looked down at his lie, then looked at his caddy. Parker's caddy dropped the bag and started toward Springer, the caddy swelling in stature as he got closer. Springer wishing he'd brought the Beretta or a Stinger missile. Thinking good gosh, look at this guy. The big guy saying, "Mr. Parker's golfing and he don't like to be interrupted. We understand each other, don't we?"

"Just be a second." Trying to look around the caddy now, which wasn't easy. What'd you feed somebody this size?

"You ain't got that long."

"Checkers," said Parker. "Let him talk." He turned to the other two golfers, arms extended, and said, "Guy who'll walk across the course to make a bet like that's gotta be some kind of interesting, don't you think? So, you think you can put the ball on the green from this spot and land within ten feet? And you're saying five gets me seven?"

Springer nodded.

"Well, hell, I can't pass that up. Pat him down, Checkers."

"Raise your arms," said Checkers.

"Checkers?"

"You got something to say about it?"

"No." Shaking his head, letting him know it was okay. "No, I don't." Springer raised his arms and said, "Is it going to tickle?"

"Keep smarting off, asshole. I love that kind of shit." Checkers patted him down and it felt like being nudged with an elephant's trunk. Checkers was going bald in front and had a messed-up eye, scar tissue running through the eyebrow and on the cheekbone, giving him a half wink. He pulled out Springer's money clip, looked through it, finding the driver's license, Checkers turned and said, "Name's Springer—"

"Cole Springer," said the familiar-looking man. Guy was six-feet, 180 pounds, capped teeth, fit. Nice tan, sandy-brown hair. Looked like a movie star. Springer had him now. California. The old days. Springer remembering Don Janzen as a sneaky asshole and sort of a bully used to shove the younger guys into the urinals while they were taking a leak. That kind of guy.

"So, Cole," said the guy. "You remember me?"

Cole put his wallet back in his pocket, nodding, "Yeah, I remember you, Don. How're you doing?"

"Not bad, Springs."

Sonny Parker said to Don Janzen, "You know each other?"

"Played ball together. Cole was a hell of a second baseman. Good stick, too. Didn't the Cardinals draft you?"

Janzen looked different than Springer remembered, not so much his looks, as his demeanor. Something about him. The smile maybe—too big, the ambience not right. Springer would've thought Janzen would be less than glad to see him. Janzen was a tricky, mean kid when they were in high school, but Springer remembered that he was also smart and tough and popular around school. Looked like he was still that way. Last time Springer saw Janzen he was lying on the concrete with a broken nose and a tooth on the ground beside him. Years pass, though, so maybe it was all behind them now.

Springer walked toward Parker, Parker handed him the pitching wedge grip first, and Springer lined up the shot, took a couple of practice swings, and then dropped the ball up on the green, and rolled it seven feet from the cup, Springer thinking sometimes you get lucky. He handed the club back to Parker.

Parker looked at Springer. Smiled. "Well, I'll be damned." He looked up at the lawyer type, saying, "You see that, Goldstein? Pay 'im."

Goldstein reached into his pocket and brought out a money clip. Springer held up a hand. "It's okay. Let it go."

"I pay my debts, Springer," said Parker.

"Well, what I really want is some information from you. I'll take that instead of the money."

"Must be pretty important information."

"Worth it to me. I want to ask about a friend of mine."

"So make an appointment."

"That's what I'm doing now."

"The way it works," Parker was saying, "you call my secretary, she looks at my schedule and then she says something like 'How about Wednesday?' Whereupon you show up at the appointed time and we converse. Doesn't seem that difficult to me."

"Jesse Robinson."

Parker smiled, looking at Janzen now and then back at Springer. "Don't know the name. You say he's a friend of yours?"

"Robinson's the one killed over the weekend," said Janzen, lighting a cigarette. "The one in the paper yesterday morning."

"Oh really," said Parker. "Now that's interesting." He looked at Springer and pointed at him with the wedge. "And you're wanting to know about him? A man who"—shrugging his shoulders, looking at his friends, lifting the wedge—"I don't even know."

"I heard you did know him. Also, even if you didn't, not much escapes your notice. So that's at odds with my information."

"You doubting my word?"

"Not if I can help it." Nodding at Checkers.

"You a cop?"

"No."

"So I'm under no legal obligation to say anything to you?"

"That's right."

Parker laughed. Guy had a nice smile for a man with his reputation. His eyes lit up and he flashed the nice teeth. Disarming. "So, not being a slave to protocol, you just show up and start asking questions. Well, that's something. Isn't that something, Goldy?" The attorney was looking at Springer. Parker said, "Well, I don't know him."

Springer looked around the course. "Well, I hear you know everybody and everything."

"Maybe once. Not anymore. I'm retired."

"Mr. Parker said he doesn't know him," said Checkers, bulling up now. "That's all you need to know."

"Well, I want to know a lot of things, so that's not entirely accurate. Don, you knew Jesse. You knew him from way back. Maybe I should talk to you about this, too. Mr. Parker, I don't mean to embarrass you and I don't intend anything disrespectful and I'll be glad to do this at a time more convenient—"

"He don't want to talk to you, asshole," said Checkers, moving closer now.

Springer put up a hand and moved back two steps. "Checkers, I'll be done here in a second, so you keep your distance. You're scaring me. Hell, you'd scare a Marine division."

Checkers reached for him and Springer slapped his hands away and danced to one side. Checkers made another grab for him and Springer feinted a left hook, shuffled right, and drove four fingers into the man's left armpit. Checker's face went green and he placed a hand on the spot where he was struck. Nobody said anything. Parker crossed his arms and watched. Goldstein moved behind his caddy. The caddy a little guy looked like he was getting a kick out of the whole thing. Checkers was wheezing and looking at Springer. "What'd you do to me?"

Don Janzen smiling now, enjoying the show, saying to Springer, "You picked up some new tricks since high school. Where'd you learn to do something like that?"

Springer could see two guys, burly no-nonsense types, driving up in a golf cart with no golf bags on the back. Way he had it figured they weren't there to offer him a gift membership. Springer said, "Well, looks like I'll be leaving here momentarily. We have an appointment?"

Parker was smiling, gesturing at Goldstein with his cigar. "Get this guy," Parker said. "You believe this?" He lifted a hand toward Springer, said, "You got balls, son. I don't see much of that anymore. Old school. Sure, be at Streamers tonight. Ten. Tell security you're there to see me. I've got a private card room and I'll have it all set up. Sound good to you?"

Springer, looking over his shoulder at the two security guys who had just pulled up, then back at Parker, said, "I'll be there."

The two security guys got out of the cart. Springer looked at them and said, "I was just leaving."

"We'll give you a ride," said one of them, a weightlifter type.

"What if I don't want a ride?"

Muscles rolled his shoulders and his shirtsleeves pulsed like pythons. "We have to see you off the course, either way."

"What I thought. So, I get to drive?" The muscle guy looking at him, unamused. You couldn't please everybody. "No, huh?" So Springer got into the middle of the cart, between the two men.

"Hey, kid," Parker said, "you like to gamble?"

"Sometimes."

"Yeah," said Parker, nodding his head. "I'll bet you do."

From the golf course Springer drove out to the city morgue. He wasn't looking forward to it even though he'd seen dead bodies before—in Iraq that time when he nailed three regulars that were shooting at him.

They checked him through and led him downstairs to a cold-air basement, smelled of chemicals and disinfectant, his shoes loud on the tile floor. They opened the drawer and unzipped the bag. And here was something interesting.

He didn't know who it was on the table.

But it sure wasn't Jesse Robinson.

THREE

"Tucson" Cody Powers quit the rodeo circuit at 3:00 P.M. at a stoplight in Conners, Oklahoma. He had thirty-seven dollars and fifty cents, a pack of Dutch Master Deluxe Coronas, and a very old .25 caliber Colt auto in his pocket. His real name was Joe Bob Powers, Cody being an alias he'd taken, stealing it from Buffalo Bill, thinking it had a nice frontier ring to it.

"It occurs to me," Powers said to Freddy McStain, the rodeo clown he was riding with, "that I don't think I want to do this shit anymore." "This" being the rodeo circuit and Powers being a bull rider and part-time rodeo clown. He was tired of wearing the crap he wore. He was a Texan and a cowboy but liked nice things and had spent two years playing football in junior college, picking up an associate of arts degree.

Freddy McStain spat a brown squirty stream of Red Man out the window of the '88 Chevy pickup and said, "Up to you."

Powers looked straight ahead through the dusty windshield of the pickup and nodded his head. "Let me out" was all he said.

Freddy pulled the Chevy to a halt at the crosswalk, causing pedestrians to walk around the front of the pickup. Powers got out of the pickup so he could get his gear out of the bed. Cars honked at the pair as he walked back to the driver's side of the truck.

"Why they call you 'Tucson'?" asked Freddy, while some guy in a beige Oldsmobile yelled for them to "move the fuckin' truck."

Powers thought about it for a minute. "I don't know," he said. "Guess I made it up."

Freddy always asked too many questions, thought "Tucson" Cody Powers.

"One more thing, Freddy," said Powers, letting Freddy see the little Colt, and leaning in the window. "I'm gonna need whatever money you got there in your poke."

Powers first stop was a local bar called the Rainy Day Bar and Grill, place looking like it had never seen rain or a broom. He sat down in the air-conditioned atmosphere and ordered a Carta Blanca and a shot of Jim Beam black.

"Seven dollars," said the waitress, as she sat the drinks down on his table.

This left him forty-dollars and fifty cents to his name, which was no longer "Tucson" Cody Powers. Freddy'd been holding out on him, coming up with only a ten-spot, that's all I got, man, is what he said, and Powers didn't believe that, but he didn't have time to go through everything back at the intersection.

"I'm going to have to get out of Conners," said Powers, paying the girl. "Either that or I'm going to have to start drinking bar whiskey." Maybe switch to domestic, too, he thought.

"Lot of people do," said the waitress.

"Do what?"

"Drink bar whiskey," she said. "And leave Conners."

Powers nodded. The waitress was knowledgeable, he decided. He would keep an eye on her. He unwrapped a cigar. Three left.

Five hours, three Corona Deluxe cigars, seven Budweisers, and four shots of some kind of well whiskey that tasted like shoe polish, Powers made a decision.

"I am drunk."

He felt good about the knowledge. He was also damned near broke, which he had mixed feelings about. He had an idea about what he could do about a road stake. He also needed to find a place to spend the night.

When the waitress returned with another red-and-white can of Budweiser, the King of Beers, Powers said, "I want to spend the night at your place."

The waitress, although only four years out of high school with ready-to-wear hips and wide brown eyes, was wise beyond her years about such things.

"Sure," she said, with a shrug. "Why not?"

Powers had an idea where he could raise a road stake. First he would rob one of those convenience stores that uglied up the landscape and then he would call a guy he knew in Vegas owed him some favors and would sometimes give him a job to do. The kind of job they didn't list in the want ads.

He had Sylvia, the barmaid, pull up to a Git-N-Go and told her, "I'll be right back. I need some cigarettes." Then he put on mirrored sunglasses like the "man-with-no-eyes" road boss from *Cool Hand Luke,* stuffed his hair under a cap that said "Shit

Happens" on it, and walked into the store, pulled the little gun, and told the mullethead clerk to "give me what's in the drawer and also a roll of those lotto tickets."

The clerk, shaking and slobbering, what an unhealthy looking shithead, went goggle-eyed on him, so Powers grabbed the guy by the mullet and dragged him over to the cash register, ramming his face into the machine. "Don't go stupid on me, boy. Get to it."

He scored $115.76, two packs of Marlboros, a fresh package of Dutch Masters Deluxe Coronas, a roll of Copenhagen, and a pint of Jim Beam in the plastic bottle. That ought to do it, he thought.

"Pleasure doing business with y'all," he said to the clerk.

The next morning, after an all-nighter with Sylvia the barmaid, and, son, could that girl turn you around, all squirmy and excited about hanging out "with a real outlaw," Powers shaved off his beard and mustache and rinsed the spray-can colorant out of his hair—summer blonde, the can had said—and restored his natural reddish-brown coloring.

He wasn't going to jail. No way. He'd been to jail before and didn't like it much. He wasn't going back. Ever. Didn't matter what he had to do to avoid going. That much he'd made up his mind about already.

He randomly left the lotto tickets around town to throw off the police, knowing they'd be tracing the ticket numbers to bums and drifters, and then he called Vegas.

Collect.

It was perfect timing, because they had a job for him. A job Powers could do. And the price was right. Five grand and a vehicle to make the guy leave town. "Guy's being a nuisance, see?" Ten if he had to kill him.

Powers figured he'd maybe go for the ten grand. What the hell, huh?

"That's him."

"You're right. So, what do you want to do?"

"Look at that. His tire hit the white line. Now, that's sloppy driving. We allow that and the next thing you know they'll be driving on the sidewalk."

"Know what you mean. So, we're hitting the siren?"

"Sure. What fun is it being cops, we don't get to use the accessories?"

Springer saw the blue lights flashing in his rearview mirror, looked down at his speedometer. He was two miles below the speed limit. He'd left the morgue, thinking about what he'd told the med techs. "Can't be sure" was all Springer told them. But he was sure. It wasn't Jesse. It was a black guy all right, Jesse's height and weight, but it wasn't Jesse. See, Jesse didn't have any tattoos. Jesse hated tattoos. Why mark on my beautiful black body, that's what he'd say when the subject would come up. And this guy had several. His skin was also a lighter color than Jesse's, but unless you knew him well, and Springer did, you could mistake the guy for Jesse. Springer didn't tell the technicians that. He wasn't sure why he didn't, but later he decided he wanted to know more about what was going on. He had a feeling about it, thinking there was something going on, that they didn't know it wasn't Jesse or did know and were hiding it. Sanborn Meeks said Sonny Parker knew everything happened in this town, but if he said he didn't know about Jesse Robinson, he had a reason for lying. One thing Springer knew about Jesse was Jesse liked to be known. Always did.

Besides, if that wasn't Jesse on the slab, why hadn't

Jesse come forward to tell people he wasn't dead? Maybe he was out of town and hadn't heard about it. But wouldn't someone, anybody, know where he was and call him? Maybe Jesse wanted people to think he was dead. Why would he do that?

Springer called the hospital in Denver to tell Nate that Jesse wasn't dead, but the receptionist taking the call told him he had checked out. Checked out? He'd been in traction. He wanted to go home is what the girl told him, that the doctor arranged for him a course of rehab and things he could do and that the doctor wouldn't have released him if he didn't think it was okay. So he tried Nate at home, but he didn't get an answer, and there was no way to leave a message as Nate didn't believe in recorders. "What kind of thing is that? Being rude to people, you don't answer in person?"

Springer pulled the Mustang to the side of the road. Sun was hot coming through the window as he rolled it down. Two cops got out. The driver was an older guy, a little paunchy, chest hairs sticking out of the top of his undershirt. The passenger cop was a younger guy. Mustache, slender, six-two, his shirt neatly pressed.

"Good afternoon," said Officer Paunchy. His name tag said Sullivan. "May I see your license and regis-tration?" The younger cop knocked on the passenger window and Springer rolled it down, the desert heat rolling in.

"It's a rental," said Springer.

"Then show me the rental papers. How hard's that?"

Springer looked at the younger cop, leaning into the passenger window, his elbows on the door, aviator sunglasses hiding his eyes. Springer thinking this wasn't about speeding while he fished out his license and got the rental agreement out of the glove box.

Sullivan said, "You know why we stopped you?"

Springer turned his head and looked at Sullivan, waited.

"I asked you a question." Looking at the license now and saying, "Mr. Springer from Aspen. I asked you if you knew why we stopped you?"

"You wanted to welcome me to Vegas?"

"Don't be a smart-ass."

"Not it, huh?"

"You hit a white line back there."

"You're kidding me, right?" This was going to be fun; he could see it right off.

"Step out of the car, sir."

Springer got out. Sullivan said, "Place your hands on the car and step back until your weight is on your hands. This is happening because you're a smart-ass," said Sullivan.

"And we don't like smart-asses," said Madison.

"Wow, tough etiquette laws," said Springer but he leaned against the car. No use arguing. These guys were looking for a reason, and Springer wasn't going to supply it. They patted him down, Springer glad he'd left the Beretta back in his motel room.

"All right, turn around." Springer did so, and Sullivan returned the wallet. "Looks like everything's in order here. You see how it is, don't you?"

"I get anything, I guess right?"

"See, you still don't get it." Sullivan looked over Springer's shoulder at Madison. "You think he gets it, Officer Madison?"

"No, I don't think he gets, it, Sully."

Springer said, "You guys work one of the comedy clubs here?"

Sullivan stuck a stubby finger in Springer's face. "You . . . you gotta fuckin' shut your hole."

Springer cocked his head to one side, shrugged.

"Just thinking you need to punch up your act, that's all I'm saying."

"I'll lay it down so you'll know how things are. You're asking around town about Jesse Robinson and it's not appreciated. You're annoying people and involving yourself in an open investigation. Probably better if you cease from that. That's why we're the police. You following any of this?"

"Who would I be annoying that would send you around?"

"Nobody 'sends us around.' "

Springer looked at Madison and back at Sullivan. "Can I go now?"

"You forgot the magic word."

Springer wanted to say something else, thought that wasn't the way to go, these guys were pissing him off, so instead he said, "Magic word, huh?"

"Tell 'im the magic word, Madison."

"The magic word," the younger cop said, "is don't fuck around in Vegas."

Springer said, "Actually, that's more than one magic word."

The two policemen looked at each other and walked to their unit. They got in and roared out, passing within inches of where Springer was standing, the wind from the unit ruffling his hair and shirt.

Springer thinking they did it on purpose.

Why did they care so much about what he was doing?

Where was Jesse Robinson? There was the question.

They were watching Springer through the casino's surveillance cameras.

"I like him," said Parker. "He's got panache. He's no cupcake, either. He took Checkers today and

Checkers isn't a stroll in the park himself. You say you know him from high school?"

Janzen said, "Yeah, he played second base. Jesse played shortstop."

"Funny you should mention the colored guy. Where'd you play?" said Parker, playful now, in that way that he had and Don had seen him use to get inside people's heads. "Left out?"

"Close. Left field. We didn't get along all that well."

"Let me guess. A woman."

Janzen sipped his drink, said, "Always the way, isn't it?"

Parker, still looking at the screen, said, "Women, huh? Can't live with 'em and you can't leave them on the corner for the garbage guy to haul off. Thing is, this guy's asking around about Jesse Robinson, and for the life of me I can't figure that one. I mean, I know who Robinson is, and I'm somewhat surprised you never mentioned you knew him from before." He was looking hard at Don, but Don let it fall off him. "But I'm hearing nothing about who cooled out his action. He wasn't a problem that I can see."

Janzen swirled the ice around the whiskey in his glass. "Jesse was getting too bold. Cocky. Maybe that upset some people. What I heard, but it's just street talk, and I don't have any real feel for what was going on there."

"Not good to have somebody iced in this town, Donald. Bad for business. You know that, don't you?" Don smiled, thinking about this old wiseguy trying to open him up with his dialogue. "Tourists don't like it. In the old days the bosses wouldn't put up with it. Vegas was a safer place then. You killed someone or even mugged them, you had to get permission first, and then you had to take them out of town. But now . . . ," his

voice trailed off. He said, "Now, with these corporate
assholes in town turning it into fucking Disneyland and
the Colombians and the Russians and the blacks running around like it's fucking Dodge City, well, it's just
not the same. No patience, no class. No style. This guy
here"—he tapped the monitor glass with a finger—
"this guy has style."

"Don't become too enamored of him. Springer's
out for himself, at least that's the way he used to be.
Interesting that he's become so handy with his fists."

"Yeah," said Parker. He held up his glass and said,
"Can I get another one of these?" Janzen nodded to his
manager and the manager called downstairs. Parker
said, "I had my people check him out. He was in the
Secret Service. High up, too. Which explains why a
guy lives in Aspen can move like he does."

"Maybe that's why he's in town."

"He got kicked out of the Service. Or he quit or
something. That part's fuzzy. He was kind of a non-
conformist type and that didn't work out so well for
him. You've seen those guys, haven't you? With the
Foster Grants standing around like department store
dummies. Hard to imagine a job where you might
have to take a bullet headed for someone else. They
even look for it, what I hear. You know that this guy
once told the president's chief of staff that he could
fix it so the guy would be sneezing in his own ear?
That's ballsy as hell."

"Well, he's certainly got those. Did you talk to our
girl?"

There was a knock on the door and a waiter handed
in a tray with a drink on it. The manager took it and
carried it to Parker. Parker said thank you, took a sip,
then said, "Yeah, I did. She's being stubborn. Besides, I
haven't really decided which way to go on this. She's
got a good business head and she does what she has to.

For instance"—being the teacher now, the old sage
with the history behind him—"the other night some
cowboy asshole, too much booze in him, starts becoming aggressive with one of the dealers. Diane's passing
by, holds a hand up to let security know she's on it,
and then asks the cowboy if he knows anyone could es-
cort her to her car. Cowboy forgets about being pissed
off, looking at her. You with me, Don? They get to the
door, she motions security and tells the guy, 'Thanks
for escorting me. Now, this is the last time you come in
here. Because next time I'm going to have one of these
security guys grab you by the balls and swing you over
their head. I hope you understand that.'" He paused,
nodded at Don, made an appreciative faraway look. "I
kind of admire her business acumen."

Janzen smiling at him, tapping his glass with a finger, letting the old dinosaur talk. Parker saying, "I'm
going to be straight with you. I don't have to tell you
that this isn't chicken change we're talking about.
Somebody fucks up, somebody gets greedy or nervous
or ballsy . . ." Parker was looking over the rim of his
rocks glass now and saying, "I'm telling you, Don, I
can go either way here. You know anything about
Robinson, or"—giving Don the cold gangster look
now, and could do it, too, no matter how long ago
that was—"if you had anything to do with it and
you're not telling me, well, that's going to cause me to
swing another direction."

"You don't have anything to worry about. My
worry is Diane. What's her take on all this?"

"She feels you should give up your end or
maybe . . . Let's see if I can get the words right." Enjoying himself at the thought. "She says, 'Maybe Mr.
Handjob needs to find a way to negotiate without getting his dick caught in his zipper.' I believe that's how
she put it."

Janzen smiled. "Well, she's always been spirited." He patted a cigarette out of a pack and produced a lighter. "Thing about Diane is, even when she's being a bitch, she still has a great ass."

"Funny the way guys think about their ex-wives. See, I look at her and find it remarkable that somebody looks like that can be so tough. Every tall pisser in town wants a piece of her." Parker looking at him now, trying to get a rise. "That bother you?"

"Is it supposed to?"

Parker screwed up his face and shrugged. "I don't know. Shouldn't it? I mean, I understand how you're a big hit with the cocktail waitresses and the showgirls around town, but I think you like it stormy, and that is one whirlwind of a woman. Hard to ride, harder to tame, wouldn't you say?" Parker raised an eyebrow and looked at him.

Don ignored the bait. Parker said, "Right now, things are what you would call 'at a sensitive juncture.' You'd agree, right? And you still have to come up with your part. Coming up with your part may depend upon you getting along with your ex. And if this deal is to work, then everybody, that includes you, has to avoid raising eyebrows at Gaming, where they seem to have begun to raise an eyebrow or two. You want to tell me why that is?"

"I'm sure I don't know."

"Then allow me to shine some light on the subject. You"—he pointed a finger at Janzen—"are calling attention to yourself with some of the people you're hanging around with."

"Meaning?"

"Meaning that fucking cretin Vincent. Somebody beating the black guy to death is right up that motherless maniac's alley."

"Sonny, I'm sorry about that incident with your

son, but we've discussed it before and you said you understood it as a consequence of the business. I would never—"

"That was before I met the sadistic fuck. You know something, Don, ten years ago I would've had the cocksucker iced. Now . . . now, I'm more philosophical about such things, but, and it's a big but, Don, some nights I think about having that giraffe-looking bastard wasted in terrible ways. And something else. When I see Vincent around, I smell Red Cavanaugh, which is fine if that's the way it has to go, but I'm not going to personally deal with that dishonest piece of monkey shit. That'll be entirely up to you."

"Sonny, Sonny." Janzen putting his hands up, wanting to calm and defuse the situation. Parker's power had declined in recent years, but his influence had not. Sonny was well thought of all over town and, for that matter, all over the state. The wiseguys liked him, and even the police liked him. Sonny Parker was no one to piss off, and Don wanted to avoid that, if he could. Red Cavanaugh was another man better kept happy.

Don said, "What are you going to say to Springer?"

"Haven't decided. Mostly, I want to look at him, see what he is, what he wants. He intrigues me. I want to find out—"

He pointed at the screen with a diamond-encrusted pinky. "Well, will you look at that shit?" He laughed. "This guy, huh?"

Don looked at the screen, and there was Springer, down on the casino floor, looking up at the ceiling.

Waving at the camera.

FOUR

Springer took the drink from the waitress. Cute Midwestern girl, always liked the type, nice smile, great hips. He tipped her two bucks and sipped the Scotch. Vegas. The one thing he liked about the town was the service. You ordered a Scotch and you got more than the regulation shot of Chivas in your glass, like doubles every time; they wanted you buzzing and uninhibited.

He walked around and got the lay of the place. Four exits all the same direction, ten uniformed security guys, twenty cameras, six security people masquerading as patrons. The undercover security guys gave themselves away whenever Springer tried to catch their eyes. They'd look away. Also, they didn't gamble. They tried to blend in, and they were usually pretty good at it, but Springer knew what to look for. They'd pan the room with their eyes and then act like they weren't watching anything, while they were watching everything, and they couldn't slack off because of the eye in the sky.

He was looking at his watch when the tap on the shoulder came. He turned around and there she was, like a time-lapsed snapshot of a homecoming queen who had blossomed. She looked even better now than she'd looked then, and she'd looked pretty damned good back then.

"Hello, Diane," Springer said.

"Hello, Cole," Diane said. She was beautiful in her dark business suit with the diamond necklace sparkling against her lovely throat. Her smile was incredible and made you want to make her do it again. It was as if the room was gathering in around her. She was the centerpiece. Always was. He knew that's the way she planned it.

"I'm surprised to see you here."

She smiled. Always had a great smile and it was nice to see again. Diane was the girl next door with the heart of a hooker. "You mean, what's the nice little girl doing in this big bad town, in this awful place?"

"If that's how you want to frame it."

"I own the place," she said.

"It's nice."

"Thank you. Where are you staying?"

He told her.

She said, "Why not stay here? I'll comp you."

He cocked his head, considering her. "Sounds okay. What's the catch?"

She moved her head side to side, like she was trying to look under his eyes. "You think that's a question to ask a lady, an old friend, who offers her hospitality?"

"I withdraw it."

"Good," she said, tracing a lock of her golden hair away from her face. "I'll arrange it with the desk. You have a minute? I'd like to talk to you," she looked around the casino, "someplace where there isn't so much activity."

She turned and he followed her. She stopped a cocktail waitress and ordered Springer another drink.

The waitress brought it and Diane presented it to Springer. He held up the drink he hadn't finished, but Diane carried it for him. He said okay and then entered a room off the main casino floor. Her office. Big room with a glass-walled view of the Strip. On the desk was a nameplate that read DIANE JANZEN, VICE PRESIDENT, OPERATIONS. That's interesting, he was thinking.

She closed the office door and walked back to where she was standing right in front of him. Close. She said, "Kiss me."

He said, "What's the hurry?"

That's when she threw the drink in his face.

He said, "I should rephrase the question, huh?"

"You like Scotch?"

"Not this much," he said, slinging his hands and trying to stand so he wouldn't drip on his pants.

"You no-good dirty son of a bitch," she said.

Springer wiped a hand across his face and said, "You know, I've been working on the dirty part. You always were . . . turbulent. What is it this time? Because I didn't kiss you?" He pointed at the desk plate. "You're married. To Don Janzen it appears."

"You left me for that bitch Sheri Daniels."

"Well, that's not entirely true," he said, smiling now, enjoying himself. This wasn't so bad. "And you dumped me for Jesse Robinson, my best friend, remember? That was kind of painful. And actually, for accuracy's sake, right after you I started up with Susan Johnson. Remember her? Extra-deadly brunette? Great legs—"

Diane took a swing and Springer leaned away from it, her hand whistling by his chin. "Just wanted to be accurate," he said. Here was a lady could hold a grudge. Sheri Daniels was almost twenty years ago. She recovered and swung again and he caught her by the wrist, so she tried the other hand, and he caught that one, too.

She composed herself and looked at her trapped hands and said, "By the way, I divorced Don six months ago."

"Okay," he said. She leaned in and he held on to her wrists and allowed her to kiss him. On the mouth, her lips warm and spicy. He pulled back and she said, "You can let go of my arms now."

He leaned back, cocking his head, considering her. "It safe?"

She smiled. "You don't like safe all that much."

"More than you might think."

"It'll be okay," she said. "There are towels in the bathroom. I'll get you one."

He released her but leaned away, wary of her, and she walked to the bathroom, looking back over her shoulder once as she did. She returned with a towel and handed it to him. "Would you like another drink?"

"No." He brushed at his jacket, damp with Scotch. "One's enough. So, you married Don?"

"And divorced him. Yes."

They sat down on an overstuffed couch. He said, "Did you hear about Jesse Robinson?" She dropped her eyes and looked at her hands. Yes, she had.

"It was horrible. I got sick at my stomach when I read about it."

"Any idea why it happened?"

She turned in her seat, looking him in the eye. "Maybe I know who did it."

Lieutenant Detective Tara St. John spread the photos, one at a time, on her desk. They were brutal. Bashed his face in and smashed all his fingers up. The ME said he had been beaten to death, but there were two types of blows. One from a blunt instrument, like a baseball bat or the handle of a tool, like an ax handle, a round one. But those blows were postmortem. The killing blows came from a sharper weapon, but still not a blade or anything like it. More like a hard, slender instrument that left U-shaped depressions under the skin.

"What leaves marks like that?" she'd asked the ME, a guy she didn't like that much, something about him, this doctor shaking his head and saying he didn't have any idea. "I've been doing this for seventeen years and haven't seen anything like it," he said.

Tara had been working hard on this case since it had fallen to her. It was her first major case since she'd made detective. She had been surprised she had caught it. It was a big case for her. She'd started off in the county sheriff's office, working as a bailiff in county court. She stood around in her uniform while the miscreants fidgeted on their benches, looking humble or scared, waiting their turn. Then, she'd applied for Vegas PD and got on, starting off on casino duty, walking around the casinos, watching for trouble, which seldom occurred, and when it did, the casino bouncers handled it.

But she worked hard, turned in good reports, and they moved her up to vice, and she made a couple of good busts, and they gave her more to do. So here she was, ten years later, a homicide detective.

The other cops had fun with her. "Man, the brass gets it all with you moving up. They get affirmative action and get the feminists off their ass all in one bold stroke. Shit, you convert to Judaism, you'll make chief." Cop talk. Cops were big kidders. She didn't mind. It was part of it. She didn't have any respect for females that bitched about the ribbing, threatening harassment action, wanting to be like the men until they were treated like one of them. She'd worked her

ass off to get here, and she meant to do the job right
and not act like a bitchy female. She'd pull her own
weight and not use sex or her ethnicity to get any
advantages. Being a black female homicide detective
didn't make her feel conspicuous, it made her feel,
well, it made her feel *distinctive*.

She'd always been the type to reach for what she
wanted. She was a track star, 200 meters, in high
school. Made it to the state finals, but lost by a hun-
dredth of a second to a Navajo girl from the Four
Corners area.

She cried all night after she lost, thinking about all
the preparation she'd made. All the dreams.

She wanted to earn respect, wanted to get the job
done in a way that would show she was the right person for the job. Her first homicide case and she was
going to close the killer out. Put him inside and turn
the key. It was important to her.

The guys teased her but it was okay; it meant they
accepted her. They invited her for drinks after shift at
their hangout, the Badge and Ladder, a cop and fire-
man hangout off the strip. Casino security guys hung
out there, too. Quite a bit of insider information was
exchanged there. She'd go once in a while and they
treated her good. She'd been asked out by a couple of
her colleagues. Nice guys, cute, too. Guys she would've
dated in a minute if they weren't cops. But she didn't
want an office romance, didn't need one, as it might
keep her from attaining her goals within the department. Any office fraternizing might come back to
haunt her, and she had already decided that wasn't going to happen. But being a police detective excluded
her from the thin pool of desirable bachelors in town
who weren't players. It was tough sometimes, but she'd
chosen and didn't regret it most days.

Her thoughts returned to Jesse Robinson. So far,

she'd learned he hung out with unsavory types. Handsome. Tall. Athletic. Popular with the local ladies and the weekend talent. He'd gone to high school with Don Janzen, a man she knew, and knew well, who had his hand in a couple of casinos and a dog track.

Janzen's ex-wife, Diane, also went to the same high school with Jesse. A couple of Vegas's beautiful people who couldn't get along anymore. Add to that the fact another man in town, Cole Springer, also went to that high school at the same time. The four of them had to know each other.

And now this Springer guy had come to town. Cole Springer, late of the Secret Service, owned a bar in Aspen, lived in Jack Carlisle's Aspen home. Jack Carlisle, the actor. Here was something else. There was a file on Springer said he had somehow gotten involved with the San Francisco mob.

And the mob came out on the short end of the deal.

Right now Springer was looking at Diane Janzen, knowing she enjoyed drama, so he wasn't ready to buy into her statement about knowing who killed Jesse Robinson. Not just yet. "Are you saying you have an idea who killed Jesse or you *know* who killed him? There's a difference."

She crossed her left leg over her right knee. "How'd you get so cynical?"

He made a face and scratched the side of his neck. "Dating, I think."

She was shaking her head, making a face herself but enjoying the moment, he could see it. Diane liked verbal jousting. "Well, you haven't lost your touch. You can still be an asshole when you want, can't you?"

He said nothing, waiting on her.

"You like this, don't you?" she said. "You never

change." She laughed, tossing her hair. She exhaled a sigh, and he was aware of her, the feel of her, the smell and rhythm of her. There were many beautiful women. There were smart women. But Diane Masters-Janzen was a smart woman who was more than beautiful. She was stunning. She had presence. She said, "You know, you do something to me. I never know whether to slap you or kiss you."

"You've done both, so what's the verdict?"

"I still don't know which is more fulfilling. Do you want to find out who killed Jesse or not?"

"Why not tell the police?"

"I thought you were Jesse's friend."

"I am. Part of the reason I'm here." Diane playing games like always. Not getting to it.

"Only part?" she said. Lacing her fingers and placing an elbow on top of the sofa, she leaned his direction. "What's the rest of it?" Wanting him to say something about her. That was the Diane he remembered.

"His father. Nate. Remember Nate? He works for me. If you know who did it, then let the police in on it. You do that and I can go back to Aspen."

She looked at him, and reaching out, she brushed hair from his forehead. He could smell perfume and expensive soap. Just like in the old days, he wanted to sleep with her. Worse now that Tobi had chased him off. There was always something urgent and palpable about her appeal. It wasn't logical, it was visceral, but that wasn't it exactly either. It was like a challenge. There it was. She was a challenge. You didn't subdue Diane Masters easily. And when you did bed her, there was this reward, this total giving of herself that was like finding the pearl after prizing open the hard shell, Diane's armor. But even then it was brief, fleeting.

Springer was never sure how much he liked her, or if he liked her, but he had always wanted her.

Even now. And wishing he didn't.

"Why do you always hold yourself back from me?" she asked.

"How about a moratorium on that stuff?"

"You've filled out, gotten big through the shoulders. You used to be so cute, this slender, funny guy. Now you're a bigger man, but you still have that funny kid inside you. You like to put people on, see how they react. Why do you keep part of yourself hidden from me?"

"I don't trust you."

"Why?"

"First, because you're a woman."

"That's a fairly antiquated attitude."

"You're a woman who wants things your way."

"What's wrong with that?"

He shrugged. "Who killed Jesse?"

She shook her head and lifted herself off the couch, as if weightless. She walked over to the office bar, opened a decanter of white liquid and poured herself a drink. She walked back and sat beside him, closer than before.

"Sonny Parker," she said. "Parker killed him or had it done."

"Why?"

"Because that's what he does." She placed her hand near his leg as she sipped her drink.

"He's the type could have it done. Had he a reason, it's plausible. But I don't see what he gets out of it." There it was, he thought, looking at her and wondering what she was going to do with it. He was quiet for a moment, waiting her out.

She said, "Well, maybe that's just my take. But I don't think he liked Jesse and wanted him gone."

"Not enough."

"You don't believe me?"

"I believe you think he may have done it, and he could have it done. I just don't see how Parker comes out on the deal. But it's a place to start. I'm supposed to meet him in his card room," he looked down at his watch, "in thirty minutes."

She placed a hand on his thigh. It was warm and light as a small bird. "So, what would you like to do until then?"

Springer thinking, funny what you'll do on a breakup.

FIVE

First thing Checkers said to Springer after opening the door was "You caught me by surprise out on the course."

Springer nodded and said, "Only way I could handle you. I let you get ready, there's no way I come out on that deal. I mean, look at you. You wrestle in college?"

"Arizona State. Was lighter then. Boxed some, too. Light heavy, then."

"Figured something like that. You put your hands on me, then I'm your pitching wedge."

Checkers smiled at him, nodding his head. "You're all right, you know that?"

He shrugged. "Believe me, I'm trying."

Sonny Parker stood and offered his hand to Springer. Springer took it. It was a good handshake. Firm, friendly. If you didn't know Sonny Parker could snap his fingers and have you killed, you could get used to having him around.

Don Janzen was there. Feeling funny about that at the moment after the workout he'd had with Don's ex-wife in her office. It was strange to be experiencing these things like he was in a time warp. Feeling guilty on top of everything else but not understanding why it would bother him for Tobi to find out. That was done; that's what she said, right?

Besides Parker and Janzen there was also a woman in the room looking like she belonged. Good-looking girl in a cocktail dress, looking bored but paying attention with intelligent eyes and sipping from a fluted champagne glass. There was another guy in the room. Tall guy, wavy hair, sunken eyes, pewter-colored suit, peach-colored shirt, no tie. Guy had a look about him. The kind of guy who you cracked him across the head with a pool cue you'd better go ahead and kill him. Crazy eyes, long neck, big shoulders on a rangy body. About three inches taller than Springer. He was staring at Springer now. Springer nodded at him and the guy nodded back.

Don Janzen said, "Cole, this is Vincent. He's a . . ." Janzen looked at Parker, then said, "Vincent is helping us out on a project. Like Checkers, he used to box, didn't you, Vince?"

"High School. City champion," said Vince. He said it the way you might say your phone number. "Got in the semis of the Gloves once."

"Look, Vince," said Janzen, his hand on Vince's shoulder. "Cole, as we've learned today, is handy with his fists. Maybe you and him should work out together, spar a couple rounds. What do you think about that, Cole?"

Springer not believing this part, but that's the way Don was, always a guy wanted to make you look bad. Always a prick in school, but he didn't have time for him now.

Springer ignored Janzen and Vince, turning to Parker instead, and saying, "I won't take up much of your time, Mr. Parker. I'd really like to do this in private." Turning to Janzen now, "No offense, Don?"

"Mr. Janzen asked you a question," said Vince, standing now and touching his hands to his shirt collar. One of those guys.

"And I ignored it. You miss that part?"

"You talking shit?"

Parker interrupted, saying, "Get 'im the fuck outta here, Don." Then he pointed a finger at Vince. "You. I don't like you so much, see?"

"I don't mean no disre—"

"Shut up. I barely tolerate your dumb ass now. You open your fucking hole again without me asking you something, which I won't, and I'll have your lips sewn together. You think you can remember that?"

Checkers stepped up and put a hand on Vince's chest. "C'mon, Vince, let's go downstairs. I'll buy you a steak."

Vince took a deep breath, let it out, gave Springer a couple of tough-guy glares, and turned to leave. Parker looked at Checkers, then at Springer, raising an eyebrow as he did. Parker turned to the girl. "Cassie, honey, why don't you go downstairs and get a drink."

"I have one, honey," she said. Big smile for him. "See?" Holding up the glass.

Parker smiled back at her. Springer could tell they liked each other. She was comfortable being asked to leave, and he was okay with her teasing him. She was with him, Springer decided. Exceptional lady. Good to be king. "Then why don't you go down, catch the rest of the show, play the slots? Take Don downstairs for a few minutes."

She stood, not upset. "Well, I've seen the show and I don't play the slots, but then I guess there's no reason to hang around here since it seems the excitement's over now." She looked at Springer. "If you'll excuse me?" Springer nodded, and she took Janzen's elbow and led him to the door, Janzen not protesting.

"All right," said Parker. "What is it you wanted to talk about?"

Springer got right to it, asking Parker what he knew about Jesse Robinson.

"Not much," said Parker, a big cigar in his hand, using it to gesture with. "Knew of him. Seen him around." Springer smiled at that, and Parker brightened, saying, "I didn't know you. You think you get ahead in life telling everything you know to people you just met?"

"So, you knew of him. What'd you know?"

"Good-looking kid. Bright. Ballplayer. Played here on the local minor-league club, couple years up at the bigs with the Angels. Popular with the ladies around town. If you're asking was he involved in anything, I couldn't tell you."

"Couldn't? Or wouldn't?"

Parker smiling and nodding. "You get right to it, don't you? I probably wouldn't tell you if it didn't suit me, but I don't really know very much. Heard he had a couple of brushes with the law, but I never heard he was into anything that might be . . . What's the word I'm looking for here?"

"Criminal."

"Such a hard word, but I never heard anything about the kid like that. Sorry I couldn't be more help."

"What about Janzen?"

"What about him?"

"Him and Jesse."

Parker tapped the ash off the end of his cigar. "You know, it's a funny thing and maybe I'm reading too much into it, but I didn't know that Janzen knew him. He never mentioned him, you know what I mean?"

"You think he was purposely withholding that information?"

Parker leaned back. "I don't see what he gains by it. He's kind of a sneaky fuck, so I don't know. Maybe it just never came up."

"What about Don's ex-wife?"

"Diane? You know her? Well, that's between them, of course. They still own the casino together."

"Who has the controlling interest?"

"Neither of them. You know, business is a funny thing. Sometimes you can be in control without having a controlling interest." He picked up a deck of cards that was sitting on the green-felt poker table and began to shuffle through them. "It's like sitting in on a game of Texas no-limit hold 'em with two guys don't like each other and would rather lose to anyone else. You know that game?" Springer nodded. "You play it right, you might not even need more than a pair, or in the business world maybe you don't even need a very large piece of the action. That connect for you?"

Springer thought about it. "I guess if a third party had a small share of a commodity or a business and two other people, let's say, didn't like each other, then the third party could play both ends against the middle."

"That's pretty good. You understand business."

"Movies." Springer picked up a blue poker chip and tumbled it over the top of his knuckles. "Clint Eastwood in *A Fistful of Dollars*. You seen that one? Clint comes to town and two factions are fighting for control of the town. Clint uses it to his advantage."

"But he had to kill a lot of people to get what he wanted. Gets beat up pretty badly."

"Well," putting the chip down, "it's just a movie."

Parker chuckled to himself, took a draw on the cigar. "Let me ask you something? You planning on staying in town long?"

"Long enough to find out what I need to know."

"Then what?"

"Whatever it takes."

"You could do better things for yourself than to rub Don the wrong way."

"Why would I do that?"

Parker smiled. "Because I think you like it."

"What's your connection with him?"

"You don't find it rude, asking me something like that? What if I don't feel like telling you anything?"

"I'll find out anyway."

"I'll bet you will, but it might cost you to find out. You thought about that?"

"All the time, but that's something you decide before you start, not halfway through. One way or another." Not to mention, he was thinking, where Jesse was and who was in the body bag down at the morgue. "Jesse's father, you'd have to know him . . . I don't find something out that will satisfy him, then he'll be upset some more, and that'll be hard for me to handle."

"And if he does, that would bring you back here again. That's the way it is, isn't it?"

Springer nodded. Checkers returned and sat down in a chair at the poker table.

"I like that," said Parker. "You know, I'm having some people over to my place Friday evening. If you'd like to come, you're invited. Rub shoulders with some of Vegas's elite, maybe a female headliner or two. You interested?"

"I could get interested."

"Bring a date, if you'd like."

"Might as well enjoy my stay."

"Okay, then, I'll be expecting you. What do you know about Aspen?"

"I live there."

"I know. Which thing I find incongruous, a guy

like you living in Aspen. The way you move. The way your mind works. Makes me wonder why that is. What I'm talking about is business opportunities. You know people there? Business people, I'm talking about people who can get things done in Aspen? City council people, those types."

"Know of them, that's all. I own a bar, barely makes the rent."

"Let me ask you something else," Parker said. "You think you could take Vince?"

Springer stood. "If I couldn't, there's always Checkers." Nodding at the bodyguard.

Checkers smiling now, saying, "Hold his long narrow ass out the fifteenth floor, see if that changes his attitude."

When Springer left Streamers and Sonny Parker, there they were, hanging around the parking lot, waiting for him. Three of them. Vince and two other guys looked like they lifted on a regular basis. Springer knew the type. Had the too-small T-shirts stretched tight across their biceps and pectorals. They were leaning against the rental Mustang. But this was Vince's show and he'd be the one to watch. The boxing thing wasn't making Springer feel any better. Vince and the goons were waiting for him, no doubt about it. First the police, and now this.

Springer stopped and looked at them, then said, "Well?" leaving it open-ended. What could he say? No use acting scared. Never helped anything.

Vince, rolling his shoulders, showy. Springer had seen guys like this before, guys who watched too much television and imitated the stuff. Vince said, "You need to be thinking about going back to Colorado."

Springer cocked his head to one side like he was thinking about it, then said, "I like it here. Thinking about buying a house or leasing an apartment. Maybe find a girl and settle down. The nightlife here is something special."

"Well, you're not welcome here, but it looks like you're going to need some convincing."

"Who sent you? Wasn't Parker. He doesn't like you. Janzen?"

"None of your business, fucko."

"Fucko? Who says fucko?" Wanted to laugh but thinking maybe not a good time for it. There *were* three of them.

"You just need to listen to what I'm saying. Time for you to pack up and take off."

"I think I know what you're getting at, but why don't you get more specific about it?"

"I'm just the messenger. Paid to give you the message. Leave town. Tonight."

"And if I don't?"

The weightlifters were off the car now and walking toward him. Vince smiled like he'd done something significant and said, "Then bad shit happens."

Springer pulled out the little Beretta .32 Meeks had gotten for him. He'd left the bigger one in his room. It stopped them. "Well, then, fellas, I want you to meet 'the bitch.'" He raised it a little higher and shook his head slowly at Vince, who was looking ballsy. "See, I call her that because once she starts talking, I can't shut her up."

"You're not gonna shoot anybody."

"Don't bet your life on it." Funny the way people thought, like Springer wouldn't take a couple shots to avoid a beating. Springer motioned with the pistol. "You won't be my first. This is Vegas. Want to lay odds on getting to me before I put one in your throat? The cops'll show up while you're lying on the pavement, gargling blood, when all you had to do was go home. Makes no sense when you think about it." He gestured with the weapon. "Move away from the car."

One of the guys who'd been leaning against the car said, "Be careful with that thing."

Starting to enjoy himself, now, liking it that he was able to turn it around. How many times do you get a chance like this? He said, "You know what Clint Eastwood would say in a situation like this?"

They looked at each other. Vince made a face and said, "Fuck you, man."

Springer raised the weapon and pointed it at Vince's nose, making Vince lean away. "Aw, come on, play along. Have some fun with it. You may never have someone point a gun at you again. Try. Live a little." He held his free hand out to Vince, entreating him. "Okay, here we go. Now, what do you think Clint would say in a situation like this? Think *High Plains Drifter*."

Vince watched the gun with his eyes, thinking about it, pursing his lips, some of the swagger gone now, shaking his head slightly, then said, "I guess . . . I guess, 'Do you feel lucky, punk?' "

"No," said Springer, brightening now, shaking his head. "Clint'd say, 'You still here?' "

SIX

Springer liked the black lady cop, Detective Tara St. John, helluva name, right off the bat.

After Kristen died, Springer more or less lost the best part of himself for a while. Whole period was dreamlike. Drinking too much, wasn't much inspired to get up in the mornings. He'd sleep late, take a handful of aspirin, washing them down with black coffee or a beer, trying to put all the snakes back in the basket. His business failing because he wasn't paying attention and didn't much care.

That's when he'd met Special Agent Tobi Ryder. Right about the time he scammed the mob out of a large amount of unreported cash the IRS would never know about. Mob money. Tobi came along, investigating him. She was Colorado Bureau of Investigation, trying to help the feds bust him, and they ended up falling in love, which is how he saw it. Well, they liked each other a lot and he enjoyed her company, but when you loved someone the way he'd loved Kristen—loved her more than he loved himself, more than he loved the way the pattern of his life was, more than he had imagined he would ever love a woman—when that happens and that person is gone, well, it's like somebody shut off a power switch inside. The women's magazines called it "emotionally unavailable." Maybe he was. Tobi had mentioned it more than once. That he had to let Kristen be dead, but it was still hard to do. He could see that Tobi was tired of it when he left for Vegas.

Going to Vegas was an excuse for Tobi. Or maybe for him to give her the chance to let him go.

So now it was another lady cop—Metro investigator—who was talking to him, and he found himself attracted, her being pretty and smart, but thinking, what is this, are you becoming a cop groupie? Two in a row. Do you have some sort of thing about women in authority, which was funny when he thought about the time he had accessed, illegally, his file with the Secret Service. The words "has difficulty with authority figures" and "noncompliant," "not a team player," were in there, so maybe being attracted to women in authority was something in his psyche that appealed to him.

Or maybe he just liked dangerous women who might shoot him they got mad enough. Which would explain Diane. What was it she said? Oh yeah, she said, "You don't like safe all that much." Could be right.

Springer had been asked to come down to the municipal building and meet with St. John. "It's a request, not a command," he'd been told. He'd also been told it was regarding Jesse. Detective St. John's mother was black, her father was white, which was unusual, since it usually went the other way in mixed marriages. Usually it was black men marrying white females, not the other way, she told him.

"Reason I called you down here," she said, after she'd shown him to her office and offered coffee, "was to ask you why you're making inquiries concerning Jesse Robinson."

Nice lady with showgirl legs and skin as smooth as

poured milk but darker. Darker than tan, with pure white teeth, bleached at a dental office, which was normal back in Aspen. Vegas, too. She was black, but the light café au lait skin and the incredible green eyes spoke of another heritage. She was striking. One of the most beautiful women Springer had ever seen outside the movies.

"He was my friend," he said. "His dad is like family to me."

"He was black."

"So was his dad. That's the way it works."

"My father was white." A challenge in it.

"So was mine. Maybe we're related."

She was working on a smile. "Okay," she said. "Let's try again. Are you a licensed investigator?"

"Not licensed."

"You need a license to make the kind of inquiries you're making."

"This is pretty good coffee," he said.

"Thanks. I grind it myself. I can't take the coffee they make out in the squad room. The last time they cleaned the pot Elvis was playing the International." She lifted the edge of some papers on her desk, serious again. "You were in the Secret Service at one time."

He said nothing, waiting on her. She said, "I see nothing in your file that suggests you have any official capacity to insinuate yourself into my caseload."

He waited some more.

"Mr. Springer, you can be arrested and charged for investigating without a license. You're aware of that, correct?"

"This is probably not the best way we could've met, you seeing me as some kind of obstacle or someone with information you need to clear up this killing." He was holding back that it wasn't Jesse down at the morgue, but wasn't sure why he was doing that.

Something to hold back, like a card up his sleeve, thinking Jesse could show up himself and explain things to the police. Springer didn't see an advantage in sharing it at the moment. At least he didn't feel like telling it until he talked to Jesse's father, Nate. "I didn't have anything to do with it. Haven't seen Jesse in five years."

"Then what's your interest?"

"His father. His heart's broken, I think anyone would understand that, and I don't enjoy watching him feel bad. I come out here to see if I can do anything that might put this to rest for him." Springer knew the old man would be glad it wasn't Jesse on the slab, but what would he tell him if he asked where he was?

"That's a tall order."

"Nathaniel, that's Jesse's father, says he wasn't a criminal. I can prove he wasn't, that'll be something."

"He was busted for drug possession. Intent. Found it in his car during a traffic stop."

"What was the stop for? You know, probable cause. Speeding?"

She started flipping through the papers on the right side of her desk. "I have it right here," she said. "He was weaving on the road."

"Hit a white line?"

"Yes," she said, looking up now. "That's one of the things police look for with DUIs."

"They write him for DUI?"

"No," she said. "No, they didn't."

"So, they didn't write him for DUI but stopped him and busted him for drugs they found in his car? That's just good police work. You know, I remember Jess from high school. He was kind of a health nut. Wouldn't even take aspirin." He smiled and looked out in the squad room. "I guess the arresting officer's name will you go out with me?"

"I'm not sure this conversation is helpful—"

"Sullivan or Madison. Either of those the arresting officer?"

Her green eyes widened briefly. "Yes." She stopped for a moment, and he could tell she was thinking about it. "As a matter of fact, it was. How'd you know?"

He extended a hand out to the side. "I'm a good guesser."

She tapped her pen on the desk, thinking. "The med techs tell me you didn't ID the body."

He nodded. She said, "You couldn't tell if it was him or not? Was he too beat up?"

He liked her enough it made him consider telling her, almost did in fact, but held back. "It was pretty gruesome."

"What's your connection to Don Janzen?"

"Knew him from high school."

"Anything else?"

"He didn't like me much."

"And you? Did you like him?"

Springer shrugged. "We didn't hang out."

She thought about that some more. He watched her. He could hear the clicking of computer keyboards off somewhere. Her desk was neat, things were stacked symmetrically, and he was thinking she could find anything she wanted without having to think about it. She was likewise neat in her attire.

Springer said, "You ever go dancing?"

"Pardon me." Shaking her head like she had something in her ear. "You asked if I ever go *dancing*?"

"That was the question."

"I don't see how it's relevant."

"Well, I like to dance and wanted to know if you'd give some thought to going dancing with me, you know, if you had the time."

She was smiling now. Full scale. It was dazzling, the kind of smile you'd need sunglasses on to look at it for long. "Are you trying to charm me, Mr. Springer?"

"Call me Cole."

"That wouldn't be professional."

"So, when you get off duty you could call me Cole."

"Okay," she said. "If I happen to run into you somewhere, I'll call you Cole. Until then we'll stick with titles. And I might have coffee with you some-time if you'll give me more background on Jesse Robinson. Help me to get a handle on this thing."

"You know," he said. "You might be able to run into me at Streamers tonight around eight thirty if you worked it right."

"Why would I go to Streamers?"

"So you could take a shot at calling me Cole," he said. "Try it out, see how you like it."

Powers was driving down the Strip at 2:00 in a brand-new Chevy dual 4×4 pickup that Red Cavanaugh had arranged for him to use. Probably hot, but who cared? Not him. The sun was high and hot and he pulled another beer out of the cooler on the floor-board. Somebody was supposed to meet him at three. Fine to be back in Vegas with a buzz on and money coming his way. Rode in a couple of rodeos here years back. Could be a nice trip. Good hotel, play some poker, find him a club gal or a soiled dove if he had to, they were lawful here. Hell, gambling, drinking, and whores. What else was there?

Partner, Vegas was a hell of a town for a cowboy who was bucks up.

Tara called her brother, Michael St. John, her step-brother actually, who was head of security at the Bel-lagio, telling him about this guy. This Springer. What was it about him? She was attracted immediately. He was good-looking, but not shiver-handsome, that wasn't it. It was his eyes. Something *in them*. They were nice eyes, kind and knowing. Eyes that smiled at you. Eyes like James Garner or Paul Newman, not the color but what they looked like when they knew something was up or something funny to tell you. They weren't the eyes of a man could shoot someone, which his file said he had done, or coolly look a mob boss in the eye and tell him whatever you wanted, which he had also done. But his eyes took her breath away, sounding silly when the thought came into her mind, but that's how it was. He looked at you and she could feel her breathing stop. His eyes were so *what*? So unambiguous. He would look at her and then he was looking right inside her, but not probing or aggressive; it was like, I'm just looking inside a little to see what's going on with you. And again she thought it was a silly thing to think.

But when you'd look into his eyes and when you tried to get past the kindness and the smile in them, there was a roadblock. You could only go so far in and then the curtains came down. But he'd been a Secret Service agent, one of those tight-lipped guys who looked at nothing but saw what they needed to. She couldn't see him as one of those guys. She couldn't see him in Aspen either. He was an anomaly and she could see he enjoyed being one.

"So, is this a white guy?" her brother asked.

"What difference does that make? You're white." In her mind she could see him smiling at that. Smiling his big Irish smile, playful and full of fun.

"You gotta watch these white guys. You go for the rogue types, that what you're telling me?"

"I didn't say I 'go for' him. Where did that phrase come from anyway? I said he had an affecting personality." Hedging a little now, keeping something back. "He wasn't what I expected. How do you figure him for a rogue?"

"You said he scammed the mob."

"I said he 'allegedly' scammed the mob."

"Cop talk."

"I'm a cop."

"You think he knows something about Jesse Robinson's killing?"

"No," she said. "I think he wants to know something about it. And, it's crazy, but I get the feeling he does know something but he's keeping it to himself. I think he'd like to find out who did it."

"And if he finds out, then what?"

"Then I think he would like to exact something."

"Vigilante type?"

"He seems too pragmatic for that. More like a settling of scores. A reckoning maybe."

"Those are romantic notions. You see him as some kind of knight in white armor?"

"He wore armor, white wouldn't be the color." Blue, dark cobalt blue, she was thinking. So blue it would reflect like a mirror in the moonlight. She was thinking like a high school girl with a crush on the quarterback. She hadn't felt like this in a long time. It wasn't like her, but she could think anyway she wanted, right? She asked Michael about Sullivan and Madison.

"They come in here sometimes," Michael said. "Act like they're checking things out, helping us out, you know? Brownnose me for free drinks, so I let them work at it. Of course, we're happy to serve the locals, good relations, you know. We need you guys from time to time and want to keep you smiling along with us. But these guys, they try to promote the cocktail waitresses, want to meet the showgirls. Regulation shitbags. How'd they get on with Metro anyway?"

"Affirmative action. An outreach to the terminally stupid."

Her brother laughed. "That's how you got on. Affirmative action."

She said, "I got on because I'm good." She stretched out the word "good." "And maybe because my big brother's the best security man in Vegas." Kidding him now.

"I had nothing to do with it. You are good, but don't let your emotions trip you up here."

"They won't." But she wasn't sure about it. It had been a long time since she'd met a man who was a man and not a hormone with legs.

"Guy sounds like a con man."

"His background is law enforcement. Secret Service. There's some con man in him, you can tell. He's easygoing and, well, he's quick with the right thing to say."

"Maybe that's his routine. Comes across affable and easy to talk to. Disarming. Lot of those guys around town."

"I'm telling you, Michael, there's nobody in town like this one."

"Oh my God. You're smitten."

"I'm not smitten. I'm not going to drag him to my bedroom and rape him, you big jerk." It was a thought, though, smiling to herself that she would think something like that. "He's just . . . well, he's interesting."

"You going to meet him?"

"Think I might. Be nice to get to know him and the added bonus of maybe learning more about Robinson's death."

"I asked around, checked with my people and their

contacts, like you asked and I'm coming up with nothing so far. You said you hadn't identified the body for sure yet."

She had been thinking about that. Springer had been cryptic. She could feel him dancing away from it, like he had something he wasn't sharing. "Keep asking anyway."

"Sure. Where you meeting this guy?"

This was the part she relished and at the same time wondered how it would affect Michael.

"Streamers?"

"You're kidding me." She could see him setting his lips in a straight line, that way he had when he was thinking about something. "Send Ken and Barbie"— meaning the Janzens—"my love, okay?"

She knew it was touchy with Michael even though that business had been cleared up. Michael had been head of security at Streamers for two years before the Janzens fired him. Michael had been cool about it when it happened. Told her how when they fired him he just smiled and said, "Since I'm not here anymore, you probably aren't interested in which pit boss is ripping you off." Letting them think about it when he left. Besides, the Bellagio had been after him for weeks before the split came, Michael seeing it way ahead of it happening.

"You did the right thing, Michael."

"It worked out in the end anyway. This is a better job, more pay. I can't believe it. My little sister finally meets somebody who can get behind the tough-cop exterior."

"Oh, stop it, Michael. Nobody's behind anything yet."

Well, not yet, anyway.

SEVEN

Don Janzen, who had decided to quit smoking a month ago, lit his second cigarette of the last two days. The phone rang and Janzen took the call. Things weren't going like they were supposed to. Springer. Like the Old West, you ask the stranger to leave town and he won't go, then you had problems. Parker was close to committing to this venture and his divorce from Diane was final, so now Springer shows up. Springer, exasperating as always, shows up at the exact wrong moment. He had a talent for that.

The voice on the other end said, "Tell me what 'it didn't turn out as anticipated' means." The voice belonged to Red Cavanaugh, a man who could turn the screws when he wanted to. Red Cavanaugh was part of the "legitimate" criminal element in Nevada—legitimate meaning he had legitimate businesses and was also an authentic crime boss—a man who controlled casinos in Reno and Tahoe and Vegas and was important to Janzen's plans.

Don telling him now, "Springer decided not to be scared. He turned it around on them."

"How did he do that? We send three guys and it isn't enough? Guy's so tough we're supposed to call the Marines have them send out a division? What are you telling me? That we sent the Three Stooges?"

"Vince is your guy, Red, not mine." Don was irritated to be saddled with Vince in the first place, never quite understanding why Red liked the imbecile.

The girl brought in his lunch on a tray. Club sandwiches and cole slaw. He didn't like cole slaw, but they kept bringing it to him. He indicated for her to set it down and then waved the back of his hand at her. She left.

Cavanaugh said, "I want to know what went wrong."

What went wrong? They sent Vince, that's what went wrong. But Don said, "Springer had a gun."

"That's why we need somebody who's not those guys. Somebody can get the job done, that's what we need. Okay, so we try again. I called somebody. He should be here today."

They talked about it some more, and Red wanted Don to send Vince to meet the new employee when he arrived. Cavanaugh was also voicing his concern about Sonny Parker, a guy, he said, was a fucking guinea prick, thinks he still runs the Strip. "Those days are over," Cavanaugh said, "but the guy ain't paying attention to it. And I want this old friend of yours straightened out."

First the moves out on the golf course, now a gun. Springer was full of surprises, but then he always had been. Springer and Don had always had this strange, almost symbiotic, relationship going. Don thinking they could've been friends under the right circumstances, but people pitted them against each other, guys telling him, "Hey, you should see what Springs is up to now." Or, "You gonna let him get away with that?" whenever Springer, the wiseass, said something

to him or when he found out Diane broke up with
him to go out with Springer. They were always competing over one thing or another, though neither of
them gave it voice, except when it had come to Diane.
He didn't think of himself as a jealous person, but
maybe he was and didn't know it. Sometimes, if he
were honest with himself, he'd have to admit Springer
wasn't competing with him and he wasn't jealous of
Don, either. Another reason he didn't like him.

Don ended up with Diane. But it was by default,
Springer heading off to college. "Never even said
good-bye, the bastard," Diane had told him that night
on the beach, after they made love for the first time
since Springer had interrupted their romance. Don
telling her Springer was seeing Sheri Daniels anyway,
hoping to make her feel better . . . or more pissed at
Springer, he had to admit it.

After ten years with Diane he was wondering who
came out on top of that deal. He didn't want Diane,
but he didn't want Springer to have her, either. Part of
the ongoing rivalry, he guessed.

And now Springer had popped back into his life at
the worst possible moment. Which is why they had
sent the three morons to tell him to leave Vegas. But
Springer wouldn't go. Springer never did what you
thought he would or what you wanted him to, Don
smiling now as he thought about it, knowing deep
down that Springer couldn't be scared off. In a funny
way, he missed Cole. Springer made him sharper,
more careful and scrupulous in his planning. So, in a
way, he couldn't have Springer around, but it was interesting to have him here, like a card game with a
high roller. Wondering if he had agreed to have
Springer roughed up so he'd stay? That's crazy.
Springer would keep pushing, keep prodding and

looking into things, because that's what the guy did. He looked too far, then maybe he'd be looking into things Don couldn't let him see.

He didn't like the attention his ex-wife was giving Springer. His floor boss had told him they had been together. Why did that bother Don? Because that's the way it was between them. He really didn't want Diane as much as he didn't want anyone else to have her. Especially not Cole Springer. In fact, the last thing in the world he wanted was to be married to Diane again. Diane was the type of woman who created the Prozac industry. And he knew Diane. She would love the attention and so much more if she thought it would wind somebody's clock, in this case Don's. She wouldn't want him as much as she wanted to show Don she could still get to him—and that she could still rope Springer in. Funny the way things worked in relationships. Maybe Springer knew how Diane was and that was his advantage, knowing better than to get involved with Diane, who was a danger zone with legs.

Then there was the message he'd gotten via the people downtown. They wanted a meeting. Soon. The kind of people you couldn't blow off, telling them you had a heavy schedule. On top of that, there was the bank calling earlier. They were considering extending credit for the deal on his financial enterprise, and would he mind coming down to talk to them about it and provide names of people in his financial syndicate, telling him his credit was extended already. Everything was on the line. Bankers going along all these years and now they were getting cold feet. Like Sonny Parker, the bank smelled Red Cavanaugh and Cavanaugh was trouble, but Don needed Cavanaugh's muscle and Parker's influence . . . for now, anyway. Don was working a high-wire act here, but if it all came together, he would be one of the most powerful men in Nevada . . . or he would be flat broke, maybe even in jail, yes, he had to consider that as a possibility. Betting it all, that was the way he liked it anyway. You either lived fast or died trying to live fast was the way he saw things.

Cavanaugh said, "Talk to this Springer guy, face-to-face. Explain the advantages of going home rather than insinuating himself into our affairs."

"He's not really that good a listener."

"Well, the guy I'm sending is convincing. Let's not fuck this up, huh?" Telling him not to screw up, when Don could tell him going after Springer was a sure way to screw things up. But the wheels were turning and it was too late to pull back.

Don hung up the phone. He ate his lunch, leaving the cole slaw—why'd they give him that crap anyway?—and called downstairs and asked for Vince. Five minutes later Vince was sitting in the chair facing Janzen.

"Vince," said Janzen, gesturing with a cigarette. "You've been working for Mr. Cavanaugh and me for what, six months now?"

"Something like that." Vince slouching in his chair, fingers intertwined just below his chest, no tie, shirt unbuttoned.

"During that time, haven't I told you to maintain a lower profile around Mr. Parker?"

"Yeah, Don, but listen, man. I can't—"

Janzen held up a hand. "Have I told you that or not?"

"Yeah," he said, lips pursed, not happy about it. "You told me. I got it, believe me." Both of them knowing what the job market was for guys like Vince. Janzen knowing he needed to get Vince squared away and once again realizing what a tough act it was handling someone of Vince's temperament. Damn, Sonny

Parker on one side, Red Cavanaugh on the other, Springer in town, and now he was having to explain himself again to Vince, a guy who thought he was in a Frank Sinatra movie.

"Parker is sensitive about you being in my employ. The incident in the ring, remember?"

Vince rolled his shoulders, a mannerism Don found annoying. "Listen, when you step between the ropes it's for real."

"That's not my point. Parker is old school, believes that this is just business, so he overlooks the 'accident' and makes himself accept the fact it was a legal bout and a consequence of the sport."

"His boy was talking shit out the side of his mouth. Saying he was going to make me his bitch. Dago motherfucker telling it to my friends. Asking me 'Who's your daddy now, bitch?'" Don not believing two guys so dumb could find each other in a ring. "I don't think a gentleman should act like that. Do you?" The moron's arms out, imploring a response. "No, baby. No way that's acceptable behavior."

"It's his son, Vince. His *only* son. You get that yet? Now the kid's lost the feeling in the left side of his face, got that Stallone thing going, which pisses Parker off, and I think anyone could understand why." Not mentioning Vince was an obnoxious moron with the way he dressed and the street lingo he'd pulled straight out of a Tarantino movie. "He's very family-oriented. Worries about his legacy, his name, the future . . ."

Vince wasn't saying anything, nor nodding in agreement. Just staring and looking bored with hearing it. Putting up with it but not listening. Don knew he was talking to himself but wanted to have it said so there was no doubt he'd given the guy a chance to save himself.

Dealing with Vince was tiresome. Don looked at his cigarette and stubbed it out. He'd talked to the guy before with the same result. Why get started again? Not much longer, anyway.

Janzen spread his hands on the desk. "Look, I need Parker right now. Mr. Cavanaugh needs him, too. Think about that. Therefore, Vince, it would be helpful to me, not to mention what it would do for you, if you would not call attention to yourself in his presence. The less he sees of you, the less he hears your voice . . . well, just shut up when he's around."

Vince said, "Not afraid a him."

Right. That's because it takes brains to be scared. Trying again. "Are you listening to me?"

"So, I'm supposed to act like some little girl hasn't had her period?" Still not getting the idea.

"No, I'm telling you that saying nothing around Parker would be the best way to approach things." Seeing the pouty-bored look on Vince's face again and trying to maintain a professional tone. "Listen"—he paused, pointed at Vince—"Sonny Parker's the kind of man, he doesn't want you, or me, around anymore, then suddenly we're not around anymore. Is any of this registering?"

"He's La Cosa Nostra." Not saying "Mafia" or "gangster"; no, this guy has to say La Cosa Nostra. Saying it like it was a revelation. Probably only heard the word lately and wanting to try it out.

Don said, "That's another thing. Don't even mention that. What's with you? Do you have some sort of biological defect keeps you from saying anything helpful? Who says those things anymore?" Don didn't even want to think about that part of it. Red Cavanaugh was bad enough, because he was unpredictable and maybe even emotionally disturbed, but Sonny was formidable in ways Cavanaugh couldn't begin to conceive of. You could talk around Red. Sonny would smile at you, dissect your words and throw them back at you. "He is a retired business-man, that's the way he wants to be thought of, so I'm going to allow that. Why argue the point? I don't know if he was a made man, you understand what a made man is?"

"Fuck, yes," Vince said, screwing up his face like Janzen had asked him the dumbest question in the world. "Who you talkin' to? I'm the only guy in the room."

What a frustrating jerk-off this guy was. Janzen said, "The people who *are* connected like him and have worked with him for decades. People cooperate with Sonny. Attorneys, law enforcement, politicians, celebrities, doesn't matter. Gaming loves him, and he has a couple of them in his pocket and the way he works is fascinating. He can strong-arm people but he rarely has to because he has charisma. You under-stand charisma?"

"Magnetic personality, yeah, sure."

"Now, I want to know you've got the other deal set up and we're good to go. There can't be any mistakes. You understand that?" Vince nodding his head. "I want people who can do it but too dumb to see what's coming. People who don't know me. Have you got that done?"

"Need one more guy and it's done."

"When you get them all together I'll tell you what to say." Thinking about that now—this was the tricky part—was worse than arranging the financing or get-ting Parker to go along. This escapade would have to work or the rest would fall. Springer. Damn him for showing up now.

Don said, "Springer's coming over to the club later and I want you there."

"I don't like him."

"And I so wanted you to like him, Vince. He's easy not to like, but take him seriously. I watched him take your buddy Checkers in a way would give you pause had you been there." That was still on Don's mind. The Secret Service angle. But their expertise was protection and limited law enforcement, like counterfeiting. Springer wasn't working for them, and even if he was, it wasn't their jurisdiction. He shouldn't be a problem in what he had planned unless he chose to be.

"Checkers is slow."

Shit, I'll tell you who's slow. Could you believe this? "He's also strong and tough and you weren't there to see it. Don't underestimate Springer." Thinking he should take his own advice.

Vince saying, "Sure," but rolling his eyes when he said it, and Don could see he wasn't convinced. Vince too obtuse to get it. What a waste of chemicals this guy was.

Hell, he was perfect for what Don had in mind.

Don told Vince there was a guy coming to town, a guy Red wanted Vince to meet and bring him in. "Name's Powers. Red sent for him and he's supposed to get here around three. Meet him and get him situated. He's a cowboy-looking guy, kind of rough but dresses like a Texas oilman. Used to be a bull-rider, then a rodeo clown, so he's used to being around animals. You won't have any trouble."

Vince holding one hand up by his head, saying, "Oh, so I'm an animal. That's the way it is, huh?" Acting like a little kid, hurt and sarcastic.

The phone on his desk rang. He picked it up. It was Diane.

"What is it, Diane?"

"I want to talk to you. Come over to my office."

"Are you summoning me, Diane? You know better.

I've got four o'clock open—" He heard the phone click and knew she had hung up on him.

Janzen looked at the phone, hung it up, looked at Vince, and shrugged.

Vince said, "Mrs. Janzen."

Janzen nodded.

The phone rang. Diane again. Without saying hello she said, "I must've hit the wrong button or something." Like she wasn't mad when she hung up. He wanted to tell her she always knew exactly what she was doing but didn't want to get into an extended argument with her. She said, "I know you're trying to get Sonny to sell you his percentage so you can use Streamers to leverage that land deal you have going, but I'm not going to allow it."

"Diane," said Don, winking at Vince, "why would I do that? I need the money, I can get it anywhere. I don't need to place a lien against Streamers. You'll benefit from this, too, and you know that. There's no percentage in fighting with each other with this on the table. Come on, you know me."

"I do know you. That's why I'm calling you. We'll talk about this later."

She hung up and Don put the phone down.

"That one," said Vince, making a face. "One ball-bustin' bitch. Am I right?"

See? Even a guy like Vince knew it.

EIGHT

Springer was losing at blackjack. He always lost at blackjack, so why play it? You were at the mercy of the draw. Poker was his game. It was a game of skill and nerve, so he liked it better, but he didn't like to sit that long smelling cigarette smoke, and the company at the nonsmoking tables was boring. He played blackjack because it was a faster game and easier to get out when the cards went cold.

At 8:50 P.M. Detective St. John showed up, looking sharper than a chorus line in a smart one-piece that set off her cinnamon-colored skin. Voices were chattering and chasing each other, the slots whistling and clanging, the casino electric with movement and humming the multicolored rhythms of Vegas nightlife, which was pretty much the same as the daytime life. Tara St. John was an exotic, the type of striking creature men would follow with their eyes and women would watch out of the corner of theirs. Springer betting she was more interested in being thought a good cop than a beautiful woman. She would be a cop first, then a woman—but a titleholder at both. Springer cashed in and went with her.

Springer said, "This an official visit?"

"Depends."

"It is, the uniform's changed."

"We're through with the badge and ribbon-striped pants. It's been done."

He gave her an up-and-down, thinking it was nice to have an excuse to be able to examine her. Looking at her wasn't a bad way to spend an evening. "Where do you hide a gun in that?"

"What if I can handle you without it?"

"Willing to chance it if you are."

She exhaled and placed her tiny tongue between her teeth. Her breath smelled of mint, her skin of soap and perfume. "I don't know if I'm ready for you. I don't do things like this."

"Hang out with potential witnesses in murder cases?"

"You're not really a potential witness. I meant dating. I don't do it very often."

He smiled, feeling good. "Me, either."

"Liar," she said, setting her perfect teeth in a line.

"Thought I'd start off with one. Keep in practice. Caught it right off, huh?"

"I'm a trained professional. Hard to fool."

"Might be fun trying."

"Hmmm," she said, her hand touching her throat. They moved to a horseshoe-shaped bar and he asked what she was drinking, she said vodka martini and he nodded to the waiter and got her one. He ordered another Scotch.

"I find myself wondering what I'm doing seeing a lady cop. You're probably wondering, too." She said nothing. "I can look around and find women who are not in law enforcement. You're a homicide detective and—"

"You're an ex-cop," she said, finishing it.

"Pseudo cop. More like a palace guard. Mostly

I stood around and played games in my head so I wouldn't go crazy. It's sort of like being on a stakeout, only wearing a suit." Nodding at her. "Long periods of inactivity. Kind of like my love life." She smiled and he liked that he could get her to do that. "You too busy to date?"

"Too picky, maybe."

"Maybe if I'm charming enough you'll drop your standards tonight."

She took a tiny sip of the martini. "We'll see."

He was thinking of something else to say when he saw Diane Masters—funny he thought of her with her maiden name—walking toward them. This ought to liven up the evening. He wasn't making much headway about what happened to Jesse Robinson, but he was attracting attention. Ironic that everyone thought he was looking for Jesse's killer when actually he was looking for Jesse. Wasn't having much luck, either. It was why he wasn't forthcoming about the one fact he had no one else had—that Jesse wasn't dead—or at least he wasn't the corpse they had. Still, he didn't know what good he was doing. Maybe he should go into the investigation business. Work for people who weren't result-oriented. If you didn't want to discover anything, he was the guy for the job.

But the police didn't roust him without direction from above, and then there was Vince and the two thugs last night, wondering to himself who sent them. His first thought was Don Janzen, but it could've been someone had information about Robinson, maybe the killer, who didn't want him around. He gave some thought to Sonny Parker, but dismissed it as too amateurish for Parker. Parker wanted him gone, he would've sent more convincing help. Not Parker then. Janzen. Or someone else. But things were picking up. It kept up, he might even accidentally learn something.

Then there was the other possibility. Red Cavanaugh. Cavanaugh had never forgiven him for his car-in-the-fountain trick. More evidence that Cavanaugh didn't have a sense of humor. Then, as now, Cavanaugh sent a couple of his "employees" to entreat Springer to leave town. Not because of the car, but because Springer wanted his ten thousand dollars and wouldn't back off. The two men Cavanaugh sent told him Red wasn't paying and they got forceful about it, so Springer broke one guy's jaw with a phone receiver and knocked two teeth out of the other guy with an elbow. The elbow shot left a small half-moon scar in Springer's elbow.

This seemed to upset Cavanaugh even more, so he had sent someone around again, not muscle this time, to tell Springer to get out of Vegas and stay gone. Springer had been back since, but he didn't take the warning lightly.

Diane said, "Two nights in a row. What a delight." She turned toward Tara. "Well, Tara, it's good to see you again. How's Michael?"

"You know, tall, good-looking, best in town at what he does."

"Are you here with my friend Cole?"

Tara, a cool lady, he could tell, said, "Not exactly." Diane smiled, then Tara said, "However, I'm considering the possibility of leaving with him."

Diane's smile ebbed ever so slightly before flashing the look that had launched a thousand daydreams. "Leaving with him? Well, you won't have to go far. Cole is staying with us." Saying it in a way that carried more suggestion than the words themselves. That was Diane Masters Janzen. "He can be a handful, don't you think?"

"I like a challenge."

"Well, good luck with that."

Springer felt like he should say something here but didn't know what it would be. Might be better to say a lot without saying much. Kind of liked watching, though.

"Mrs. Janzen—," Tara began.

"Call me Diane. Please."

"All right. Diane, did you know Jesse Robinson?"

Diane's hand went to her diamond necklace. "Is this an official visit?"

"You know, that's the same thing I asked her," said Springer. Tara gave him a shut-up look that was better than summer lightning.

"Hardly official," said Detective St. John, "but I wanted to come around and ask about it and thought now was as good a time as any."

"Yes, I knew Jesse, but I haven't seen him in years."

"When did you last speak with him?"

"I told you. Years." Getting edgy now. Diane preferred to be in control, not liking to be on the defensive. Diane was a baseball player, she'd be the designated hitter. Now Tara tapped a perfectly manicured finger against her lips. "So, you went to high school with a man that you never spoke to even though you both live in the same town. You're sure?"

"It's a big town," said Diane.

"Not really. I'd say Los Angeles was big, Denver and Chicago are pretty good sized, even Salt Lake City is of a size, but Vegas is a relatively small city. I bump into people all the time. You ever notice if he came into your casino?"

"I would've noticed that, yes."

"Well, he was in here, twice, in the week before he . . . disappeared."

"How do you know that?"

"That's the job, Diane. Noticing things."

"Well, if he was here, I missed him. I don't have

time to talk to or see every customer that comes around."

"I've been watching you and you seem to move about the place and don't seem to miss a thing. But you missed Jesse. That could happen, I suppose. Hard to understand, though. First, you knew him, and second, he was black. I'd think he'd be hard to miss, but I don't know much about the casino business. Maybe you're looking for other things when you're on the floor." Tara looked around the casino. "Not many of the brothers here tonight, I notice."

"Well, I didn't see him."

"What about your husband?"

"Ex-husband. You know my ex-husband, don't you?" Something else in that, crackling in the air like static electricity. Springer didn't miss it.

"Do you think your ex-husband has been in contact with Robinson within the past, let's say, month or so?"

"I'm not in his confidence, so you'll probably need to ask him."

"I will."

"Am I excused?"

Tara laughed and said, "I'm not detaining you, Diane."

"How kind of you. Well, enjoy your evening and let us know if there's anything we can do to make your experience more enjoyable." In hostess mode again. You blinked, Diane could change on you. "Have a nice evening. Good to see you again, Cole. Stop by the office later, I have some more on that situation you were asking about."

She left them.

He whistled lowly. "I don't think she likes you all that much. What do you think?"

"She doesn't like it I'm here with you, either, does she?" said Tara.

"And yet, I continue to live."

"Are you seeing her?" asked Tara, suddenly becoming Detective St. John again.

"Old girlfriend. Everybody's old girlfriend, actually. Jesse Robinson's also."

"Really?"

Springer nodded, said, "Who's Michael?"

"He's my brother. He used to work here before the Wicked Witch of the West had him canned. What about you?" Tara cocked her head to the side. The sounds of the casino filled the silence. "Her disposition suggests she thinks your relationship is more recent. And what is this 'situation' she mentioned?"

Springer sipped his Scotch. "Something I tell you, maybe you start acting prosecutorial all over again."

"Jesse Robinson?"

"Could be."

"I think you should be more forthcoming."

"Why ruin the evening?"

"How about you? When was the last time you spoke with Jesse Robinson?"

"I already told you that."

"Tell me again."

So he did.

She said, "You hadn't seen or talked to him since."

"Nope."

"And yet, here you are. Why are you so interested in this man you hadn't seen in years?"

"Told you that, too." Boy, was this woman ever a cop.

"There's something else there, something you're not telling. Do you feel guilty about Jesse's death?"

He was thinking maybe he would feel guilty if that had been Jesse's body lying there in the morgue. He hadn't seen Jesse in years, not since the time years ago when Jesse seemed different, more worldly, not the guy who used to sneak into the movies free and go to the 49ers games so they could watch Montana throw to Rice. Nothing he was hearing sounded like the person he'd known. But then the body on the slab wasn't Jesse, either.

He said, "You want to know what I know about Jesse Robinson and I want to know what you know about Jesse Robinson. And I want to know about you."

"So, what is it you want to know?"

"I want to know what's going on here with the Janzens. Maybe there's a connection to Jesse." He wanted to know about Sonny Parker and Don Janzen. Something was up with them. Was he poking at something they wanted left alone? How had he managed to rub somebody the wrong way? Right now, he wanted to know what made this lady smile, what she looked like in blue jeans hiking up a trail.

"Join the club," she said.

"Here's something. Last night I was accosted by three thugs in the parking lot." That was interesting to her, he could see it. "So I'm asking myself why that is."

"Robbery?"

"Nope. Told me to get out of town by sundown."

"They said it like that?"

"Not exactly, but it's fun to say it that way. I'm telling you I was lucky to get out of there without sustaining multiple contusions. Two of the guys bench-press twice what I weigh."

"How'd you manage to get out of that?"

"I'm two yards of molten lava." He smiled at her. "Here's something for you, maybe. Janzen sent a guy around, wants me to come out to his fitness center tomorrow."

"So?"

"He doesn't like me."

"You do have a way about you. Anything else?"

"You want to see my room?"

Big smile now. "Maybe. Maybe I'm not that kind of girl."

"It's got a sauna and a beautiful view of the Strip."

"I don't think so."

"Another time then?" he said.

She shrugged and gave him a look. "We'll see."

Well, she didn't say no.

Vince, using his cell phone, made the call he'd been waiting to make, telling his man, Nicco, what was what. Nicco not so sure. Vince, to reassure him, was saying now, "The man trusts me. You worry too much, baby. He thinks I'm just a punchy ex-boxer he can talk down to. I'll cover this end."

"What if something goes wrong? Then what?"

"Part of it, bro. Do something relaxing. Get drunk or stoned or something and wait on the word. You just do as I tell you and it will work out. You wanna be rich, you gotta roll the dice, baby. It's like boxing; you know what you can do and maybe you don't know what the other guy can do, so you just step into it."

Vince snapped the cell phone shut and walked down the street to buy a drink, feeling good about himself. "Fuck Janzen. Cavanaugh, too."

NINE

Springer tried to call Nate again, but no answer. Springer wondered if he was staying at his sister's house. She lived in Denver. Couldn't remember her last name but it would come to him. Even if he wasn't there, maybe she could get hold of Nate for him. Springer could leave now, he knew that. But first he wanted to know where Jesse was. Besides, he didn't want to go back and face Tobi just yet. Aspen would be lonely without her.

He hung up the phone, pulled a Red Stripe out of one of those college-boy refrigerators hotels stocked so they could take inventory and charge you for what you drank, thinking first how handy it was and then maybe too handy. Everything in Vegas was handy.

The phone rang.

"Hello."

"Hey, Springs, guess who this is?"

He knew. It was funny; he wasn't surprised when he heard Jesse's voice. Like he expected it. "You sound just like a guy I know couldn't field a ball of yarn wearing a Velcro glove. Now, he can't even get dead right. How hard can it be? Where are you, Jesse?"

"That the way you start a conversation with your main man? 'Where are you?'"

"How about this instead? Who's lying on a slab at the morgue with your name on the toe tag?"

"I don't know. Some black guy about my height, I guess. You thought it was me?"

"Knew it wasn't you when I saw the body."

"How?"

"Guy looked too good."

Springer heard him laugh. Jesse Robinson said, "Thing is, whoever did it thought it was me. That's why I'm keeping a low profile. It sucks, babe. Have to stay inside, not give any the local bitches a chance."

"Tell me where you are and I'll come over."

"Okay," Jesse said. "You tell Pop it wasn't me?"

"Haven't been able to get hold of him."

"Don't tell him just yet. They get me, there's no use upsetting him twice."

Jesse was staying out at the Super 8 on Boulder Highway, close to Lake Mead. He was sitting by the pool with a cooler full of beer beside him. There were a couple of decent-looking females sunning themselves, one of them facedown, her top loosened in the back so she wouldn't have a tan shadow. "Being dead ain't so bad, Springs."

"Doesn't anyone here recognize you? Your picture was in the paper."

"All us black guys look alike, bawse."

"Except for the ugly ones. You guys stand out."

Jesse offered him a beer; Springer accepted it and sat down on a lounge chair. It was hot even in shorts and a T-shirt. Springer's T-shirt said "Colorado University" on it. Casual today. Springer sipped the beer, put his elbows on his knees, and looked at Jesse.

Jesse said, "You got a pretty good tan, Springs."

"I golf. Some hiking. You've got a pretty good tan yourself."

"Yeah, been working on it since the day I was born. Seems like I don't hardly have to do nothin' and it just come along fine by its own self."

Springer looked over the top of the motel complex, into the bright sunshine. He squinted.

"Good to see you alive, Jesse."

Jesse smiled, again. "Yeah, it's good to see you, too, man. Specially now. And I ain't kidding."

They talked about people they knew, about high school and the baseball team. About NFL football. Two old friends drinking beer and taking in the sunshine.

"I been thinking about splashing water on that one girl," said Jesse. "See what she got when she jumps up."

"Why don't you just go ask her for a look?"

"Been thinking 'bout that, too."

Springer said, "Jesse, what the hell have you gotten yourself into?"

"Man, I don't know. But whatever it is, it's sure pissing people off."

Springer wasn't sure he believed Jesse didn't know. Jesse was smart. Springer asked him about Chewy, Jesse telling him that pimp motherfucker got mouthy with a lady I was with and then got to mean-mugging, but nothing came of it. Telling him to back off or Chewy would have to change his nickname. Springer asked him about what he was doing for a living, and Jesse said he was speculating.

"On what?"

"Land. Do some gambling. Own some rental property."

"People are telling me you're in the extortion business."

"Who's telling that?"

"Doesn't matter. Are you?"

"That's why you came, to make insinuations about me?"

"No, I came because your father's made himself sick mourning over you and believing in you. He thinks you're not a criminal."

"I'm not." Jesse sitting up now, crossing his arms.

Springer shrugged, gave a nod to his left.

Jesse said, "You think I'm a criminal? That it?"

"Are you blackmailing the Janzens?"

"Why's it called blackmailing? Why's black got to be the operative word?"

"How about it on the evasive bullshit, Jesse? I've been threatened twice since I've been in Vegas and it makes the visit stressful. I don't know why I'm being threatened. You going to answer the question or not?"

Jesse looked down at the beer in his hand, chewed on the corner of his mouth. "I had a business here. Good business. Men's clothing. Was doing good, too, making it. Wasn't no millionaire, but I could afford a nice place in a good neighborhood, go out when I wanted, date nice ladies. Anyway, I got squeezed out. Couple years ago. Investment syndicate's buying up stuff and wants to buy my place. I don't want to sell. Kinda people not used to hearing no. Price wasn't bad, but I liked what I was doing, you know. Next thing I know, I start getting ordinanced by the zoning commission, OSHA people coming down on me. I fight through that, and then somebody comes by, throws shit through my window. I'm not talking they threw a rock through my window, like that. I'm saying, after breaking my window they threw cow shit into my store, man. Stinking cow flop." Shaking his head at the thought.

"Then came the phony assault charge, the dope

charge. I don't do drugs, Springs. You know that. I take care of myself. Beer's the worst thing I put in my body. Two cops—"

"Madison and Sullivan."

"Yeah." Jesse leaned his head back and looked at Springer. "Anyway, people stop coming into my place, the Gaming Commission puts me on suspension, tells me I can't go in the casinos for a year. I'm a criminal, the casino people're not supposed to consort with me. Shit like that." He stopped, looking at Springer now, his face angry. Springer stayed impassive, waiting him out.

"And, fuck you, Springer. What do you know? These people be fuckin' with me so I just be fuckin' 'em back."

"How're you doing that?"

"Man, I don't know if I trust you."

"Maybe you ought to rethink that. Eventually you've got to get your life back. If you're right, and somebody killed a man thinking it was you, then what happens they find out they killed the wrong guy?"

"Yeah, I thought about that."

"And what were you going to do about it?"

"I don't know."

"Maybe there's a way out of this."

"Yeah? What way?"

Springer shrugged, looked at the two girls basking in the hot sunlight.

Jesse said, "You?"

"Why not?"

"You and me?"

Springer shrugged again.

Jesse got out of his chair, walked to the side of the pool and dove in. He swam to one end of the pool and back. He got out and walked to his chair, dripping onto the concrete, leaving a damp trail behind him.

"It was hot," said Jesse. Springer looked up at him. Jesse ran his hands back through his hair, slicking the water out, saying now, "I've been blackmailing Diane Janzen for the past year."

That caused Springer to raise his head. "For what?"

"Why is a better question."

"Okay, why?"

Jesse sat down. "Because when I looked into this financial syndicate drove me out of my place, I found Don and Diane fingerprints all over things."

Springer got another beer out of the cooler. Two in the early afternoon, plus the one back at his room. He opened it and looked at the sweat beading on the can. "You think they were behind it?"

Jesse nodded. "Sure. So I'm taking them down if I can. So Diane pays me."

"How's that?"

"Something that happened."

"What?"

"I can't tell you, man."

Springer laughed to himself. "What'd she do? Father your child?" Jesse looked at him, panic in his eyes. "Oh, no," said Springer. "You're kidding."

"Man, I didn't say nothing."

"When did this happen?"

"Springs, I told you I'm not gonna say what I got on that woman. Besides, how I know you not still pissed off about me taking her from you?"

Springer didn't say anything.

"Dammit, Springs, you a bastard. Digging into things, you gonna mess everything up. I didn't ask for your help, you know."

"No, you didn't. Your dad did."

Jesse stopped and he looked off toward the building.

Springer said, "You want to go to prison or end up dead, that's your business. Nothing to me. But it does mean something to Nate, and Nate means something to me."

Jesse set his mouth, his teeth clenched. He pointed his thumb at his own chest and said, "So, what am I?"

"That's the other reason, Jesse. You're my friend. I don't want you screwing your life up, but I'm not going to force myself on you."

"What can you do?"

"Two's better than one. I know you're brave and I know you're tough. Seen it. The times base runners were trying to take you out. I'd flip the ball to you and you'd stand in, make the throw, and take the hit."

Jesse was smiling now. "Yeah." Nodding his head thinking about it. "Seen you do the same."

"Teamwork is everything."

He slapped at a gnat. "I've got something on them. Something juicy. It'll fuck 'em up. Better than the other thing I had. They not sure I got it, but I do." Springer giving him a look. "Yeah, I had something else, but this is better. Or worse, I guess, since they into killing over it rather than paying."

Springer nodded, didn't say anything. Swallowed beer. No use pushing Jesse. Jesse was smooth and would come to it when he was ready, just like when you tossed the ball waist-high over second base without looking. Jesse would be there. A safe bet.

"How come you not pressing me about why I'm blackmailing these people?"

"You'll tell me," Springer said. "When you're ready."

"Maybe I just like being a thug and shaking them down."

"I don't care. They're trying to kill you, and it offends me."

Jesse's eyes softened and glistened. His mouth was working. "These are some tough people," he said.

"What fun would it be if they weren't?"

Jesse was laughing now. "Oh, Springs, you my boy. Damn. We might just be able to pull this off."

"Even if we can't, it'll be something to do."

"I'm broke, too."

"Might be able to do something about that, too, you don't mind shaking down a few small-time criminals."

"Let me think on it some. I'm in room 107," pointing with his finger. "Over there."

"Sure," said Springer, getting up.

"Springs?"

Springer turned around. "Yeah."

"She gave the kid away. Didn't even ask me. She never told me until he was grown I had a boy. He won't talk to me, thinks I ran out on him. What she told him. Then, her and her man drove me in the ground like I was something stuck to the bottom of their shoes."

"You tell Nate?"

Nate shook his head. "Pop don't know. You know how he is, into Jesus and all. Hurt him too bad knowing he's got a grandson he didn't know about and can't go see."

"You don't give him enough credit maybe. Catch you later, buddy."

As he was leaving, Springer walked by the young lady with the top off and splashed water on her. She jumped up, calling him a name. Jesse, across the pool, held up a beer and said, "Thanks, bro."

"Teamwork," said Springer, lifting a hand above his shoulder, without looking back.

Two o'clock Thursday afternoon, Springer showed at the Desert Fitness Center and was led to a large room that had hardwood floors, mats, and large windows. Hearing the clash of steel zipping and singing as he walked into the room. The girl that had led him up pointed toward a man in a powder-blue body suit that she said was Mr. Janzen. Off to one side, Vince was working on a speed bag, making it blur like the spokes on a bicycle going downhill.

Janzen was fencing, dueling Springer guessed, with another guy in white tights. Both were advancing and retreating, parrying and thrusting, neither saying anything, the only sounds the shuffle of shoes on the floor and the jingle-clink of the épées and the speed bag beating a rhythm.

Invited Springer here so he could see it, always wanting you to be impressed, that was Don. The kind of guy back in school always had the best clothes, the most expensive baseball glove, and wanted you to know it. Springer could remember Don getting a new aluminum bat, Don telling him and the other guys not to touch it or he'd be pissed and somebody wouldn't like what happened after that. So, with Don on second base, Springer picked up Don's bat, weighing it and waving out to Don on second, and went up to hit. Don looking angry and gesturing, kicking at the base and pursing his lips. Then Springer smiling at the guys in the dugout before he stepped up to the plate and singled Don home. That was fun, especially when the coach got on Don for complaining about somebody driving in a run. Afterward, in the dugout, Springer telling Don that deep down he knew Don was a team guy, willing to make the sacrifice for the team. He could remember Jesse laughing, throwing his head back, slapping his hands together and telling Springer he was one crazy motherfucker.

Now, Janzen feinted with his épée and made a thrust that touched his opponent on the chest. Janzen removed his protective mask and shook hands with the other man, who left the room.

"You ever fence?" he asked Springer.

"Never liked digging the holes."

Janzen smiled thinly, then placed the button of his épée against Springer's chest, Springer looking down at it, then up. "Touché, Don."

"Would you care to try your luck?"

The noise of the speed bag stopped and Vince walked up to them. "Or perhaps you'd care to try your luck with the gloves on?" Vince said.

Springer looked back and forth between them. "How about," he said, looking at Don, "I spar with you"—shifting attention to Vince—"and duel with you?" He spread his hands as if to punctuate the question.

"Vince's not too bad with a sword in his hands."

Springer said, "Might as well be good for something."

"You," said Vince, slapping a gloved hand against his thigh. "I hardly know you and I don't like you."

"Tastes vary. What did you call me down here for, Don? I mean, now that I've seen your flashing blade and Vince got to scare me, can we get to it? You made the appointment."

"You said you wanted to ask about Jesse."

"I do," he looked at Vince again. "But not in front of the kids."

Vince said, "Keep talking, big shot."

"Aw, develop a sense of humor, huh?"

"You better watch your mouth, baby, before things happen to you."

"Now I don't know if I can even talk, what with my chin quivering and all."

"You think you can talk this way 'cause we're in a public place. That it? You think I'm the kind of guy likes that shit?"

"I don't think about you at all. Things'll go better

you stop thinking about me." Vince was staring at him and Springer met it without blinking.

"Vince," said Janzen, "why don't you see about getting me and Springer a couple of bottles of water? Okay?"

Vince shot a look at Janzen and then, as if deciding something, slammed his gloves together in Springer's direction. Springer made a show of brushing the back of his hand. Vince left. Janzen removed his fencing gloves and led Springer to a table near the huge windows. The view was the distant desert, heat shimmers rising up in the distance.

"I wouldn't bait Vince, I were you," said Janzen.

"Passes the time."

"Don't enjoy it too much."

"He's a cheap bully who wears his tough-guy image like a badge that gains him access to other people's lives. Guys like him are always surprised when someone brushes them back from the plate."

"You like Vegas?" he asked.

"Less than some places. You ever talk to Jesse?"

"Couple years ago. Why?"

"What've you heard?"

"Like I said, not much."

"You have any business dealings with him?"

"Why would I?"

"The word I'm getting is that you took the time to run him out of business. Why would you do that?"

Janzen smiled and wiped the back of a wrist across his eyebrows. "You always were creative. I don't see any reason to entertain your imagination. Where did you get information said I had anything to do with Jesse's business downturn?"

A college girl brought two bottles of water and plastic glasses. Janzen thanked her and she left.

Springer said, "Night before last, three thugs tried to run me out of town. You know anything about that?"

"Why would I know anything about that?"

"Hell, I'm just stumbling around trying to find things out. It's your town. Maybe these guys work for you. Reason I ask is that Vince, who works for you and was there, seems to find me objectionable and his dislike seems to meet with your approval, you know, kind of like somebody with an attack dog that isn't chained. Honest businessmen don't usually hang around with thugs. Now, I don't care if he doesn't like me, and I don't care if you don't like me, but I draw the line at being told to leave town as a threat rather than a reasonable request. And I'm getting sick of Vince, too. He keeps acting tough around me, I'll stick him in a culvert."

"You think you can do that?"

He shrugged.

"Aw, Springs, come on." Giving him the smooth salesman act now. "You know I like you. I don't know what you want me to say. Vince doesn't like many people, so there's nothing to be read into it. He's socially retarded. I'll talk to him, okay? As for the men who attacked you, I don't know about that. Did you report it to the police? No, you wouldn't, would you. Not you. Not your way, is it? Why not ask Vince who sent him? And what reason would I have for running Jesse out of business, whatever that business was?"

"You tell me. Jesse lived here the last five years, so I think you would've run into him or talked to him or heard something about him. But you and Diane both act like he's invisible. And I believe maybe you had cause to wish him harm."

"You're delusional. I told you, I did talk to him, a

couple of years ago." He brushed at something on the sleeve of his fencing suit. "Look, let's get to the reason I wanted to see you. You're here because of Jesse's dad. Can't remember his name right now—"

"Nate."

"Yeah, that's right. Nathaniel Robinson. I remember him at the games. Never said much except when Jesse would do something his dad would call embarrassing."

"Not embarrassing. Jesse didn't embarrass his father. Nate didn't like it when Jesse didn't keep his composure. He thought it was undignified. Nate's a man of integrity. Look the word up sometime."

"Listen, I don't know who killed Jesse and I don't think we'll ever know."

"We'll see."

"But I can tell you this, and it'll make Nate feel better. Jesse wasn't a criminal. Tell him that."

Which is what Springer had told Detective St. John, and now Janzen was mentioning it. And after telling Springer he hadn't talked to him for two years, Janzen was saying he knew Jesse wasn't a criminal. Why would Janzen say that?

"I will tell him that," Springer said. "So, why did you ask me here?"

"Look, Springs. Things are at a sensitive juncture here. People, important powerful people, are involved, and they aren't happy to have you around."

"You want me to leave town, that it?"

He cocked his head, looking like he didn't wish to say.

Vince returned, showered and dressed in slacks, his cheeks bright with health and shower heat, still focusing his street-tough glare on Springer. He wasn't very good at it. "Anytime you want to strap the gloves on, you know, be a man, I'll be around. You won't always have your gun handy. Then we'll see."

Springer looked at Janzen and raised his eyebrows. There was a dueling mannequin, a padded dummy with a heart-shaped target on its chest that Janzen probably used to practice thrusting his sword. Springer stood, reached into his pocket and brought out the .32 Tomcat, sighted in on the mannequin, and squeezed the trigger. The crack of the small weapon was sharp in the large room, echoing and fading.

"Dammit, Springer," said Janzen. "Are you deranged?"

"You're fucking crazy, man," said Vince, his nostrils wide, the whites of his eyes showing.

"See, I will shoot." Springer said, "And, I'm always ready for guys like you, Vince. Think you can remember that?"

"I'll see you again."

"You're not careful, you'll see me one time too many."

TEN

Detective St. John found Springer coming out of the fencing club in midafternoon. She was a little upset. Did he know? He smiled when he saw her.

"I've been looking for you," she said.

Smiling at her now, being a smug jerk. Like he was thinking, yeah, you and a hundred other women. But now she was thinking the smile wasn't as smug as it was playful.

"The man who was murdered isn't Jesse Robinson."

"Wow," he said.

"You don't seem too upset." Trying to look into those roadblock eyes now. "Or surprised."

"Why be surprised? You're good at what you do."

"You knew."

"Body was too beat up for me to tell."

"Bullshit."

"Okay, I knew it wasn't him."

"I want to talk to you. Officially."

"Anyone ever tell you you're cute when you're being official?"

She looked at him, letting him know the charm act wasn't playing.

"Okay," he said. "Do we have to stand here in the heat? You can glare at me inside just like out here."

Damn, he could be annoying.

So they walked to a nearby water hole and she ordered a Diet Dr Pepper and he ordered a beer. Good town for beer. He made a comment about the heat and she said, "Talking to you is like listening to talk radio. Lot of noise but you don't learn much. When did you know it wasn't Jesse?"

"Right away."

"Why didn't you say anything?"

He shifted in his seat, held the beer bottle between the fingers of both hands like he was going to give it a spin. "Nothing to gain by telling you. Besides, maybe Jesse's dead. I'm asking myself, if he's still alive, why not come forward to clear this up? You have any thoughts on that?"

"Maybe he's scared."

"Maybe he doesn't know anything about it. Could be out of town. Who knows?"

"You do," she said. "You know more than you're telling. Where's Jesse Robinson, Cole?"

"Let's pretend I know where he is. I tell you, I'm just going to have to tell everyone, and I'll get worn out doing it. Then you're going to want to talk to him. Why do you want to talk to him? I don't understand that. He hasn't committed a crime. And if he's still in danger and you talk to him, then the bad guys'll know he's alive and maybe try again." He turned a palm up on the table. "Naturally, this is all hypothetical and has no practical application in the present circumstances." He smiled at her, enjoying himself. She could see it.

"We could protect him if he needed it."

"How long? Round the clock until you found out who wants to kill him? Like he was protected when he was being run out of business? Who would you assign? Those two idiots pulled me over? Madison and Sullivan? No, we both know how it works. After a while your department would pull people off him, and then what?"

She stood and looked down at him. "I think you like having power over people by hoarding information. You like being obscure and clever. Laughing at people on the inside. But you're cynical about others. You know, Cole, whether you want to believe it or not, there are still honest people in the world. One of these days maybe you'll trust one of them."

"You talked to Don Janzen about what I said." He said it flat, and she knew he meant it as an accusation. It didn't sound like a question to her. Where did that come from? Sometimes he could be a spooky man. Nothing you said ever knocked him back. He kept on whatever subject he was interested in, pulling rabbits out of his hat. What was he getting at here? She said, "Why do you say that?"

"Because I never told anyone but you about my intentions regarding Jesse, and Don mentioned it. So I put it together."

"Yes, I talked to him. I had to talk to him about Jesse. He knew him."

He was smiling now.

She said, "What?"

"So who likes having power over others?"

"I'm a police officer. Does that connect for you? I'm the person in charge of the investigation. Not you, not even if you have the background, not even if you're connected to the victim, who, as it turns out," a fist on her hip now, "is not really the victim. Right now I'm trying to understand why I'm even telling you this. I will say this. If you know where Jesse Robinson is, and you're withholding that information, I will burn you down."

"If he wasn't the victim, then his whereabouts, even if I knew of them and didn't tell you, isn't a crime. And you know that. So why're you so angry?"

"I'm not angry."

He laughed to himself, looked around the place, put his chin in hand, looked at her, and waited.

"Okay, so I got called in, told not to annoy people. I was advised to, quote, 'be more judicious in my line of questioning and more aware of disturbing people not directly involved in the investigation.'"

"The Janzens?"

"You're so perceptive. You must be clairvoyant."

"They called you in about talking to Diane Janzen?" He filed that away. Diane had some juice in town.

"My gut feeling is someone wants this swept under the rug." She made a sweeping hand with an arm.

"But you won't do that."

"No. And, don't get in the way of this. You screw me around and I'll put you inside with some other clever people."

"What are you doing Friday night?"

"You're asking me out?"

"Sure."

She was shaking her head now. Looking away with her eyes and exhaling. "Boy, you are something. I just threatened you with jail and now you want to go out with me? Why would I go out with you?"

He shrugged. "Because I've got a dazzling personality?" She gave him a look, and he said, "That not it? Could be because you're beautiful and I like beautiful women. Or maybe you should go with me because the date is a party at Sonny Parker's place and some people you're interested in, officially, will be there. Never hurts to learn more about people you're investigating."

"What makes you think I'm investigating the people there?"

"If you're not, you will be, eventually."

"You think there will be people there that know something about Jesse Robinson?" She placed an elbow in a hand and touched the corner of her mouth with a fingernail painted a light mauve color, which matched her shoes and bag. Thinking about it now.

"You coming along or not?"

"I'll think about it and let you know."

He said, "Anything else on your mind?"

"What the hell does that mean?"

"Something's not being said here. I think it'll go better between us if you're up front about it."

She was ready to turn around and leave him sitting there, wondering. But she decided to say something. It was a cheap shot, maybe, but she wanted to get a reaction out of him. Putting him off on Friday night didn't do the trick. Nothing seemed to move him off his mark. She wanted to sail one under his chin.

"Okay," she said. "I had an affair with Don. Before the divorce. I'm not proud of it, but it happened. Do you feel better now? Or worse?"

And she left him there, sitting behind his drink, and headed out into the sunlight. But she could still see his eyes—alive like a schoolboy's who'd just watched the teacher jump after sitting on the thumbtack he'd placed on her chair.

Powers rubbed his belly, walking out of the Lone Star, full of steak and beer. He got in the big Chevy pickup and drove across town to Streamers, but when the deskman rang the room nobody answered. He asked where Mr. Janzen was and they told him he was usually at his workout club in the afternoon. Powers got the directions and headed across town listening to

Dean Martin singing on the stereo. Liked the way the guy sang. Wanted to ask Janzen where he thought this Springer dude would be. They'd given him a picture, so he knew what he looked like.

He stopped the truck in the parking lot and saw the guy they'd told him about, Springer, talking to a black girl, kind of a high yellow actually. Good-lookin' woman, Caucasian face, everybody mixing things up nowadays. In her case it worked out. She looked mad and walked off. The Springer guy, got in his car and drove back toward town. Powers followed him.

Springer saw the man, one of those big thick-bodied guys, get out of a dual-tired Chevy pickup, and walk toward him, Springer wondering what he wanted. Guy was all shoulders and long legs, wearing a dress-up Stetson and an expensive western-cut business suit.

"Hey, partner," the cowboy said, pushing back the front of the Stetson with a thumb, "got a minute? I'm not from around here and I'm looking for the Stardust. You know where that might be?"

He was thinking how to tell him when the man walked up and sucker punched Springer right in the breadbasket, Springer not seeing it in time, and the impact doubled him over. The cowboy produced a leather sap and snapped it between Springer's shoulder blades, Springer feeling the pain pulsate down his spine and into his thighs. His legs buckled and he shrank to the pavement. The cowboy kicked him sharply in the ribs with the pointed toe of his cowboy boots. Springer gasped.

Springer tried to cover up, but the man cracked him on the point of the shoulder with the sap and Springer's arm went numb. He tried to kick at the man but missed, and the cowboy, quicker than he looked, stomped his knee. The cowboy grabbed a handful of hair and jerked Springer's face up close to his, Springer sucking his breath in.

"Don't listen good, do you, partner? You have trouble paying attention in school?" Springer could smell the mixture of aftershave and tobacco juice, rank in his nostrils. "You were asked, real proper and nice, to get outta Dodge. But, you're a cute boy, right? Don't have to do what you're told. So they sent me to ask again." He gripped Springer's hair tighter and shook his head like a rag doll and he could hear and feel hairs ripping along his scalp. "You listenin' to me, boy? You better. This time, ol' pard, you get the message or I come back. And I'll do this again. Next time it'll hurt. *Comprende?*"

Springer said nothing, trying to think how to get out of this jam.

The cowboy saying now, "I heard you're carryin' a popgun." He made a clucking noise in his teeth. "That's not neighborly. Where is it?"

"Don't have it on me," he said, between gritted teeth.

"Don't lie to me."

"Wouldn't think of it."

The cowboy cuffed him, playfully almost, on the ear. "You gettin' smart with me, boy?"

"Waste of time. I'd have to keep explaining it," said Springer, his eyes closed in pain.

The cowboy boxed him sharply behind the ear with his knuckles. Springer's vision spider-webbed into stars and lines with the impact. He felt the cowboy's hands on him, patting him down, searching him. He found the Beretta and held it up to Springer's face. "Oh," Springer said, choking the words out, "you mean that gun."

"Well, you sure got you some cojones, don't you? Talking back just like you were a swingin' dick, when

all you are's some city bitch can't hack it. Sort of respect that, but don't back-sass me again, son, or I'll
bust your spleen and you'll drown in your own blood.
I'll say it again, so maybe even a slow learner like you
can get it. You saddle the fuck up and ride into the
sunset and we won't have any need to talk again."

"I was leaving anyway." Tell him anything to make
it stop, he was thinking. It was taking an effort not to
start crying from the pain.

"Well, that's good to hear. You'n me, we be partners then. Whaddya think about that?"

Springer huffed and said, "What's it taste like when
you're blowing your pet goat?"

Springer felt a meaty hand pushing down on the
back of his neck and then the sun-heated pavement
crunching into his face, tiny pieces of grit grinding
into his flesh.

"That's some mouth you got on you, boy," the cowboy said, his laughter deep inside him like the grunt of
a bull. "You ain't in control here, which you don't
seem to be able to keep your mind settled on. One
more time, so clean the shit outta your ears and listen.
You're leaving town. That's all there is to it. Today. Or
tomorrow I'll be back to see you again and I'll hurt
you real bad instead of playing with you like now."

He twisted his hands in Springer's hair and turned
his face toward him and spat tobacco juice in his face.
It was pungent and clammy, running warm and rank
down his face.

Springer felt his anger rising and said, "I see you
again, I'll square this. Count on it."

The cowboy backhanded him and it felt like being
smacked with a sack of rocks. Springer tried to roll
with it and the big man kicked at him, aiming at his
balls, but Springer covered and rolled. The boot caught
him just above the pelvis, and the pain was electric.

The cowboy was kneeling now, one leg up, the other on the ground, a wrist on raised knee, his hand dangling casually. He pushed back the front of his Stetson, folksy, and said, "Well, I hate to leave when we're having so much fun, but there're things I gotta tend to." He pinched Springer's cheek between his thumb and forefinger and gave him a gentle shake. "I'll think about what you said. When you heal up, if you're still all fired up to get together again, let me know and I'll accommodate you. Adios, city boy."

Springer heard boots crunch across the pavement, then the pickup firing up and leaving. Glad he left.

Springer rolled over and sat up against his car, his left arm limp, trying to clear his head. He made a mental note to keep his mouth shut next time somebody was beating the hell out of him.

ELEVEN

Springer limped back to his room and, with an effort, peeled off his clothes and threw the damaged shirt in a wastebasket. He called down to room service and asked for ice, lots of it, and a fifth of Chivas, telling them to bring it in thirty minutes, no sooner, and started the shower. He stood under the torrent and felt it stinging the abrasions on his face and knees and hands. His knee felt like broken glass where the cowboy stomped it and the impact aggravated the cartilage damage.

He toweled off, wrapped the towel around his waist, and looked at his face in the mirror. His cheek and nose were raw and scraped and his head was jangling with pain behind his ear where the cowboy had hit him. He shook four Advil from the bottle and swallowed them.

He put on a pair of running shorts, gingerly, slowly tugging them up over the injured knee, and a T-shirt; his shoulder pulsing with tiny pinpricks of icy lightning, leaving him unable to lift one arm above his ribs.

The phone rang and Springer answered it. It was Nate Robinson. Jesse had told him his aunt's name and Springer had left a message for Nate to call him.

"What did you find out, Cole?"

"Nate, I want you to brace yourself for some good news. Jesse is alive and well."

The other end was silent for a moment, then Nate said, "Tell me you wouldn't lie to me to make me feel better. Tell me."

"I talked to him and he's fine. I've been trying to get hold—"

Springer heard a shriek of joy followed by, "Praise the Lord. Praise the Lord Jesus. Cole, you bring my boy to me. You hear me? Bring him to me so I can see him and touch him. Can you do that?"

"I think so. But I think it's possible he's still in danger, so I'll have to do it quietly."

"You just get him here. Get him here and I'll fight the devil himself. God bless you, boy. God bless you, Cole Springer. You're my true friend."

"I'll get him back to you, Nate." He hung up the phone and felt better about things.

The ice and Scotch arrived and Springer tipped the bellhop, the boy staring at the abrasions on Springer's face but saying nothing. In Vegas the help learned not to ask questions. Springer mixed up a tall Scotch and water and settled into a chair, placing his leg up on a table and icing the knee. He'd never been beaten like that before. The guy handled him like he was a child. It was chilling to know he could be handled so easily, so brutally. Something to think about. Something else he'd been thinking about, rolling around in his head like a marble in a glass bowl was the corpse that was mistaken for Jesse Robinson. Did the killer think it was Jesse, or was there another possibility? Maybe the killing was unrelated. And maybe there was a connection—one that was so obscure that no one saw it.

So far he'd managed to piss off someone who'd sent a sharp-dressed cowboy after him. If Jesse

Robinson wasn't dead and they knew it wasn't him, then why send muscle? If they thought they'd killed Jesse and found out they hadn't, would they be back to try again? Tara St. John was a young investigator. Maybe someone with influence had put her on the case hoping she'd fail—if that was their thought then they'd made a big mistake. She was going to keep probing and pushing until she found the killer. Would that put her in jeopardy?

After twenty minutes of icing the knee and shoulder he limped back into the bathroom, filled the tub, freshened his drink, and turned on the whirlpool. He slipped gingerly into the swirling water. It only felt wonderful.

Walking back into the room, the towel wrapped around his waist, there she was, sitting on his bed.

Diane Janzen. Wearing a terry-cloth robe, and it looked like that was all she was wearing. There was a pair of shoes on the floor beside the bed.

"Well, what happened to you?" she asked.

He looked at her for a moment and clutched his towel a little tighter. "How'd you get in here?"

"I own the place. I can get in anywhere."

"Hmm. Well, look, don't take this personally but I'm not in the mood for anything like . . . Well, I'm not in the mood for anything."

"You expecting the colored girl? That it?"

His head hurt. "Some other time, huh?"

"Sure," she said. She walked over to him and pressed herself against him and he could feel her breasts floating against his skin. It made his breath catch in his chest.

"There," she said. "That's just a harbinger of things to come. You get some rest and I'll come back later."

She left.

Vegas was getting to be a complicated place. But kinda nice.

An hour later, feeling better but far from copacetic, Springer heard a knock at his door. It was Sanborn Meeks.

"You look like you jammed your face in the garbage disposal," said Meeks. "What happened?"

"Nothing." He took another sip of the Scotch. His third.

"You drunk?"

"Working on it."

"Got any for me?"

"Help yourself. You got anything I can use?"

Meeks poured Scotch and looked thoughtful, as if deciding something. "Yeah. Something juicy. But it's going to cost you. Beaucoup bucks, babe. And there ain't gonna be any discount coupons on this one, either."

"Look, Sanborn. You're always wanting to do some detective work, right?"

"Yeah."

"Well, I got some for you. You tell me what you've got for me and I'll put you on the payroll, just like Jim Rockford. Give you a per diem and pay your expenses. It'll be better than scamming promiscuous wives."

"No shit?" He took a healthy swallow of the Scotch. "Sounds good. You're doing the right thing here. Nobody knows Vegas like Sanborn Meeks. Man, I can go places no one knows about. I'll have to get me a gun. One that's unmarked. I know somebody. We need to smoke anybody—"

"Hang on, Marlowe. We're not going to shoot anybody. We're just going to get somebody out of a jam. I need your eyes and your contacts. I need you for surveillance only."

"Sure, I can do that. But I can do much more than that."

"Look at me now, Sandy," Springer said, holding up a finger. "Are you listening to me?"

"Yeah, yeah, you got my ears, Springs."

"You'd better do exactly what I say. You got that?"

Sanborn put a hand out, palm up. "I'm listening, what the fuck?"

"Okay," said Springer. "Here it is. Your first directive. Don't detect anything. Okay?" Sanborn started to speak, but Springer stopped him. "Don't bother anybody. Don't ask any questions. No secret agent crap, no heroics, no kidding."

Sanborn's mouth was working into a disgruntled frown. "You know what, Springer? You're no fun sometimes, you know that? What is it? You ain't getting laid enough?"

The information Sanborn Meeks had was interesting and maybe even worth the price they had haggled over.

According to Meeks, there was a street buzz that a sham robbery was going to occur within a matter of days involving some big names in Vegas, but Meeks didn't have those names yet. It sounded like an insurance scam and Springer said so.

"They're going to make a claim on the money then double-dip by keeping the money that was stolen," Springer said. "Do you have an idea how much is involved?"

"Guy I talked to said seven figures. In cash."

That sounded like a casino robbery of some sort. But which casino? And who was involved? Robbing a casino only happened in the movies. It was like trying to break into the Pentagon. So maybe not a casino. What were the odds that Streamers and the Janzens were involved? Probably astronomical. But it might be worth intimating to them that he knew of this enterprise. If they weren't involved, they'd merely ignore him. But if they were . . .

"Your contact. He a player or just some small-time hood?"

"Name's Murphy. Calls himself Murph the Surf. Murph, he's not much, ya know? I mean, I know the guy for over five years and he's never been into anything big. He hustles, does favors, been up a couple of times for dipping some fat cat's wallet. That kind of thing. I can't figure why they'd use him."

Springer thought about that. Why use a small-time crook for a venture like this?

"Can you find out the people involved in this thing?"

Meeks was nodding his head like he was a bobblehead doll. "Maybe," he said. He rubbed his thumb across his fingers. "I got the know-how if you got the cash, baby."

"You're on the clock."

"This could be dangerous shit, man. I could use some hazard pay."

"What's hazardous is your attempts to shake me down."

"How about it, Springer? Shit. We're buddies, right?"

"Maybe I can do better than hazard pay."

"What's better?"

"What if you got to keep part of the take?"

"What, I'm a criminal now, right?"

Springer held up the Scotch bottle and Meeks held his cup out. Springer poured the Scotch and said, "Don't act offended. It doesn't work for you."

Detective St. John was concerned about the identity of the John Doe in the morgue previously thought to be Jesse Robinson. So who was this man? She didn't understand why they had been unable to ID the body and more striking was the fact that they had so readily accepted that it was Robinson. And where was Robinson? She figured Springer knew, but she would need some leverage to get him to say. Since Robinson was not dead and had no warrants out on him, there was no binding legal authority she could employ to force Springer to tell her the whereabouts of Robinson.

Now she was cursing herself for telling Springer about her affair with Don Janzen. It had been impulsive and vindictive on her part, and she didn't like it that Springer could get to her. The affair hadn't been much. Janzen was handsome and charming and going through a divorce. She'd been on the rebound from a long-term romance and was looking for comfort. Don was there, that's all. She called it quits after only two weeks.

She called down to the morgue and asked to meet with the ME who had performed the autopsy on the John Doe. She had called him before and he had begged off, saying he had other commitments. This time when she called she wasn't going to listen to it. When she got him on the line she told him, "I'll be there in ten minutes. Stay there." She hung up before he could protest.

The medical examiner was Dr. Milton Moore, a fiftyish man with bushy eyebrows and thick hair on his hands. Dr. Moore had been with Metro only a few weeks, he explained to her, and this was really a new line of work for him. He'd moved there from Detroit, thinking the desert heat would be good for his allergies. Besides, he'd grown tired of the cold Detroit winters, the wind blowing off Lake Huron.

"I want to know about the John Doe incorrectly identified as Jesse Robinson."

Dr. Moore rubbed the down on the back of a hand

and said, "I've only got a few minutes and then I have an appointment regarding another case."

She wasn't waiting for more excuses. "Why did we ID the corpse as Jesse Robinson?"

His eyes moved left as if lost in thought or as if choosing his words. "I'm trying to remember why that was. Oh, I remember now. It seems that he was wearing a necklace of a type that someone had identified as belonging to Jesse Robinson."

"Who was the person that identified the necklace?"

"I don't know. My job is to ascertain the cause of death. Affixing the individual's name is Metro's province."

"But you gave them the particulars. Height, weight, approximate age. I read the report and you have now amended your report. In the original report you say the corpse was a man in his early to midthirties and now you have changed that to"—she flipped over a page on her clipboard—"a black male in his midforties." She looked up and waited a beat, then said, "Why did it change, and how did you miss it so badly? I don't understand why a DNA print wasn't run."

"Not every person has submitted to a DNA print. We'd have to have a sample from Jesse Robinson and we don't." Dr. Moore's busy eyebrows knitted. "There has been much controversy on DNA. And, there were indications that the police knew the man."

"Who were the officers that thought they knew him?"

Dr. Moore held up a finger, saying, "Just a moment. It's actually one officer. I've got the name here someplace." Flipping through some pages. "Ah, here it is. The officer's name was Sullivan. Said he thought he knew the corpse. Does that help?"

"It would've saved a lot of trouble had we known it

wasn't Jesse Robinson. Is there anything else you can tell me about this person besides his approximate age and cause of death, which I already know about?"

"I can tell you that the necklace on the body had the initials J.R. inscribed on the back."

"Maybe his name was Jack Reed or Jerry Rankin."

"The assumption, I guess, is that that was enough corroboration for a preliminary identification. And I believe Mr. Robinson has not made an appearance to dispute that claim. Mrs. St. John—"

"Detective St. John," she said, correcting him. "And I'm not married and have never been married."

"I apologize. But I've done what I can without new information or a positive ID."

She knew that. Sullivan. That was interesting.

Tara St. John held up the black one-piece dress and looked at herself in the mirror. Not bad. Then she held up the gold evening gown. Girl, you look good, she was thinking, then smiling that she was acting vain. The big question was what to do with the gun. She was required, by department regs, to have her gun and badge with her at all times. So she always needed a bag big enough for the gun.

But this was a society party. Semiformal to casual dress, Springer said. She had a little five-shot Colt auto that didn't weigh much, and she could put it in her bag or wear it under a jacket. Too hot for a jacket this time of year. Anytime of the year in Vegas for that matter. She could wear slacks and a blouse outfit and place the weapon under the blouse. What a pain it was, sometimes, being a lady cop.

By the time Springer showed up, she had decided on a skirt and sleeveless shirt, the gun in her bag. She opened the door and was surprised by the abrasions on his face.

"What happened to you?" she said, as he stepped inside.

He reached up and touched his cheek. "What? You mean this?" He was smiling, like it was something funny happened. "This is nothing."

She looked at him and waited.

He said, "Long story."

"So give me the short version."

"They sent somebody to ask me to leave town again. Somebody better at it than before."

"Did you report it?"

"You know, if I didn't know better, I'd think I was pissing people off. But, you know, I'm usually more charming than this so I don't—"

"You didn't report this, did you? When're you going to learn to go through proper channels? This isn't the Wild West and you're not John Wayne."

"You got anything to drink? Is it always hot here?"

She blew air between her lips. Gave up. "There's beer in the fridge."

"Rather have a Coke."

She walked to the kitchen and brought back a red can. "Here. Now, I want you to report this incident. To me, if you have to."

"I'll do it if you'll let me kiss you."

She smiled, put a hand on her hip, and shook her head. This guy. "Maybe I don't want to kiss you."

"Sure you do. You've been wanting to do it since the first time you saw me."

"You're certainly sure of yourself, aren't you? What makes you think that?"

"I don't know. Maybe because I want to kiss you enough for both of us."

She cocked her head to one side and considered him. He *was* nice-looking and he was working her with those eyes of his. He was right, she did want him to kiss her, but even though she was a cop, she was still a woman and he could wait.

"Maybe later."

He fluttered a hand on his chest like his heart was breaking. What a clown.

"Guy was a pro. Big guy. Cowboy in a red Chevy pickup." He recited the license plate. She said, "Wait, I'll get a pen." He said she could write it down later but it wouldn't do any good. She asked him why that was.

He said, "Because he'll have a couple of guys that'll swear he was someplace else at the time of the assault. That's the way it works. You know that."

"But at least we could ID him and take him over the hurdles. Run him through NCIC and see what we come up with. Might help if we knew his name."

"That's not bad," he said, putting the Coke can down. "You ever think about getting into law enforcement?"

"Shut up and kiss me," she said.

"I don't know. It could lead to other things."

"Well," she said, pulling him toward her, "let's hope so."

TWELVE

"Whaddya think, Cas?" said Sonny Parker, from the walk-in closet. "I go with the blue suit? Or the tan?"

Cassie Parker said, "I like the tan, if you're talking about the bone-colored one which you call tan. It sets off your eyes."

"I still don't get it about the ice sculpture. How long you think it'll last in this heat."

"I know what you mean. It's so extravagant. But what good are you if I can't waste your money?"

"Another thing, I can't believe you invited Red Cavanaugh, that sack of shit, to be here tonight."

"Helps to see your enemies up close. Remember what Marlon Brando said, 'Know your friends, but keep your enemies close.' And I don't appreciate your language."

"That was Pacino said it. He was saying that his father, Don Corleone, that's who Brando was, said it."

"I guess I should trust you on gangster data." Playing with him.

"You take care of the caterers?"

"They're already here, dummy. You look outside the window, you'd know that."

"Always busting my balls. Why do that? You know I can have you iced for talking like that."

"Oooh, you're so sexy when you're acting the killer. But I prefer the hot tub, you big thug, you."

He'd never met anyone like Cassie before. She was gorgeous for one thing, but the town was full of gorgeous girls. No, that wasn't what made Cassie. Cassie was smart. Business smart. And savvy. She could read people like all the information was written down and handed to her. He put on the bone-colored suit and walked into the bedroom and put his arms out showing it to her.

She was looking at him in her mirror, making kissing noises now. "I could just eat you up, baby." She kept putting on her makeup.

"What did you think of Springer? You know, the guy came up to my card room the other night?"

She turned around to look at him. "He's something," she said. "I looked at the tape of him talking to you and the exchange with Vince. Vince's an idiot if he thinks the man's afraid of him. Of course, it's a given that Vince's an idiot. I'll tell you this much. Springer decided to be a poker player, he'd clean this town out. When he's not kidding around, he'll mean what he says. You can see it. But you can only go into him so far and then there's like a roadblock. He's affable. Knows he's charming. Confident. Underneath the nice-guy smile there's a dangerous guy inside. I wouldn't underestimate him. There's more there than he lets on. You want him on your side, I'll tell you that much."

"Can I trust him?"

She turned and checked her eyeliner. "I'll let you know after tonight."

When Springer and Tara showed at Parker's place, the night stars were sparkling like diamonds on velvet.

Springer was feeling pretty good, glad to have Tara with him. When he showed up at her place he could feel they were through playing games with each other and they were going a different direction with each other tonight. She said hello and he kissed her and she kissed him back and it went from there.

They had a couple of drinks afterward, her asking him why people liked to smoke after sex. He said he didn't know, because he didn't smoke but would remember to ask someone who did, and why ask, did she feel like smoking? She said no and laughed, first time he'd heard it. It was a nice laugh and it was good to hear.

On the way to Parker's she'd asked him if he could think of anything else that might be helpful in learning the identity of the cowboy assailant. He told her yeah, he's not from Vegas. Sounded like a Texan. Had that drawl, not Midwestern and not a Southern drawl but a hint of both. Could be an Okie, but he thought Texas. Dressed well. Western-cut suit. Dress Stetson, like the ones LBJ used to wear. More like a businessman than a cowboy but the cowboy underneath it all was unmistakable. She asked would he recognize him if he saw him and he said yeah, six-four, 240 pounds, blue eyes, dark brown hair, curly under the edge of the hat, a scar beneath his left jawline, one ear had a tiny piece missing, nose'd been broken more than a few times, two of his teeth had been replaced, knuckles on the right hand messed up from fighting or bull riding, stank of Brut aftershave, and was in his early forties.

She'd leaned back, looking at him sideways and said, "That's all you could remember? You should've paid better attention."

"Well, I've been out of practice."

Cassie, Parker's wife, greeted them when they

arrived. When she shook his hand, Springer noticed that she was giving him an appraising look. It wasn't sexual; it was more like someone checking produce at the grocery store or weighing something. She looked like a dancer or a stripper, but her eyes were intelligent. He was thinking people would see her and underestimate her.

He introduced Tara but Cassie knew her. "Hello, Tara. How are you tonight?"

Tara seemed happy to see her. They hugged and when they broke their embrace Cassie said, "I used to work for her brother at the Bellagio. Security."

He was looking at her. She laughed and said, "I was a dancer before that. Didn't like it much. No rhythm, but I had nice boobs. That's how I met Sonny." She put her hand to her mouth. "Oh," she said. "Not because of the boobs. I escorted him out of the Bellagio one night. He was being an asshole and it was my job to get him out. None of the others wanted to do it. He's still kind of an asshole, when you think about it, but kinda cute.

"Anyway, the way it went was I've got Sonny by the elbow, smiling sweetly at him, and he's telling me how I'm emasculating him in front of his friends. Real pissed off about it, you know." She paused, then said, "So I told him, oh, Sonny don't worry about it. You don't have all that many friends."

Tara laughed and Springer was smiling.

Cassie said, "So, he said I had to go out with him or he'd look bad. We dated, I liked him, and so here I am."

"Good thing he liked you," Springer said.

She waved her hand, dismissively. "Oh, he's nothing. Just a big teddy bear. All that tough-guy stuff is in the past. He's out of the life."

"You know that?"

"Sure," she said, leading them to the backyard. "He wasn't, I'd kick him right in the balls." She batted her eyelashes, theatrically. "In front of all his friends, too."

The backyard was about the size of a hockey rink and strung with lights. There was a large table heaped with hors d'oeuvres, and in the middle of it all was a huge ice sculpture, a swan, melting in the night air. There was a bar set up and Springer got a glass of chardonnay for Tara and Scotch with a lot of ice for himself. Drinking too much lately, he was thinking.

He ran into Don Janzen at the bar and Don was expansive, glad to see him. "What's up, buddy? Whoa. Looks like someone's been working out on you."

Springer said, "Thought I'd get out and see what the beautiful people are doing." He lowered his height and moved his head side to side looking at Don's mouth.

"What the hell are you doing now?" Don said, amused by Springer's antics.

"You can't even tell they replaced the tooth."

Don laughed to himself. "After you knocked it out, I picked it up and went straight to the dentist's office. It came out by the root. He put it back in, stitched up my lip, and I was good as new." He sipped his drink. "If you're trying to get at me, Cole, I'm a big boy now, and I've forgotten all about it."

"Why would I do that?"

"Because that's what you do. That's what you've always done. You enjoy pissing people off. You think I had something to do with Jesse Robinson's death, so you're working out on me. I didn't."

"Not even because he had a thing with Diane for a while?"

Janzen's eyes narrowed an eighth of an inch. "I

knew about that. She told me. Yesterday's box score, Springs."

"Well, I didn't know about it," said Springer, lying about it, seeing if he could unnerve Don a little. "I was just guessing. Until now, that is."

Janzen placed his tongue against the back of his upper teeth. "You know, Springer. I don't see any reason for you and me to get in each other's face."

"Then get the thugs off me."

Janzen placed a hand on his chest, leaning back slightly. "Why would I do that?"

"Why not? First, you don't really like me, never have, and second, I think there's something floating around, something you know about and are part of. Way I figure it is you're looking to move up, financially and socially, and that means you need capital. I've also got some scuttlebutt about a money scam involving some players here in Vegas."

"That's news? Hell, this is a town on the make. There's always some financial scheme being cooked up."

"Well, just thought I'd go fishing. Wouldn't worry about it, I were you."

Janzen laughed. "You just go on speculating and annoying people. It's what you're good at. You have a nice evening." He started to turn away, then turned back and said, "Oh yeah, beautiful lady you're with. I used to see her."

"She told me," Springer said. "Said she didn't know which was of less use, your brains"—he held up his Scotch—"or your dick. Cheers."

Janzen started to say something, hesitated, laughed, and walked off to be received by some casually well-dressed people.

Springer took his drink and Tara's back to her. She was talking to a couple looked like tourists, but told him later was the mayor and his wife. He handed her the drink and she excused herself and pulled Springer aside.

"Saw you talking to Don."

"Yeah, that was Don all right."

"Well?"

"We decided we still don't like each other. I'm crushed, of course." She gave him a look that said quit playing around. He said, "I told him to get the thugs off my case."

"Right at him." To herself, she said, "Amazing." Then back to him she said, "What good do you think that'll do?"

"I don't know. Maybe none, but I don't know much about what's going on, and I thought I'd serve something up see if he hit it back."

"He say anything about me?"

He told her what he'd said to Janzen. She covered her mouth with a hand. "You," she said. "I don't know if I can take you places."

"Already violated you, what do I need you for now?"

"I'm carrying a gun, you know."

"I'll keep it in mind."

"Also handcuffs. So be a good boy, okay?"

He raised his eyebrows and smiled. She smiled back and touched his chin with a finger.

She introduced him to a few people she knew, and while they were talking to a lady Tara knew that was a pit boss at the Grand, Springer saw the guy: big guy, his back to Springer, wearing a dress Stetson like LBJ used to wear, talking to a man with thinning red hair and a nubile blonde on his arm. Red Cavanaugh. Well, that settles that, he thought. Sonny Parker and Cassie were there also. Parker was talking to Cavanaugh, animatedly, not looking glad to see him. Checkers was nearby, being unobtrusive.

Springer walked that way, picking up a bar towel and a slice of coconut cream pie on the way. Tara called to him and began following him. Springer wrapped the bar towel around his left hand. When he got close enough, Springer smashed the pie against the cowboy's back.

The cowboy said, "What the—" as he turned, but that's all he got out. Springer threw a left cross into the side of the guy's jaw that knocked the man across a serving table.

Cavanaugh said, "The hell's going on here?" Parker's eyes were merry, and he was smiling. Cassie was, too.

"Hey, Red," said Springer, looking at Cavanaugh now. Aware that his hand was hurting now. "Guess who's back in town?"

Tara grabbed Springer by the shirt and said, "What do you think you're doing?"

Springer was slinging his hand in pain. "That's him," he said, pointing with the good hand. "That's the guy."

Then he stuck his hand in an ice bucket.

THIRTEEN

"Maybe pointing him out was the better choice," said Tara. Being sarcastic. Couldn't say he blamed her. There were at the police station. She had arrested the cowboy, whose name was Powers, a.k.a. Joe Bob Powers. Powers had a warrant in Oklahoma. She called it in, and a uniformed officer came and took Powers in. But the warrant was a misdemeanor and Springer knew they wouldn't keep him for that. They'd left the party after the uniform cuffed Powers. Springer had to go along, too, also in custody. Springer still had the ice bucket, his hand inside it.

She said, "You know, something like, 'That's the man who attacked me. I'd like to register a complaint.' Not as dramatic, but a polite alternative."

Something you can say when you haven't been mugged in a parking lot, Springer was thinking, but kept his mouth closed. She didn't appear in the mood.

She said, "You didn't give him much of a chance."

"I'm not giving anyone looks like that a chance. He wants a chance, he can buy a lottery ticket."

"You realize assault charges may be filed against you."

"You know better." She wanted remorse from him;

he could see his reaction had jarred something loose inside her. Her cop sensibilities or need for order. Something. "He's a hired thug. They don't use the legal system. They avoid it like a communicable disease." He took the ice pack off his hand.

She was shaking her head. "Why go to all this trouble?"

"Trouble?" he said, looking at the soda machine and deciding whether to go with a cola or bottled water. "What trouble?" She was looking at him funny, so he said, "Like you said. I wanted to know his name and now I do. And I have a connection. Powers was talking to the redheaded guy. Red Cavanaugh." He told her about the difficulties he'd had with Cavanaugh, then asked her, "You know him?"

She told him every cop in the state knew who Red Cavanaugh was. Springer told her he'd seen Cavanaugh talking to Janzen and then Cavanaugh was talking to Powers.

"Well," she said, "at least I get something out of attending the party."

It wasn't the best idea he'd ever had, but he felt better. Parker didn't mind, either. In fact, Parker liked it. After Springer slugged Powers, Springer heard Sonny Parker say to Cavanaugh, "See what happens you bring dog shit to my party? Like it's not enough I gotta live in the same town with you without you bringing one of your mental defectives to my home."

And after Cassie had come up to him, looked down at the cowboy who was rubbing his jaw, and she said, "Nobody can say my parties aren't fun." Then she looked up at Springer, her eyes sparkling. "I made that pie myself, you know."

He said, "I thought it could use a little more vanilla."

They released Springer and Powers when neither

would file a complaint. Springer told the booking officer that he had Powers mixed up with another guy. The cop looked at him funny and asked him how many guys he knew looked like that. Powers glared at him some as they left, but it went like Springer thought, no charges filed against him, either.

"So far, this has been a pleasant evening," said Tara.

Springer shrugged and said, "I'm not going to put up with the likes of him."

"That's certainly macho of you."

"I was just trying to liven things up."

"Nobody can say you didn't do that."

Leaving the police station Springer spotted the red Chevy pickup. At a red light Springer edged the rental up next to it where he could see Cody Powers, sitting at the wheel, his dress Stetson perfect on his head. Springer rolled down his window.

Tara said, "What're you doing now?"

"Having fun. You like to have fun, right? Trust me." He honked his horn.

Powers lowered his window and said, "You want to finish this?"

"I'm giving you forty-eight hours to clear out of town."

It amused Powers, who said, "You're a fascinating sumbitch. I'll give you that. What're you gonna do, partner, if I choose to do otherwise?"

Tara tugged at Springer's arm. "What are you doing?" she said. Springer gave her a hand gesture, hand flat out, palm down.

Springer said, "Clock starts now. You want to synchronize your watch?"

"I owe you one, you know that."

"You'll just get frustrated you dwell on it a lot."

Smiling, shaking his head now, Powers said, "What good is it to talk that shit to me? You think you can talk this way because you got the law with you? Good-lookin' filly for a peace officer. Kinda light-skinned for a smoke. That the way you like 'em, boy?"

Tara was getting mad now, but kept her composure. Springer liking her poise. A very cool, fully realized woman. Springer said, "Just thought I'd give you fair warning, so you'll know what's up and have time to do the right thing. It's this: you're going down for a murder charge. I'm going to see to it. Oh yeah, one more thing, are you listening? I'm taking twelve hours off the time limit because you insulted the lady."

"Well, old hoss, I ain't killed nobody, so go piss up a rope." The light changed. Powers smiled and smoothed the brim of his hat and pulled away.

Tara was looking into the windshield. She didn't say anything for a few moments, as if frozen on some speck on the windshield. Finally, she said, "What makes you do these things? You are crazy, aren't you? And I'm with you, so that makes me crazy, too."

"He's a bad guy and he needs to know I'm serious."

Tara said, "He calls me 'smoke' again I'm going to change his worldview with a nightstick."

"Next time."

"You think you have to protect me?"

"Nope. But go ahead, be mad at me, not him. That makes sense."

She didn't say anything for a few seconds. He could feel it building in her. "This is crap. This doesn't even happen anymore. What have you got planned if he doesn't leave town in two days? Or thirty-six hours?"

He shrugged. "I want him thinking out of his anger. He's dangerous, not dumb. He'll be less dangerous if he's not calm. Besides, I wanted to know something."

"What's that about? Murder?"

"Somebody killed a man. Brutally. I'm thinking

because they thought it was Jesse. I think it was a hired guy. Maybe Powers."

"And?"

"I don't think it's him now. What I wanted," he said, turning left, "was to see if I could shake him up. He didn't seem very shook-up. You saw that, right? Besides, I never planned anything in my life," he said. "When I think about it, I realize I've never even rehearsed anything."

Springer dropped Tara off at her apartment. She didn't ask him in. Already did that, she told him, maybe next time. She'd had enough excitement for one night, thank you. Springer knowing she was ticked off at him, but what could he do about it?

He wasn't having a lot of luck with women lately. He was 0 for three in the appreciation department.

He took the elevator up to his room. As the door opened, he thought he heard someone running down the hall. He moved quickly down the hall, trying to be quiet, but saw no one. He opened his door and immediately was struck with the sense that someone had been in his room.

He stepped back outside and saw two men walking into the elevator he'd just come up in.

Feds. No doubt about it. He could smell it on them as if they were flipping out their IDs.

Why were they there?

As if he didn't have enough problems thinking about Red Cavanaugh and Cody Powers.

He slept with the Beretta under his pillow.

Sanborn found out a couple of things for Springer. One, that Vince was associating with an independent hire named Nicco. Nicco he'd known from before. Nicco was an imported tough guy knew how to handle

himself, and the talk was Nicco done a guy once. Sanborn followed Nicco into the High Dive, a bar off the
Strip.

There was another guy with him, a guy Sanborn
knew. The guy Sanborn told Springer about called
himself Murph "the Surf" like the DJ from the fifties.
Murph was a real oddball, even for Vegas.

So, what were they up to? Was this something to do
with the tip Murph had given him about a job going
down? Springer would like this info, maybe even pay
a little extra for it, then thinking, the guy was too
much of a hard-on to do anything thoughtful.

There were two of them. They always came in pairs,
Sonny Parker was thinking as they sat down in his office and identified themselves. Agent Tompkins and
Agent Johnson. White guy and a black guy. White
guy with one of those tennis tans and the black guy
looking like an accountant who ran five miles a day
and liked it.

They badged him and asked could they talk, Parker
asking what choice did he have? The white guy smiling, flashing a $600 bleach job. One of those new
guys the Bureau was turning out, college boys who
joined health clubs and didn't eat red meat. The black
guy was trim, with wire-rimmed glasses and a serious
expression. After talking to them for a few minutes,
Parker realized the black guy was smarter, but the
white guy, Tompkins, was in charge. He'd do the
talking, and the black guy, whose name, was Dubois,
would do the listening and make observations. But
the feds, particularly the FBI, weren't people to monkey around with. The idea that Hollywood put out,
that Bureau guys were dummies, was way off. The
guys Sonny had met when he was in the life weren't
stupid, and these guys wouldn't be stupid either.

Tompkins asked him if he knew a man named Cole Springer. Parker, more from memory and a sense of humor, put his palms out and shrugged, enjoying himself.

"You've been seen with Springer," said Tompkins.

Parker raised a finger and said, "So, knowing that, you ask anyway." He looked back and forth between them, his smile bigger now. "You guys wanta get to it, or do you want to jerk me off some more?"

"We're not after you, Mr. Parker," said Tompkins.

"So," said Sonny, leaning back and extending a hand, smiling at them, "then this must be some new kind of law enforcement technique. How's it work? You ask questions you know the answers to about people you're not interested in? That it?"

"Mr. Parker—"

"Call me Sonny. But I like your formality. Not enough of that anymore. These new street guys, huh? They watch MTV and hold their guns sideways, like who could hit anything with the gun turned that way?" He arched his salt-and-pepper eyebrows. "Not that I know anything about it but I watch TV. You know, *The Sopranos*? Somebody in the life's advising on that one. They're real close on it. But, like I said, not that I would know the difference." Putting them on, something he couldn't do so much in the old days. No, then it was serious. They could throw you inside, but now . . . now he was a citizen, an authentic businessman, one of those guys who paid federal salaries with his taxes.

"We, that is, the field men who have worked this area before, have great respect for you. They say you never went back on your word." Parker had to admit it was flattering to hear those words, but these guys wanted something. "All we want to know from you is what you know about Springer."

"You wanta know what I know?"

"Yes."

"Almost nothing." Thinking about it now, Parker realized that was exactly what he knew, nothing. In fact he didn't know anything that the feds wouldn't already know, but they wouldn't be satisfied with that answer because suspicion is what they were best at.

So, Parker was thinking, there was even more to this Springer guy than he thought. There ought to be some way to use that knowledge to his advantage.

"Love to help you but I don't see how I can."

"We think you can do better than that."

"If I could, and I can't, I still wouldn't, and you know that. This is a dry run, boys."

Tompkins looked at Dubois. Dubois reached a hand up and adjusted his wire-rims and said, "Mr. Parker, we don't have anything on you, or even on Mr. Springer. That is, we have no warrants. His movement is of interest to the Bureau, that's all. He's someone we . . . uh . . . monitor. Of course, we would prefer that you help us of your own accord. But we're prepared to use certain . . . uh . . . leverage if we must."

Parker tossed a hand at him. "How many times you think I've heard that? Huh? Like I was some cherry has to have an ID card to buy a six-pack." He laughed and stood up. "You guys'll have to excuse me because I got things to do. No hard feelings, though, right?"

They left and Sonny lit a cigarette. Thought about Cole Springer. Thinking he hoped Cassie was right, the guy could be trusted.

Red Cavanaugh pulled out a big cigar and looked over the flame at Don Janzen. Janzen thinking how theatrical

the guy was, acting the mafioso, never mind he was
Scots-Irish. He said, "Why was Springer there?"

"Sonny invited him."

Cavanaugh turned to Cody Powers, who had a blue
welt on the side of his jaw that looked like bad meat.
"Correct me if I'm wrong, and I could be way off
here, but it looks like the guy hasn't left town."

"Sucker punched me," Powers said, and Don could
see he didn't like Cavanaugh's tone. Powers would be
the kind of man not used to being talked down to.
Cavanaugh carried a lot of weight in town, but the
big Texan wasn't the type who'd care how formidable
Cavanaugh was if Red pushed too hard.

"You said he was going."

You could see it coming if you knew Springer. Cavanaugh not understanding in his thug mind why they
shouldn't push Springer, and now he shouldn't push
Powers too hard either. But that was what had always
worked for Red, muscling people. Don had told him
about Springer before, and was telling him again,
"He's stubborn. The more we push, the more you're
going to see"—gesturing at Powers—"that."

"I'll convince him," Powers said. Yeah, that'll
work, thought Janzen. He was working with scholars.
Janzen knowing that short of killing Springer, nothing was going to stop him now. "He thinks I killed
somebody."

"Have you?"

Powers smiled. "Not lately. And not here."

"I don't like the guy. Never have," said Cavanaugh.
"He's trouble and a pain in the ass. I told him not to
come back to this town after that other thing. The
balls on that guy. And you"—he pointed at Powers—
"you stay out of trouble. Right in front of the mayor
and the police." Not stopping for a moment to consider that none of this was really the cowboy's fault.

Red had told him to rough up Springer and then took Powers along to the party when the guy didn't really want to go. Red had taken him as a silent insult to Parker, knowing Sonny Parker didn't like Red bringing along muscle. Red was looking at both of them now. "He brought a cop to the party with him. You give that some thought. You think they won't remember that, the guy shows up at the hospital now? Then it'll come right back to me. I want that asshole gone, but now we have to leave off him for a time. So"—he pointed at Cody, Don could see the guy's cheek muscles tighten up—"you keep your nose clean. Nothing here in Vegas, y'understand? You're going to have to learn to have a little imagination, you know? And you'd better not have done anybody here in Vegas, or maybe the same thing happens to you."

Cavanaugh looked at his cigar, and then said to Janzen, "So what are you telling me about this guy? I don't like it that you didn't tell me you know him. If you know him, why don't you try asking him to leave or buy him off?"

Still not getting it. So he'd try again. "You can't buy him off and he won't leave until he's ready."

"Why?"

"Because he thinks somebody tried to kill his best friend."

"The black guy?"

Don nodded.

"Well, he's going," said Cavanaugh. "He just doesn't know it yet. You think I can tell some guy to stay out of Vegas and have them ignore it? You think that's the way I do things?" He threw his hands out and ash dribbled off the cigar and floated to the floor. "Just not now."

So, was he going or not going? Not going now was not going until he was ready, but it would wear you out trying to illuminate each contradiction. "There's another problem. It has to do with Jesse Robinson."

"Well, what's that? You get some kind of thrill out of keeping me in suspense?"

Sure, keeping a psychotic sadist in suspense was high on his list. Go at it another way. Janzen said, "The problem is, Robinson and Springer were close at one time. Best friends. That's the reason he's poking around. Why provide a reason to look at other things?"

Cavanaugh pushed his lips out, exhaled. He looked at his cigar, watching the smoke trail upward. "So, maybe we're looking at another way of dealing with this problem."

He was beginning to understand.

"What about Parker?"

That was a good question. But Don was in too deep to fold now. He knew that. He knew it the minute he threw in with Cavanaugh. The gambler's dilemma. "He's in."

"But he don't like me, does he?"

Don touched his forehead, looking down, and said, "He's mentioned that."

"I can do business with him, though. I don't like him, but he'll do his part."

"He doesn't like the muscle stuff. Which is why Vince and Powers here have to maintain lower profiles." Cavanaugh looked at Janzen, and Janzen shrugged. What could you do about it? You had to say these things so later no one could say they didn't know.

"That's cause he's gone soft. Used to be, he was a tough guy, somebody you had to mark and be careful of. Now . . . that security girl with the boobs, she domesticated him. Speaking of women, what about your ex? You got her part yet?"

"Working on it."

"Working on it? You better get it done."

"It's a lock." But thinking it wasn't and he'd better make sure.

FOURTEEN

She called again, telling him she would be free at about three, Vince thinking this was it; he was going to score this time. This doll was probably ten years older than the girls he dated, but she was something else. Like a movie star, not so much in looks, which were extradeadly, but she had a way about her. You know, glamorous. Like those babes in the movies with Dean Martin and Frank Sinatra. A young Debbie Reynolds or a Tuesday Weld, like the girl next door, only sexier than either of those. She had a way of holding herself and looking at you that was almost scary. Dangerous. No way to know what she was thinking, keeping him cross-wired all the time. He got a boner just thinking about her. She also irritated him because, as yet, she hadn't come across. Just wait until the right moment, that's what she said.

He was meeting her at . . .

Starbucks, Diane Janzen ordering iced coffee with a shot of espresso, stirring a half spoonful of sugar into the espresso. Springer. She didn't like being turned out like he had done to her. Beat up or not. She sat down in an overstuffed chair near the corner of the coffee bar so she could watch the man come in.

He was a nice-looking young guy. Lean and tall and tanned. Now, if he would just learn not to talk, she could see herself getting involved with him. An affair, not a relationship, but there were plenty of young boys in Vegas. It was too bad he was so obtuse. They could have so much fun.

Here he comes now, dressed retro Vegas, a young guy forty years out of time, but it was cute. It would be better if he'd button the shirt a little further up, like Dean Martin did or James Garner did in the *Rockford Files*, instead of like he was a disco-roller king.

"Hey, doll," Vince said, starting to sit down. She hated it when he called her pet names like she was some bimbo cheerleader.

She held a hand up. "Order yourself some coffee."

"I don't want any this late in the day."

"Get some anyway and just hold the cup. You want it to look like we're screwing each other in the afternoons, don't you?"

See, that's the other thing she did, make remarks that got him hot, then nothing. "That might not be so bad. Maybe you should give that some thought."

"Oh," she said, as if he hadn't said a word. "Would you bring me back a blueberry scone? That would be lovely of you."

He gave her a look, deciding whether to let her boss him around or not. She could see it working on him. Put his hand on the back of the chair as if to come around, stopped, looked at her momentarily, then turned around and walked to the counter. Priceless, just priceless. Maybe she'd let him touch her breasts this time. She was getting him right where she wanted him.

She sipped her iced coffee and felt the jolt of the doctored stimulant hit and tingle along the back of her neck. Feeling good now. He'd do just fine for what she needed.

Officers Madison and Sullivan picked up Springer at 4:30 P.M. in his room at Streamers. As they were leaving, his phone rang, and they gave him permission to answer it. It was Jesse.

"Springs, what's going on? I just had the *po*-lice here at my place."

"I know what you mean. I had the same phone solicitor call me. I just hang up when they call, but they managed to catch me in my room today. Go figure why a phone solicitor would call your hotel room."

"Are you telling me something?"

Springer smiled at Sullivan and Madison. "They just keep rattling on until you just have to hang up on them. Just avoid them whenever you can. Know what I mean? First they call you then they call me."

"The cops are there?"

"Yeah. That's right. Look, I've got to go. I'll give you a call on your cell phone when I get a chance. I'll tell you how things are going with the folks. We need to talk about this. Soon. How about that?"

Jesse said, "Yeah, it's cool. You need me to bail you out?"

"No, no. Nothing like that. You know that's bad for you." Officer Sullivan was giving him a funny look now. "Don't take that stuff without the doctor's advice. You know better than to mix medications."

Sullivan said, "Who're you talking to? Give me the phone."

Springer put a finger on the receiver button. "Whoops, they hung up." He held the phone out slack in his hand like it was a dead thing.

"You think you're cute, dontcha, asshole?" said Sullivan.

"Everybody says that, but I don't think anybody really believes it."

Springer asked for an attorney when he arrived at the station.

"You're not under arrest," said Detective Tara St. John. "Yet. So take it easy."

"You send the two morons who rousted me before and you wonder why I think I could use a lawyer?"

She was holding something back from him. "They were the only available officers. Otherwise I wouldn't have sent them."

"Your phone broken?"

"Meaning," she said, placing a finger alongside her temple, "why didn't I just call you? Maybe I was afraid you wouldn't come. You know why you are here?"

Springer shrugged.

"Because we believe you've had contact with Jesse Robinson since I talked with you last."

"Okay."

"What did he say?"

"About what?"

She looked up from her notebook and gave him an irritated look. "This will go faster if you'll expand upon your answers."

"You have me at a disadvantage."

"You come to town," she said, leaning forward on her desk, Springer eyeing her throat, which was a creamy light mocha, and remembering how good she smelled the night before. It was a different smell than Tobi, but had the same effect. He was starting to miss Tobi, and she was working her way into his dreams again, "to see if he had been killed, you realize it's not him, and then you somehow locate him when we can't, and now you think reticence is helpful?"

He sat quietly. He wasn't going to help her. Not yet. Not that he didn't trust her; mostly it was because of his Secret Service habits, where his motto was "Don't just do something, stand there." Also, she was law enforcement, and they wanted to know things. Any feelings for him would mean nothing if he got in the way of her investigation. She had said as much herself.

She waited him out. She was no ingénue at this. But he knew better than to start talking to fill the dead air.

She sipped her coffee, not offering any. Okay, so the romance is in remission. Tapped a pencil on her desk, looked at him some more, and then said, "Robinson was involved with Diane Janzen. Did you know that?"

"Suspected it."

"Are you sleeping with her?"

"Are you inquiring officially or is this just something you'd—"

"I don't have time for this crap, Cole. You want to answer the questions straight up and informally, or do you want to go in the tank and wait for me to get around to you?"

"Gee, so emotional."

"You think this has something to do with Jesse Robinson's disappearance?"

"I think it has something to do with Jesse's son."

"What makes you say that?"

"He indicated as much."

"So you have talked to him," she said, leaning back. "When were you going to give this to us?"

"I just did."

"Every response doesn't have to be cryptic, does it?"

He waited.

"Why do you keep showing up whenever things are happening?" she asked.

"Serendipity?"

She looked at him for a moment. Opened a file on her desk, then turned around to her computer and typed in some letters. The computer screen flashed.

He said, "Can I go now?"

"You'll go when I say."

"Sure."

She turned back around in her chair. "Don't patronize me."

"What do you want me to say? Tell me, I'll say it, and then we can move on."

She started to say something else, he could see it, but thought better of it. He was irritating her and there were better things to do than get sideways with a high-ranking law enforcement officer, especially if you were sleeping with her. Wasn't trying to annoy her—well maybe a little, he had to admit it—but he didn't know what he could do about it. She was a cop and she was on point. He didn't want to open up everything to her right now, and nothing he could say would get her off where she was going, so he didn't try.

"Where's Jesse Robinson?"

"At the Super 8 last time I saw him. But he's not there anymore."

"When were you going to tell me that?"

"When it was germane."

"It was germane when we thought he'd been murdered. But you decided differently. Why is it germane now?"

"Because whoever it was may try to kill him again."

"What makes you think—" She stopped and looked in the direction of the uniformed cop that had entered the room. She was wearing a silk skirt that hit her above the knees. She had spectacular legs. She turned back around, gave him a look, and said, "Are you looking at my legs?"

"No." Now she was smiling. He could feel it. "Maybe. I'm not sure it's germane."

She looked away and then back again. He didn't know if she was composing herself or just tired of him. "Mrs. Janzen, if I'm following you, has a son fathered by Jesse Robinson." Not a question.

Springer nodded.

"I'm not going to ask how you knew that or when you were going to tell me because I don't want to watch your evasive act, which you find so entertaining. So, Diane Janzen and her ex and you and Jesse Robinson all attended the same high school. Mrs. Janzen used to be your girlfriend." She raised an eyebrow but he didn't help her out. "She married Don Janzen, and now it appears she had a child by Jesse Robinson. So Diane Janzen has slept with all three of you?"

"Past tense. Not currently. You can see me sitting here, can't you?" She didn't smile at that. Oh well. "She could be sleeping with the others. I don't know."

"How nice." Quick flash in her eyes.

"Always glad to help out the law."

There it was, that look again. The one that said she'd just about had it with his smart-ass remarks.

"So, where is the son?"

Springer said, "I don't know. I hope he's not in a drawer down at the morgue."

Tara let out a breath. "Oh my God."

He shrugged and nodded. He knew he wasn't, but wasn't ready to tell her why he wasn't.

Let her think about it for a while.

At 4:00 P.M. Las Vegas Metro, via dental records, determined that the corpse at the morgue was one Clarence Tangent, a.k.a. "Styles" Tangent.

Springer wasn't ready to give up on the thought that the killer or killers, whoever they were, thought they had killed Jesse Robinson. Even Jesse himself thought it. Otherwise, why hide out? There was some connection here they were missing. It wasn't a random killing. First, it was for a reason, and second, it was personal, because the beating had been so vicious. Powers didn't seem too concerned about being connected with a murder.

Oddly enough, he no longer thought Cavanaugh had anything to do with it. He didn't know why; it just didn't seem right to him.

Maybe Jesse didn't even know the reason someone wanted to kill him, or maybe he was holding something back. He mentioned blackmailing the Janzens. It would certainly explain the severity of the attack on the John Doe. But a scandal involving an illegitimate child? In Vegas? So what? It might make Don Janzen angry enough and jealous enough to have it done. He'd had Vince brace him in the parking lot, or had he? The relationship between Don and Vince didn't seem very warm. Don was a lot of things, but stupid wasn't one of them. However, Vince was stupid, yet wily and street smart, a thug who thought himself a Vegas personality. No, there was something wrong in the interplay between Don and Vince. It was almost as if Vince had been attached to Don to keep an eye on him.

Who would want that? Sonny Parker? No, he detested Vince. Red Cavanaugh. There it was. He was satisfied that that was the connection. So what was the connection between Cavanaugh and Janzen, and what was their interest in Jesse? And he didn't discount Diane Janzen. She had a way of looking at things first as what was best for Diane. It had always been that way with her. But when she was around, he felt the pull of her. What was it about her? It had always been there and it was there now.

Tara St. John had asked him to wait while they checked records to see if the corpse was Jesse Robinson Jr. Springer knowing it wasn't, asked if he could have some coffee if he was going to have to wait. She'd nodded at a break room and told him to help himself and it wasn't a hotel. He told her that was a relief because he was beginning to wonder about the service. She didn't smile, but he could see her holding back, a dimple forming in her mocha cream cheek.

When they had determined it wasn't Jesse Jr., Detective St. John returned and said, to Springer, "Did you think it was Jesse's son when you went to the morgue?"

"Didn't even know he had a son at that time. So who was it?"

Again she asked why Springer wasn't forthcoming about Jesse Robinson and he asked if they wanted to chase that rabbit some more. She said she just wanted to know what he knew about the situation and he told her everything he knew, and wasn't it just easier to ask that?

A uniformed officer entered the office and handed her a computer printout. She looked at it and Springer looked at her. She rattled the paper. The officer said, "The body in the morgue is a guy we know. Clarence Tangent."

She was surprised by that. "Tangent? I know him." She looked frustrated. "He's nobody. A runner for some local bookies, petty theft, small-time drug dealer."

Springer said, "And you're wondering why you didn't know that before?"

She said, "There have been a few mistakes made."

GET UP TO 4 FREE BOOKS!

You can have the best fiction delivered to your door for less than what you'd pay in a bookstore or online—only $4.25 a book! Sign up for our book clubs today, and we'll send you FREE* BOOKS just for trying it out...with **no obligation to buy, ever!**

LEISURE HORROR BOOK CLUB

With more award-winning horror authors than any other publisher, it's easy to see why CNN.com says "Leisure Books has been leading the way in paperback horror novels." Your shipments will include authors such as RICHARD LAYMON, DOUGLAS CLEGG, JACK KETCHUM, MARY ANN MITCHELL, and many more.

LEISURE THRILLER BOOK CLUB

If you love fast-paced page-turners, you won't want to miss any of the books in Leisure's thriller line. Filled with gripping tension and edge-of-your-seat excitement, these titles feature everything from psychological suspense to legal thrillers to police procedurals and more!

As a book club member you also receive the following special benefits:

- **30% OFF** all orders through our website & telecenter!
- **Exclusive access to** special discounts!
- **Convenient** home delivery **and 10 days to return any books you don't want to keep.**

There is no **minimum number of books to buy**, and you may cancel membership at any time. See back to sign up!

*Please include $2.00 for shipping and handling.

YES! ☐

Sign me up for the Leisure Horror Book Club and send my TWO FREE BOOKS! If I choose to stay in the club, I will pay only $8.50* each month, a savings of $5.48!

YES! ☐

Sign me up for the Leisure Thriller Book Club and send my TWO FREE BOOKS! If I choose to stay in the club, I will pay only $8.50* each month, a savings of $5.48!

NAME: _____

ADDRESS: _____

_____

TELEPHONE: _____

E-MAIL: _____

☐ **I WANT TO PAY BY CREDIT CARD.**

☐ VISA   ☐ MasterCard   ☐ DISCOVER

ACCOUNT #: _____

EXPIRATION DATE: _____

SIGNATURE: _____

Send this card along with $2.00 shipping & handling for each club you wish to join, to:

Horror/Thriller Book Clubs
1 Mechanic Street
Norwalk, CT 06850-3431

Or fax (must include credit card information!) to: 610.995.9274. You can also sign up online at www.dorchesterpub.com.

*Plus $2.00 for shipping. Offer open to residents of the U.S. and Canada only. Canadian residents please call 1.800.481.9191 for pricing information.
If under 18, a parent or guardian must sign. Terms, prices and conditions subject to change. Subscription subject to acceptance. Dorchester Publishing reserves the right to reject any order or cancel any subscription.

JOIN NOW!

"It's Styles, right?"

"What?" It surprised her and even angered her a little. He could see it. "What makes you say that?"

"That's his nickname, isn't it? Clarence Tangent is Styles."

She had a pen in her hand and she threw it at him. It bounced off his chest and fell to the floor. "I'm getting damned sick and tired of you releasing information in the form of slow leaks you imagine as dramatic. Or amusing. You'd better start dealing the cards faceup, Springer, or I'm seriously considering charging you with something. Anything and everything I can think of. You're pissing me off, and that's not a good thing for you. How did you know his street name was Styles?"

"Jesse told me."

She sat back in her chair, as if exhausted. "You knew this all along, didn't you?"

"I only suspected it. You, and two of your officers, the two that brought me down here as a matter of fact, warned me against involving myself in an open investigation. A more paranoid person might even consider the warning a threat. If you were me, who would you trust?"

"You bring Jesse in, and you do it today."

"No."

"Then I'll have you charged with obstruction of justice."

"Okay."

"You want to go to jail?"

"Been there before."

"Why are you doing this?"

"I don't trust those two officers that brought me in. Do you?"

She looked back over her shoulder, thinking about it.

She said, "Then take me to him."

"I'll give it some thought. But you and no one else. I want your word you won't pass this information on."

She hesitated and he could see it working in her eyes. Weighing the possibilities. She was a beautiful, remarkable woman, but still a cop. And, he would guess, an ambitious cop. This was too juicy for her to risk not being able to close it herself. She was a minority female and had risen quickly and she would do everything within her power to erase the thought that she had risen because she was a minority female. No, she would be the type wanted to earn her promotions to satisfy herself for her own reasons.

"Okay," she said. "Just me."

"I said I'd give it some thought."

Her eyes blazed up. "What makes you think you have any bargaining power here?"

"I know where Jesse is and you don't."

"We'll find him."

"I'm sure you will. Or somebody will. It may take some time, or maybe some junior officer will find him. He's the key here. I don't know why, but I think he is."

"You don't trust me," she said it flatly. It wasn't a question.

"I didn't say that." He trusted her, not her emotions. "I'm going to put Jesse first here. It trumps all other concerns, even for myself. Even over you. I have to talk to Jesse about it. He's the one who's in danger."

She thanked him and told him he was free to go, but he could tell she was put out at him.

"No need to take it personally," he said.

"Why would I do that?"

"I'm going back to Aspen soon, if you need anything else."

"I don't think I will."

"Okay."

"Always want the last word, right?"

"Me? Why would I do that?"

"Or, you answer a question with a question."

"I'll confess to that one."

"You talk to Robinson. I need to talk to him, Cole." Her eyes softened. Looking at him imploringly. Not above using her charm to get what she wanted. He didn't blame her for trying.

"I'll see what I can do." He put his hand on the door handle, stopped, and looked back at her. "Don't have anyone tail me. I haven't completely forgotten the things they trained me to do. Sometimes that stuff comes in handy."

She set her teeth, shaking her head. He scratched his forehead, deciding not to say anything else, and left.

What else could he do?

FIFTEEN

Jesse Robinson walked out of the meeting. It was a crazy meeting. Bunch of thugs wanting to pull a robbery. How Springer got wind of it he didn't know. Lots of things about Springer he didn't know about anymore. Springer told Jesse to look up a guy named Murph the Surf, not believing that name, and then go with the guy to a meeting. Said he had it already set up.

After that, Jesse drove back to his apartment, but was careful about it. He'd checked out of the Super 8 as he and Springs had discussed. Time to go live. Get hold of Springer and tell him he wanted to get out of town for a while, like Springer suggested. Go to Aspen, visit his dad, and plan what to do next.

He was thinking about that when he saw the police cruiser pull up. Watched the two uniforms walk to his apartment section and up the stairs to his place. Shit. There was a knock on the door. He didn't answer it but watched them through the magnifying peephole. They knocked again, identifying themselves as police officers. He didn't answer. After a few minutes they left and he watched the police unit pull out of the parking lot.

Find Springer. Right fucking now.

Springer got a call from Jesse and told him to meet him at Pinky's. Jesse said okay, but did you know that's a gay bar? Springer told him not to try anything with him then. Then Springer told him to wear sunglasses and a hat, something to disguise himself. Jesse said, "Oh, I got me a disguise."

By the time Jesse arrived, Springer already had three drinks sitting in front of him, the Scotch on the rocks he bought himself, a beer bought by one guy in a Hawaiian shirt and a Scotch and soda sent over by another guy in an Armani suit and a silk T-shirt. Armani suit had waited until the drinks arrived before approaching the table.

"Hello, stranger," said Armani suit. He was wearing rose-colored granny glasses on a lavaliere chain that dangled from his neck.

Springer nodded, said, "Thanks for the drink."

Armani suit gave him a funny look, then leaned away. "Oh my, you're not gay."

"What gave me away?"

Armani suit cocked his head to one side, put his forefinger alongside his chin, and flipped a hand at him. "Oh, honey, we know who you are."

Springer snapped his fingers and said, "Hoping I could blend in."

"Well," Armani jacket said, "then change the wardrobe, sugar. Nobody, and I mean nobody, shops the racks." He gave Springer an appraising look. "What a shame, though."

That's when Jesse walked in, or at least Springer was pretty sure it was Jesse. He was wearing a black leather jacket, Ray-Bans, and a black silk mock turtle T-shirt. Springer said, to Armani jacket, "My date."

"Oh baby, good choice," he said, lowering the granny glasses and eyeing Jesse over the top of them. Springer spread his hands and shrugged. Armani jacket smiled and walked back to the bar.

Jesse walked up, strutted actually, obviously enjoying his role. He pulled up a chair and sat. Springer said, "Let me guess, Tubbs from *Miami Vice.*" Jesse saying Tubbs never wore this shit, where you been you don't recognize the John Shaft look? Springer said wearing a leather jacket when the temperature was a hundred degrees wasn't conspicuous at all, and Jesse told him when you this cool you can wear whatever the hell you want.

A waiter swished over, a dozen studs biting into each ear, and Jesse ordered a beer.

Jesse, looking at Springer's three drinks, said, "Looks like you're a hit with the den-i-zens."

Springer took a sip of the Scotch and soda, said, "They were still trying to identify the body down at the morgue and they want to know where you are. I narrowly avoided being maced and beaten with nightsticks."

"Well, might do you good, somebody work on you. You always a little self-satisfied."

"Jesse, where's your son?"

"Why?"

"They considered that maybe the body at the morgue was your son."

"They thought that, then they wouldn't have thought it was me in the first place. Junior's white. Well, at least, he looks white. He's got my blood in him, though."

"What are the chances someone wanted to kill Jesse Jr. instead of you?"

"Why would they do that? And how could they confuse him with the man got killed?"

Springer told him about the necklace they found. Jesse said, silver with my initials on the back? Surprised Springer, who then asked him how he knew it was his and how did the guy come by it.

"It was stolen," said Jesse. "Yeah, some guy stole it out of my car 'bout two weeks ago." Jesse took a drink of his beer, set it down, and smiled.

"What about the meeting you went to?"

"Did like you said. Found the burnout, Murph the Surf. Yeah, no shit, that's the dude's name. Tells me he got a job for me and to be at this meeting just like you said. Man thinks my name is Styles, so I go with it. This Murph a real character, too, boy, all vibrating with whatever he's on, his eyes swimming and shit, and he tells me, 'Man, you look different in the daylight, bro. Where'd the Shaft wardrobe get off to?' Like that. Like all us brothers look alike and dress like Shaft. So I figure I'll find me some Richard Roundtree threads and check this meeting out—"

"Or maybe Samuel L. Jackson's Shaft look. You see that one?"

"Yeah, I saw that one. The leather duster was sweet. I like the part where he fronts the spic gangster and his boys and when he's leaving the place he fakes a move on one of the bodyguards and the guy flinches."

"Then Jackson laughs."

"Jackson as Shaft, right. Anyway, I go to this thing and there was this guy, Vince"—Springer was interested now but didn't say anything—"running the show, and another guy I'd seen around town, a half Eyetie named Nicco, a real badass and some fat guy." Nicco again. The same guy Sanborn had told Springer about. "I'm sitting there listening to this thing and can't figure why this Murph guy, who is, I'm not kidding you, Springs, this Murph the Surf is not firing on *any* cylinders. I'm thinking to myself, first, what are these guys talking about and why is this burnout involved and why aren't they checking me out. Then it hits me—"

"Maybe he's a patsy," said Springer. "Take the weight if things go wrong. Maybe both of you."

"Yeah. That's right. They gonna do the little dude or me, as Styles, of course, or both, and let one or both take the weight."

"Nobody there recognized you, right?"

"No. Thought I was this Styles guy. Why's that important?"

Springer brought him up to date, telling him about his conversation with Sanborn Meeks and how Meeks had talked to Murph the Surf. Springer told him everything that transpired, leaving out his romance with Tara St. John.

"You punched out a button man? At a big-shot party? Damn, Cole, you've gotta get your temper under control."

"Jesse," said Springer, "you know who was killed, don't you?"

Jesse nodded. "Figured it out anyway. It's Styles."

Springer pushed his Scotch glass around with a knuckle, thinking. "I'm pretty sure they were trying to kill you. Vince didn't recognize you, and neither did this Nicco character."

"And this Nicco, he's the one to watch. Nasty eyes."

"We need to know where your son is, because I'm still not sure they weren't after him, maybe after both of you, despite the fact Jesse Jr. is light-skinned."

Springer thought on it some. Jesse drank more beer.

"Tell me about this meeting."

"These dudes are brain-fucked," said Jesse. "From what I could gather they're going to steal something and give it back to the owner, you can believe that crazy shit. Some kind of insurance scam. Not so bad an idea when you think about it, so it couldn't be these brain-damaged motherfuckers came up with it. These guys are all smalltime thugs. Nicco is muscle all the way. Ain't no burglar. His eyes, you know? Killer eyes. Like he ain't seeing nothing. And the one guy, Vincent, who you know, thinks he's smart, but isn't, you know, and got issues with his thought processes, like he quit school in the fifth grade. Didn't say what we're doing, just where to be and when. Only he and Nicco know what's going down, and they ain't sharing. No, somebody else planning this. They don't even ask for anybody to vouch for me even though I don't know anyone in the room."

"They tell you they've got inside help?"

"Not in those exact words but you could read it, him saying it was a lock. They were supposed to give the take back to the people they were stealing it from, but he's got another idea. He said they gonna keep it for themselves, and what're those guys gonna say about it?"

"Plenty," said Springer, "if it's Red Cavanaugh involved." And found himself thinking he was hoping that Sonny Parker wasn't involved in this scam but that may be wishful thinking, since he was partners with Don Janzen. And what was Janzen's part in all of this? Maybe Detective St. John could help him out there, that is, she didn't pistol-whip him when he asked.

The waiter brought over another beer, a Corona with a lime in it, and set it in front of Jesse. The waiter indicated the guy at the bar in the Hawaiian shirt, who was now talking to Armani suit.

"The hell's that for?" said Jesse.

"The Shaft look," said Springer, slowly shaking his hand side to side, thumb and little finger extended, "a little swishy."

"Man, fuck you, I don't look gay. Shaft ain't no puff."

"Tell those guys."

"Ain't nothing gay 'bout what I'm wearing."

"Well, I'm talking about Shaft, so I thought you could dig it."

Jesse looked at him for a minute, started laughing a little, sipped his beer. "That's more stupid than funny." Jesse held up his bottle to salute Hawaiian shirt. "I'm only laughing to make you feel okay about yourself. And because I'm getting scared. What have you got me into?"

Springer looked at the three drinks in front of him. Moved the Scotch and soda with the back of his hand, took a sip of the beer, set it down, and watched a sweat drop slide down the side. Light beer. No good.

"You're thinking," said Jesse.

Springer nodded.

"So," said Jesse, "what you got in mind?"

Springer thought about it for moment before saying anything. "I want to know where and when. Then we'll take it from there."

SIXTEEN

According to the *Las Vegas Sun* it went down like this.

Las Vegas—Vegas Metro is looking into the robbery/murder of two armored-truck guards during a robbery in the parking lot of Streamers Casino. Metro Captain Robert Meadows had this to say about the daring daylight robbery, "We're checking eyewitness reports and our files to see if there is any connection between this incident and the armored-car robberies last year." Meadows was referring to last year's armored car robbery at the Desert Inn and the attempted armored car heist at the MGM Grand that was thwarted by MGM security guards. MGM suffered a similar incident in 1998.

Police have received leads on the two shooters and the getaway-car driver responsible for the killings of guards Frank Maguire, 36, and Perry Jameson, 32. An unidentified white male was also killed during the robbery. At this time police are unable to determine whether the dead man was part of the gang or an innocent bystander. No arrests have been made as of this morning.

Las Vegas police, who are being assisted by the FBI, sifted through evidence and continued to search for the men responsible for killing the driver, Maguire, and his partner, Jameson. Maguire is the father of three children.

"I have every confidence that we will make an arrest. We will continue to work at this until we apprehend these men," said Captain Meadows.

Police say at about 4:25 p.m. Friday the guards pulled up in front of Streamers Casino. The pickup was a special one, commissioned by Streamers President/owner, Don Janzen.

"We are, of course, distressed and horrified, by this heinous and cowardly criminal action," said Janzen, 36, following the incident. "Our thoughts and prayers go out to the families of these men." Janzen appeared visibly distraught when informed the guards had been killed.

Apparently, the ambush had been planned and set up hours before. The robbers used a Dodge minivan and a Lincoln Navigator SUV in the robbery. The robbers waited in the vehicles, both stolen and chosen because of their heavily tinted windows, until the Safeguard armored car had parked and was returning with the cash bags from Streamers. According to eyewitnesses the robbers backed the stolen minivan in front of the armored car. When armored guard Jameson stepped forward to instruct them to move their vehicle, the occupants of the second vehicle roared up and a gunfight ensued with Jameson able to discharge three shots from his gun before the robbers' shots killed him. Frank Maguire, a 15-year Safeguard armored car veteran, emerged from the armored car in order to protect his partner. He exchanged fire with the robbers and was gunned down. Both men died at the scene. Captain Meadows said bullet-resistant vests were unable to protect the two men from the type of weapons used by the robbers.

Witnesses say they were unable to determine when the third, unidentified man was shot. He was pronounced dead upon arrival at Las Vegas Municipal Hospital.

The robbers fled with six bags of money—one that Jameson had in his hand and five others out of the truck. Police would not reveal how much cash was taken.

"The perpetrators had information beforehand," Meadows said. "They knew the truck was coming and knew where to park the stolen vehicles to best approach the armored car. This was done by professionals."

The robbers fled the scene in a white Dodge minivan with Idaho license plates and a Lincoln Navigator with California plates. The killers drove only a half mile to a parking lot by a J.C. Penney store at the Galleria at Sunset mall and got into another vehicle, either another minivan or SUV.

According to police sources, the two stolen vehicles were part of a fleet of vehicles stolen last month from National Car Rental. The license plates on the two vehicles were also stolen.

Inside the abandoned Navigator police found bloodstains from an apparent gunshot wound inflicted on one of the gunmen.

"It appears to be a wound that would require medical treatment," Meadows said. "Due to the possibility of death or bullet shock, we have contacted hospitals in Arizona, Utah, California, and Nevada."

LV Metro also reviewed surveillance tapes

from businesses near the robbery and at the Galleria at Sunset mall where the Navigator was found, but none of the tapes reveal many clues. The getaway vehicles were parked in an area store where apparently the security camera wasn't turned on, or had been disabled, Meadows said. The surveillance cameras at the Streamers parking lot were being replaced and there were no tapes available from Streamers Security force.

"Detectives were pretty sure the tapes would have revealed something," he said.

Anyone with information in this case is asked to call Metro Police at 555-9002 or Secret Witness at COP-5555.

Vince tore off his ski mask and said, "The fuck was that, Nicco? We're pulling off an inside job and you turn it into the O.K. Corral. You do understand what *inside* job means, right? That's where it's a setup, get it?"

"Quit crying like a bitch, Vince," Nicco said. He had never put on his ski mask, which is something that should've registered in Vince's mind at the time. Like, he wasn't going to need a mask because he wasn't leaving witnesses. "What'd you think, they start shooting? You think I'm gonna sing 'em a song, maybe send 'em a nasty telegram? When'd you get to be such a pussy? Whaddya think, Chewy? Man's acting like a bush, ain't he?"

The black guy driving the car looked at Vince and smiled.

"What about you, Lunchbox? He's cherry, huh?"

The heavy old white guy, sitting in the backseat, looked straight ahead, saying nothing.

First, the black guy, the one that looked like Shaft and was vouched for by Murph the Surf—there's a name for you, and a live demonstration of why this thing had gone bad—had not shown up, so Nicco said he had a crew, and so he shows up with this street pimp Chewy and another wop old guy he called Lunchbox, who, like Nicco, has no fucking compunction about shooting people down in the street. Vince asked Nicco why he called him Lunchbox and Nicco says, "Hey, tell 'im why they call you Lunchbox."

"Because I like to eat," the guy says, like that was something funny to say instead of sounding like a dumb shit, hair growing out his dumb shit ears. Guy was a freak show.

Vince knew that shooting was a possibility but freaked when Murphy was shot, and then, as a diversion, put the Springer dude's room and phone number in Murph's pocket. Put them on his trail for a while. That was Vince's idea, and pretty crafty when he thought about it, like Frank and the rat pack in *Ocean's Eleven*, the real one, not that fake shit with Clooney and a bunch of squares who wouldn't know cool if you dropped them at the North Pole.

Diane Janzen's idea, however, was to deliver one of the bags of money to her. Let Don think about that one, she said, stroking his neck with her fingers after balling him blind. Wishing he hadn't told her about the plan. Wanting to impress her as a bad guy. She was a looker, but there was a heinous brain inside that cute head. Thinking of her as cute, rather than beautiful, until she took her clothes off and he saw the goodies inside. Like a movie star or a playboy centerfold. Incredible hooters, thinking they were plastic until he touched them. Her telling him how she had a bag of the money, Don would think twice, no, he would think *all* the time about not pissing her off. Vince wondering if she was using him to get what she wanted, but thinking maybe that wasn't all bad because all kinds of people could use you and you got no pussy, either.

The black guy, Chewy, was saying, "Any you crackers know how we gonna open those bags? They be locked and sealed, you know."

Nicco saying, "First we have to get somewhere we can do that. Not here in the daylight."

So now they had loaded up in the getaway car and stopped in a parking lot to change cars then headed for a motel room to open the money and then after, honest-to-God, back to Streamers, where Nicco had checked in. Nicco saying who expects that shit, them staying at the very place they'd just robbed? But Vince wondering if the guy had more balls than brains and how guys he knew inside said and did stupid shit and then wondered how they got caught.

But that wasn't the worst thing yet.

The worst thing while they were getting ready to change cars was when the Springer guy and the black guy showed up, the one Murph the Surf had recommended.

And they had guns.

SEVENTEEN

"The best part of the plan," Springer was saying, after he got the car stopped and had the Beretta in Chewy's face, fun to see him again, "was that you guys had to get rid of your weapons in case you were stopped. That's why we waited. And, Chewy, what a surprise to see you here, you not being a criminal and all."

Chewy made a face, looked at the floorboard, shaking his head.

"The fuck is this guy, Chew?" said a dark-haired man Springer took to be Nicco, the badass, from Jesse's description. Jesse was a little nervous at first, but he was warming to the occasion.

Chewy said, "He's a guy likes to annoy shit outta folks."

"Damn, Springs," Jesse said, looking into the car at a nasty-looking guy with gray hair, "you didn't say this was gonna be fun. Hell, you didn't say it was gonna be this easy."

"Well, you gotta figure, with Vince here involved, it was going to be a little screwed up. You look upset, Vince. Why is that?"

Chewy started to move around in his seat. Springer jammed the pistol into his cheekbone and said, "I told you to keep your hands inside the spokes of the steering wheel. You do that again and they'll be picking your teeth out of the upholstery. Think you can remember that?"

"It's cool," said Chewy. "I ain't fucking moving. Chill with the gun, huh? You can see me not moving, right?"

"He ain't gonna shoot nobody," said the gray man.

Springer removed the pistol from Chewy's face, pointed in Lunchbox's general direction and squeezed off a shot that buried itself in the seat next to Lunchbox. It also nipped a piece of the guy's rear end. Lunchbox screamed and the others clapped their hands to their ears and yelled in surprise.

"Hey, shit," screamed Lunchbox. "The fuck's wrong with you?"

"Oh, did I shoot you? I'm sorry. I was aiming at the car. Pretty quiet, don't you think, when it went off? It's a little gun but it still hurts, doesn't it? Anybody else think I won't shoot them? I'm all warmed up now."

"There's no place you can hide, asshole," said Nicco. "No place. I'll find you. You think about that."

"That's all I'm going to do for the rest of my life, think about you looking for me," said Springer. "If you're through scaring me, how about turning over the bags in the trunk."

"The hell you think you're doing?" said Nicco.

"We're robbing you. Haven't you been paying attention?"

Vince saying now, you can't get away with this, we know who you are. Chewy saying to the windshield, this the way this man acts, comes to town and start fucking with everybody.

"However," Springer said, "we're not greedy. We're going to leave you two bags."

"Why you doing that?" said Vince.

"Because," said Nicco, not looking scared or upset, smarter than the rest, "that way we can't fuck with 'im. We turn him in, then he tells the cops we were all in it together and we got two bags. And they're looking for four guys not just two guys. Use your head for something, huh?"

Springer nodded.

He made them pop the trunk from the inside button. Jesse unloaded while Springer held the gun on them.

Springer said, "While we're waiting, Vince, I want to know something. Who're you working for? I know you don't work for Don Janzen."

"I don't gotta tell you shit."

"Well, actually you do, or I'm going to shoot you like I did Lunchbox. You know I'll do it."

"What the fuck, huh? It don't mean a thing. I work for Red Cavanaugh. Anybody can tell you that." Vince laughed. "Think about what that means. Baby, you have shit in your nest here. Red's not gonna like this."

"Why's that, Vince?" said Springer.

"Yeah," said Nicco. "I'd like to know that myself. Why's Cavanaugh not gonna like this? How many people know about this shit? Fucking amateur-hour cocksucker."

Springer could see Vince knew he'd said too much.

"One more thing," said Springer. "You've got fifteen minutes to abandon this car because I'm calling the police and giving them a description of the car and you guys. I know what you're thinking, how do we get another car and transfer the two bags in the next fifteen minutes? But you know what? I'm going to be so busy worrying about Nicco here coming to get me I'll just leave that up to you."

"You motherfucker," said Vince.

Springer, looking at his watch, raised a hand, saying, "Starting—"

"You think you're cute, dontcha? You better—"

"—now." And dropping his hand like he was starting a race.

Springer and Jesse left them sitting in the car.

"We know who he is," said Vince. "We can find his ass."

"Yeah, like I wanta find him," said Chewy.

"What's that mean?" said Vince.

"Man strikes me," said Chewy, "kinda dude don't give a damn we find him. You know the kinda dude I'm talkin' 'bout? Man a badass. You get that yet? Shit, I don't want nothin' to do with that white boy. I hope I never see him again. You on your own. I am done with this shit. I'm heading back to St. Louis, where I'm from."

"You believe this shit?" said Vince, looking at Nicco.

"I'll tell you what I don't believe, palooka," said Nicco, pointing at Vince. "The guy knew my name or you miss that? Also, I think the smoke with him was Styles. Remember Styles? The guy you let in on this thing that didn't show up at the robbery?"

Cassie Murphy Parker was stunned. She hung up the phone, missing the cradle the first time. She put a hand to her face, which felt warm. She'd just got off the phone with her sister, Kelly. Kelly had been notified that their little brother, Brian, had been shot, murdered, and was possibly involved in the Safeguard Armored robbery she'd heard about on the radio. They'd called Kelly in Sacramento, for Pete's sake, when Cassie lived right here in town. She asked them why they did that, and the police said checking

Brian's sheet—they even called it that, a sheet—said checking his sheet Kelly had been listed as next of kin.

She started to fix herself a drink, a stiff one. Boodles Gin, straight up, that's what she was thinking, but instead she sat down and started crying.

Then, after she did that awhile, she made the drink and called Sonny. What the hell use was it being married to a guy like Sonny if you couldn't use him when you needed to.

They watched Springer drive away in a burgundy Mercedes Benz, Vince thinking the car looked familiar to him but didn't know why.

Only two bags, thought Vince. Damn. Diane wanted one, and there was no way the guys were going to let him have one. Don would ask where his money was, and he would tell him Springer had it, and that would set the guy off. Diane Janzen thought she was getting a cut and the guys would want an equal four-way split. The part with Don Janzen was cool because he was going to screw him anyway. But you didn't screw Red Cavanaugh by not telling him you were hitting an armored car and then laugh about it with the guys at happy hour downing shots and beers. Red would want to know why he wasn't informed and, more to the point, why he didn't get a cut.

Red wasn't going to like it that his "legitimate citizen" deal was on the outlaw trail.

Red could go Arab if he found out Springer, of all people, had the money. So that was another reason to never tell him about this. Red didn't like Springer. Don didn't like Springer. He could see Nicco didn't like him, either. Almost nobody, when he thought about it, liked the asshole, but he kept showing up and getting in the way. And then Chewy, to make things worse, was convinced Springer was some kind of supernatural being.

"Man, I had 'nuff of being 'round that dude," Chewy said. "Man be showing up way too much. Showing up everywhere like those *Star Trek* dudes, beaming hisself around. You wanta be chasing around after unsociable types, you welcome to it. You hear what I'm saying to you? Man be too spooky for me." He told them how he'd met Springer a few days ago, him asking about Jesse Robinson and now Robinson shows up with him. He thought the guy was dead.

"Who did you say that was?" asked Nicco, suddenly interested in the conversation.

"Man's name is Jesse Robinson."

Nicco looking funny now.

"I'll tell you who's the spook around here," said Lunchbox, grimacing as he leaned against the seat back, having a time getting comfortable and bleeding on the seat. "You are. You're the spook, boon."

Chewy screwed up his face and turned around in his seat. "Man, I said 'spooky,' not 'spook,' in the first place. Then, I already overlooking the comment, sounding like Chewy being dissed, you calling the brother a spook. Adding 'boon' to it gonna get your ugly, too-much-linguine ass kicked. I ain't for takin' a lot of other bullshit from you greasy guinea fucks. Just sit there and bleed out your ass, dummy."

"Who's a guinea fuck?" said Lunchbox, forgetting his wound. "I don't like that talk."

"I know you don't. I don't like being called spook, you dago piece a shit. So now we even. Anything else you got to say?"

Getting a little tense in the car now. Vince glad they ditched the guns so these guys wouldn't be popping caps at each other, though he'd've liked to have had one when Springer came up on them. Pull out the nine and send one through the guy's perfect teeth. Who the hell was that guy, and what the fuck was he doing there?

Nicco said, "Fuckin' shut up, the both of ya."

"I been shot, Nicco. And it hurts. He called us dagos."

"I heard him. So what? And he's right, you started it. You want to tear each other up, call each other names like a couple kids in a sandbox? Let's keep it together for a little while, okay? There's gotta be what, a few hundred thousand in those two bags? Think about that."

Vince knowing there was more than that in the bags. He hadn't really given a lot of extra thought about what to do after they took it. He'd sort of looked at the thing like this goal that was unrealistic, like a dream was never going to happen, but now it had. So he had no follow-up. Don Janzen had planned everything.

Asking himself now, what were you going to do with the money, you got all of it? Skip town, right? So take what was left and do that. But that was before Springer showed up, took the money, shot Lunchbox, which didn't break his heart, and before he, Vince, had involved Diane Janzen.

And that was all before they opened the bags. Everybody staring when they dumped the stuff on the bed. Air escaping from Vince and thinking . . . sshhhiiit . . .

No money. Not one cent. It was all casino chips and flyers for cathouses.

Chewy started laughing. "This the most fucked-up enterprise I *ever* seen."

Lunchbox said, "Son of a bitch," holding a motel towel on his wounded butt. Nicco got all pissed off and frothing at the mouth about the whole thing, saying

how the cocksucker with the mouth was going down
'cause he didn't take that shit off nobody. And Nicco
was right. The guy standing there with a gun on them,
smiling and making fun of them, making a big joke out
of it. Chewy telling Vince you brought this miserable
fucking white boy into our lives, and now look what
happen. Nicco asking him how could he let some off-
the-street black guy into their planning session and then
him show up with Springer.

But there wasn't any money. Meaning Springer
didn't have any money, either. So where was the
money?

Yeah, it was a mess. And it was Springer's fault.
And he'd have to pay.

At least the guy left him his car.

But still thinking, man, that car they left in looked
familiar. Where had he seen it?

Springer was thinking, well, that was funny. Back at
Jesse's new motel room at the Holiday Inn Express,
Springer started laughing when he opened the first
moneybag. It was full of casino markers and prostitu-
tion brochures.

"Man, I'm glad you can find humor in this," said
Jesse, picking up a handful of brochures and then letting them cascade between his fingers onto the floor.
"A real source of satisfaction for me, knowing you
can laugh at it. Damn, risked my life for this shit."

Springer shrugged. "What else you have going?
You were hiding out at the Super 8 when I came to
town." He looked at the bags sitting there. "Might as
well open them all. See if they're all the same."

"You think hooker catalogs some kind of hot item
in Vegas? They so valuable we cart 'em around with
armed guards? Because if they are, then we done hit
the jackpot."

"Think of it like a box of Cracker Jack. Sometimes there's a prize inside."

Jesse had his hands on his hips. He snorted. "And sometimes it ain't worth a damn what you find either. You always did—"

Springer ignored him and dumped the contents of the next bag out. More brochures, casino checkers, and then thumping out on top of the pile . . . bundles of cash with Streamers bands around them.

Jesse's mouth was open. He reached down and picked up a bundle, thumbing through it. Picked up another one and thumbed through it, too. Springer scratched his cheek and smiled. Jesse said, "Damn, must be a hundred grand here."

"Around two hundred thousand, be my guess," said Springer. "Twenty-five in each packet."

They opened the other bags but there was no money in any of them, just more fliers and markers.

"What's this about?"

"It means Don Janzen kept the money himself. This must be the payoff to the morons we robbed."

Jesse stood there, slowly shaking his head for several seconds. "This is trouble. No doubt about it. This a damn mess."

"Maybe. But, I've about got this figured out."

"*You* got it figured out?" Not looking like he believed it.

"All except the part about why they want to kill you."

"So, what do we do with this car you stole? Can't believe we did that."

"That? Already got it figured out. I think you're going to like it."

This time Tara St. John wasn't nice. She just called him and told him to get his narrow ass down to her office or she'd have him arrested as a material witness. He was thinking maybe he needed to get a room closer to the station so he wouldn't have to keep going across town. When he got there, Springer told her they had already gone over all this and he didn't know any more about who it was in the morgue even though he figured that wasn't why she wanted to see him.

"I'm not talking about that," she said. "You know a man they call Murph the Surf."

"Yeah, he was a DJ back in the fifties or sixties that turned to crime and went to prison." He knew what she was talking about but waited for her to flesh it out for him.

She looked at him for several moments, her lips pursed at one point, creating tiny dimples in her chin. She placed her elbows on her desk and made a tent of her fingers. "Do you know what I'm talking about or not?"

"He's an acquaintance of a friend of mine."

"Who's the friend?"

He shifted in his chair, wondering where she was getting her information, knowing the police seldom asked questions unless they already knew the answers, so he said, "Sanborn Meeks."

"Meeks. He's a low-life bunko artist."

"Licensed detective's what he told me."

"How is it you know someone like that?"

"I make friends easily." He smiled at her, hoping to keep her from getting any madder at him but not holding out much hope it would work.

"I hope you're not using him to investigate—" She stopped, thinking about it now. "Just what *would* you *be* investigating?" She pushed back from her desk and stood up. She had a pen in her hand and gestured at him with it. "If you obstruct this investigation, I'll put you inside with the crackheads and the drunks for so long you'll forget your middle name. You're going to start being forthcoming or that's where we're going."

He could see she wasn't just talking.

He told her that Meeks knew Murph, a.k.a. Brian Murphy, and that's all he knew about the guy. She said he *never* told her all he knew about anything, and he shrugged. She asked him why he was hanging around Vegas if his friend wasn't dead and didn't know where he was and that she thought somehow Jesse Robinson was the key to all this. He wanted to say the key to all of what, but kept it to himself, not wanting to set her off again. He didn't always say the wrong thing; sometimes he kept the wrong thing to say to himself.

She asked him why Murph the Surf had Springer's name and hotel room number in his pocket. He asked her why she was in his pockets, not trying to be smart, but maybe she took it that way. And, well maybe, he *was* trying to be smart. Then he told her he didn't know why that was, and that was the truth.

"We have Mr. Murphy in a room under heavy guard where he's recovering from gunshot wounds. He's in critical condition, and it doesn't look good for him."

He asked why he was recovering from gunshot wounds, and she told him that he was involved in the Safeguard armored car heist. "He was the unidentified third man."

"Paper said he was dead."

She smiled, not a happy smile.

He said, "You want them to think he's dead."

She nodded.

"That's not bad. One way to do it."

"I have my days." She moved closer to him and sat on the edge of her desk. "Now, tell me, lover, why is it he had your name and room number in his pocket?"

Wondering that himself.

EIGHTEEN

Chewy said, "You think Vince is stand-up?"

"You mean, will he turn us, he's caught?" said Nicco, thinking about it. He lit another cigarette and looked at the bottles of liquor displayed back of the bar, in front of the big mirror. He'd already had a Manhattan, thinking he'd just try it, but it was a little too sweet and had an aftertaste he didn't care for, so he ordered a double Jack on the rocks with a splash of water. He drew on the cigarette and blew a cloud of smoke. "He'll be okay."

"Man don't strike me as the wittiest white boy ever."

Nicco turned in his stool. "Those clothes, the way he talks. Yeah, like he's Dean Martin instead of Jerry Fucking Lewis with muscles. You see his eyes when I said we were leaving the hippy? Voice got all high-pitched."

"Hippy? You mean the little dude. Murph. Why'd you do that anyway?"

"Because he's a guy would turn us, for sure. You see his eyes? He's a juicer and a doper, too. He doesn't know us, but we take him with us, he eventually would have. Besides, we needed a diversion. Get people looking some other direction. I don't know why we had to involve him and the black guy, one that didn't show up. Why'd we have him along? Guy dressed like some guy from one of those black movies you people like so much. Leather jacket, turtleneck, turned out to be with the wiseass and turned shit around on us. Never liked the way that was going."

"You wondering about Jesse Robinson." Giving Nicco a look. Going to let the "you people" thing pass. For now.

"You saying something?"

"You knew who the dude is. Name meant something to you. Tell the way you looked. But you didn't know before I told you. Why's that?"

"The fuck's it to you?" Nicco spat on the ground. "Couldn't believe it. Vince starts talking about the job right in front of a guy he never knew five minutes before. Then when I ask about it, he says the Murphy guy vouched him, so it was cool. 'So how is it the Murphy guy is somebody giving out recommendations?' That's what I said."

"Man's not right in his brain, that's why. Got bad wiring, you see? I was there, I coulda told you who the dude was. I came in late to the show."

Nicco nodded, but he didn't look right to Chewy. Something bothering the man. Nicco saying now, "I got it figured out. Vince didn't plan this thing. Somebody else did. That's why there's no fucking money in the bags, just casino checkers. How we knew when the truck would be there and where to park. Vince had all that, but he couldn't put it together. He only has two reactions. Pissed-off or fucking stupid."

"You think Vince's in on it? Shucking us?"

"Naw. We knock the seal off the bag, he looked like somebody just opened a coffin. Actually shut his fucking mouth for two minutes. Somebody's fucking with him, too."

"Who do something like that? It don't make no sense."

"It does, you think about it. Lot of money is stolen. At least, that's what everybody thinks. Instead, you hand over a bunch of bags with nothing in it and keep the money. You see what I'm saying here?"

"Collect the insurance." Chewy thought it over, drinking his lime and Perrier. He didn't like booze when he was thinking things out. "But, those armored car guys, they check the contents before they roll, don't they? I mean, how you fucking know what you're carrying, you don't look."

"Say they do," said Nicco. "That means either the guards were in on it or the bags have to be switched at some point. How you do that, that's the question."

"The question being, in my mind, is who did that?"

"That's not even a question. Vince's a soft brain. Too many shots to the head. He ain't sharp enough to plan this thing and no way he pulls the bag switch." He tapped his forehead and then pointed a finger upward, shaking it. "The casino owner, Don Someshit, can't remember his name, he's done it."

"You sure cool 'bout this. You ain't pissed 'cause we got hosed?"

"It don't help things, so I don't do it. Just need to think it out."

Chewy said, "Somebody got a sense of humor, that's all." Now he was holding up a chip. "You think these'll play inside Streamers? I mean, we got 'em."

Nicco wasn't listening. Mostly, Nicco was thinking about the black guy, Robinson. Man, it couldn't be, could it? He was also thinking about the casino guy and was there a way to use it to his advantage. Then he thought of it. The guy, Janzen, had the money. He had to put it somewhere and he couldn't put it in the bank and he couldn't put it back in his own vault at Streamers.

So where was all that money?

There was a way to find out, he thought about it long enough.

Vince said, "No money. Paper fliers about hookers and casino chips inside. That's why we shot two guards and maybe get put in the butt-fuck dormitory the rest of my life."

Don Janzen, smoking a cigarette again, damn he wanted to quit those things, and looking at Vince, standing there looking pissed-off, Don saying now, "You thought I'd trust a bunch of thugs with fifteen million dollars? You think that's how I got here, not thinking things all the way through."

"Listen, baby, this ain't the way you laid it out, dig?"

"Who talks like you?" said Janzen, tired of hearing the guy's voice. Actually, he was tired of it the first time he heard Vince speak. "Nobody I know. This isn't a movie and this isn't the old Vegas. This is the new corporate Disney World Vegas. This place isn't even real, except in the accounting books, so you introduce your pseudo-reality to a place . . ." He could see Vince wasn't following what he was telling him and was wondering why he was trying to explain abstract concepts to a functioning moron, so he gave it up. "Dammit, did I tell you to shoot people? You're a little dense, aren't you? The guards were *in* on it. I'd think you could've remembered something like that, you fucking . . ." he trailed off, throwing his hands up. Janzen's voice was rising slightly, not as cool as he normally sounded. Vince's face was coloring, getting mad, but Don didn't care. He was frustrated. "I had them paid off, and you and that band of morons you assembled shoot them."

Vince's head was nodding and he pointed a finger in his cigarette hand at Don. "Hey, man, don't be talking to me like that? *Capisce?*"

Capisce? Now the moron thought he was a wiseguy. He didn't know which made him madder, the fact that Vince screwed up everything or the way Vince talked. Maybe he was just frustrated because he wanted to punch him, but knew better. Don said, "The police are going to be all over this. You think about that."

Vince did think about it. He also thought about the bag he wasn't going to be able to turn over to Mrs. Janzen. Funny that he thought of her as Mrs. Janzen at this moment. He'd bet all the chips in the bag he was holding she wasn't going to be happy about this. What would she do with the information now? She could turn him. Turn all of them. He pulled his snifter out of his pocket and took a blast. There, that was better.

Don was looking at him take a hit off the coke inhaler, not believing his eyes. "Are you on that shit? That's real smart. No wonder you can't think straight. Where are you getting that?"

Vince, feeling better now, feeling the stuff rush to his head, said, "The fuck's it to you. You windbag piece a shit. You fucked us."

Don said, "What are you upset about? You got paid."

Vince said, "What? Man, you're talking bullshit. There wasn't any money."

Don smiled at him. Amazed at how simple he was. The boxer and lounge lizard who hired himself out to Red Cavanaugh, who thought if he smoked cigarettes a certain way and talked in some pop-culture lingo, that would make him cool. Now he was snorting coke in broad daylight and involved himself in a setup robbery, a simple thing that had turned to murder.

"What I don't understand," Don said, "is how you could screw this up so badly. Did you have something else in mind besides giving me my money back?" Vince was looking evasive, Don thought, knowing he was right. "Were you going to keep it for yourself? That it? Or were you going to give some to someone else? Cavanaugh?" Now he was on to something. "Does Cavanaugh even *know* you were doing this?" Don nodding his head now. Smiling. "Doesn't, does he? And you working for him." Don feeling better now, in control again. "That's a lot to think about, isn't it, Vince? If Red doesn't know and I ask him about it, then he'll think you're holding out on him. That might be interesting. How do you think he'll react to something like that? I know how he's reacted to disappointment in the past." Don looked down at the floor, raising a finger, then looking at Vince. "You know what, Vince, I think you're going to do things my way or some really unpleasant people with guns and razors are going to visit you. I wouldn't be in your shoes for anything."

"So where's my pay?" said Vince, trying to be a tough guy again. Don had to admit he could pull it off sometimes, with that nose that had been broken more than once and the prominent bones under his eyebrows that hooded his eyes. But who in the hell gave this cretin coke?

"I put it in one of the bags. Didn't you open all of them? Two hundred grand split any way you want. Go back and look."

Vince looking uneasy now. He sat down in a chair and pulled out a cigarette, stuck it in the corner of his mouth, and left it there unlit. He took another hit on the sniffer and his eyes rolled back in ecstasy.

Don looking at him, knowing something was wrong. He said, "Are you wanting to tell me something?" Vince's mouth was working. Whatever he was going to say wasn't something he wanted to tell.

Finally, he said, "Springer showed up and ripped us off. Took everything except two bags had nothing in them."

Don closed his eyes and let air escape between his lips. Could you believe it? Why? He sat down in a chair, his arms dangling down the sides. Now he had to worry about what Springer would do when Don turned this over to the adjusters. This is what he got, dealing with recidivist morons and being too clever. But he was right not to leave the real money in the bags, as it would've been too much temptation for Vince and his crew. Also, now too many people knew about the phony robbery. He needed the money plus the insurance money to do what he needed to do, which was ace Red Cavanaugh and Sonny Parker and especially Diane out of this land deal. The money. He would have to do something with it now. Move it.

Vince took a drag on his cigarette, blew out smoke and with his head rocking and his leg bouncing, and said, "I get a chance I'm gonna beat that cocksucker blue. Bet on it."

Then it got worse. Vince told him there was a black guy with Springer also. A guy Chewy, the other black guy, knew about.

"What was his name?" Don asked, crushing out another cigarette.

Vince told him he thought the jig's name was Jesse something. "Robinson, yeah, that's what Chewy said."

Don didn't bother to ask who Chewy was. Don ran both his hands through his hair from his forehead to his crown. How did it get like this? Don put a hand to his head and massaged his temples with thumb and fingers.

Vince said, "Hey, something I want to know. How'd you switch the money in the bags?"

Don removed his hands from the back of his head and looked up at him. "You think that's the toughest thing I've had to do lately?"

NINETEEN

Sonny Parker had never seen her this way. Cassie was vacillating between being pissed off—really pissed off—and breaking into tears at the hospital. He didn't even know she had a brother living in Vegas, but knew better than to ask about it right now—say, how come I didn't know about this?—while she was crying and talking about wanting people's "balls cut off and placed in a jar," not wanting to be on that list. Brian, the brother, wasn't dead after all and had slipped into a coma, and Cassie's sister, Kelly, was flying in from California, and now Sonny was on the phone, calling in favors, wanting to know anybody might pull a job like the armored truck heist at Streamers, all the while thinking, hey, this is an odd moment for something like that. Why Streamers? Why now? He didn't like coincidences. Never did. Acts of God, sure. Not coincidences.

Wondering what was going on besides the shooting of his brother-in-law that he didn't even know was in town until this moment.

Women were hard to figure. Cassie hadn't mentioned Brian much, just saying he was a lazy, spoiled brat, working in L.A., the whole time the guy was in

Vegas. Was she ashamed of him or something? Sonny couldn't figure it, thinking maybe it was an Irish thing, you know, with them fighting with each other but if you said something about one of them, then they'd all turn on you. No, then the micks circled the wagons. Crazy that way.

While he was checking on the guys that hit the armored car, he also asked around about Brian, who he learned was also called Murph the Surf. Where did guys get names like that? He learned that Brian was a doper and a small-time criminal who'd been inside county and Vegas lockup a couple of times for shoplifting, car theft, real penny-ante stuff, once catching a six-month fall in L.A. for hitting a 7-Eleven, Sonny wondering why, if you were going to be a hood, why not go for the big felony, not understanding how somebody could risk county time and a record for a fucking car you couldn't keep or could only get a nickel to ten cents on the dollar at a chop shop. That was for drunken teenagers and joyriders. It didn't make sense.

Nothing, lately, made any sense to him.

Pretty soon, even the cops, God bless 'em, would realize that Brian wasn't the brains of this operation, or any operation for that matter. Sonny didn't see it as a coincidence. Why was Brian Murphy, this low-rent crook, in the parking lot of Streamers if he wasn't part of the robbery? Then those guys, whoever they were, blasting away on the streets like it was a TV show or something. Hoods had no imagination anymore. The whole profession was given over to guys that thought with their cocks. Everybody shooting at everybody all the time. Wasn't the first time this had happened in Vegas but was happening more frequently in recent years.

Used to be, you didn't do that or somebody buried

your ass in the desert. Lot of guys buried out there in the desert. He even knew where some of them were.

After making a few calls, he got a line on one guy. Guy named Nicco, somebody Sonny knew about, loosely connected with the Frisco crew a few years back. Nicco would do wet work, enforcer stuff, hadn't done nobody of any account, though, and had hit a couple of banks, they thought, one in a little place in Colorado and one in Idaho a few years back and had done time for the Colorado job. The word was Nicco wouldn't give a second thought to pulling a trigger, he thought it would help things out. The two bank robberies didn't involve guns, but that didn't matter, they told Sonny; the guy was dangerous. And violent. And cold. A real piece of work.

Sonny hung up the phone and thought about things. Thought about the Springer guy. Since he'd come to town things had been popping. Cassie said you could trust him. Cassie was good at sizing people up. He counted on her for that. Had a good business head. Maybe get in touch with Springer, see what he knew about things. What he knew about Don Janzen.

But first he dialed the number of a guy he hadn't talked to in six years, thinking, you never could get away from who you really were.

TWENTY

Powers was smiling as he turned the pickup off the main drag and headed back to talk to Cavanaugh. He had to give Springer credit. The man was one wily hombre.

Funny thing about Cavanaugh's Mercedes. Cavanaugh ranting and raving only that morning about his car missing. Cavanaugh found it parked at Streamers, wondering who had it, but knowing Springer had been at Streamers frequently of late. He'd already heard the tale about Springer, years ago. How Red wouldn't pay off a bet, so Springer stole Red's Cadillac and drove it into the fountains at one of the casinos and, boy howdy, was that man ever gonna go loco violent when he heard this one.

You had to give Springer that he had large cojones. Powers appreciated the irony of the situation. Stealing the ramrod's vehicle again.

Red was gonna love this.

Damn, but you could get to liking this Springer. He rubbed his jaw and felt the bruised skin. But things were how they were, and the sonuvabitch had something coming back to him. Sooner or later, all the bastards acting that way had it coming.

* * *

When Bureau men, agents Tompkins and Johnson, came through the door, Detective Tara St. John knew the Metro robbery guys weren't going to like it, because they wanted a shot at the armored truck heist and knew the feds would hijack the investigation. Not to mention the gaming authorities nosing around, the print media and the broadcast media all over it. There were even inquiries from Fox News and CNN and a couple of the networks.

Which is why she had latched on to Springer so fast. She was homicide, and with the feds and the media all over the place, it wouldn't be long before Captain Meadows would take over the shootings and the FBI would start walking all over her murder investigation. She knew she should share that she thought Springer and Jesse Robinson would know something, but she held it back. For now, anyway.

Why was she doing that? Acting like Cole Springer was what she thought, keeping things to herself.

She was being selfish and ambitious. She knew that. So what? What would the other guys here do? The same damned thing if they thought they could pull it off. Half hating herself for it, but she had worked hard to get where she was, and this situation could make her career.

She had the ballistics people give her the caliber and make of gun, turned around and had some of her people do a computer check on any gun robberies in the area. She called her brother at the Bellagio and asked him to check his sources.

"I want to know if there's any street talk about this," she told him. "Invariably, these things get bragged about."

That done, she ran her files on recent armored car robberies. There had been three in the last five years.

Only one had been successful, but when she ran it it came back that they had the suspects under surveillance and would soon bring them in, but her source told her the men in question had been tracked to North Carolina and would soon be in custody, and no, they hadn't been in Vegas since the heist they pulled.

The fact that the robbery had taken place at Streamers just as she was working an angle there was too delicious a coincidence to be ignored.

Then the bombshell.

She had made a request to have Springer's file made available and was met by an administrative block, telling her that only authorized federal officers could view it. She tried bribing a Secret Service agent she knew in Vegas with dinner, but he said he couldn't risk it. She tried NCIC and same result. She kept pounding away, looking for something when she got lucky.

She located a DEA man in Denver who'd had a run-in with Springer over the agent's ex-wife. He didn't have much he could tell, and again she had run into the "classified" information roadblock. Agent named Ryder. The ex-husband of a Colorado CBI agent. He told her he couldn't say anything about Springer that was official but there was a rumor going around, not part of his official file, that Springer had "hit" some crack houses in Denver.

"It's just a rumor," said Agent Ryder. "After he left the Service he got low on cash, and when he did . . . well, thing is, this is what I've heard anyway, and it's from one of my CIs, says Springer would find a crack house and take it down."

Tara said, "What do you mean, 'take it down'? How would he do that?"

"Well. The way it was told to me, is he would go in heavy, locked and loaded, pretending to be a fed, which, of course, he would know how they do it. He may have even shot one or two of them but never reported because those guys don't have the best rapport with law enforcement. No deaths, but he's supposed to be like some sort of crack shot. A deadeye dick type, emphasis on 'dick.' He takes the cash and destroys their product, thinking he's Robin Hood or something. I know the guy, he's kind of a wiseass but you can't take him lightly. I can't talk about it, orders from above, but you wouldn't believe the people he maneuvered over here. Runs a bar he about lost and then, next thing you know, well, he's up and going again and . . ." The man paused before saying, "Craziest thing I've ever seen."

"How reliable is your information?"

"You want to know how reliable this is?" said Ryder. "Awful damned reliable. It was my fucking jacket he uses when he pretends to be DEA. When I asked him about it, he wanted to know if I wanted my jacket back because he was 'done with it.'"

She hung up the phone and thought about it. Got up and made coffee and while it was making, thought about it some more. Here's what she came up with:

He'd robbed at gunpoint before. Robbed criminals, but robbery was robbery.

And he was a shooter.

But he wasn't a killer. Not according to this report. Wounded the men in the crack houses, not killed them, if you could believe the rumor. The killing of the Safeguard guards was brutal and ruthless, and they had only gone down after several shots were exchanged. Springer, if Ryder was correct, was a dead shot and wouldn't have exchanged that many shots. What she knew of him, and you couldn't always go by what you thought of someone—how many times had police turned the key on killers that their friends and family would swear they could never have killed anyone— was that he seemed too affable to kill, even for money.

Also, he was smart. Resourceful. If Springer decided to do an armored car robbery, it would've been clean, nothing messy. He decided to be an outlaw, it would be white-collar stuff or you'd never know he had pulled it off. But she remembered from the on-site officer's report, the robbery had been well planned, just not well executed, what with all the shooting. However, the robbers had disappeared, and they didn't have a clue who they were.

Their only hope seemed to be Brian Murphy, a.k.a. Murph the Surf, who was in a medically induced coma uptown under heavy guard.

Springer. Robinson. The Janzens. All connected from high school. Twice Springer had been threatened and once brutally assaulted. He had punched out a known leg-breaker and suspected button man, Powers, and gave the man forty-eight hours to get out of town, like they were in the Wild West. But then, maybe he wasn't wrong about the Wild West part.

His high school friend, Jesse Robinson, was in hiding and had yet to emerge.

So many things pointed to Cole Springer. Not least, the love quadrangle involving himself, the Janzens, and Jesse Robinson. So where did she go with all this? She had to move quickly because it was only a matter of time before Captain Meadows would bump her, if not for the glory, but because the Vegas community would pressure him for results.

Sanborn Meeks.

There it was. She knew Meeks. She could press him and he would give her something. But what? Would Springer entrust a guy like Meeks with any pertinent information?

She had to get Springer to take her to Jesse Robinson or find him herself. That was primary. But first Meeks, and see where that took her.

TWENTY-ONE

Red Cavanaugh poured her another drink, Scotch and soda, funny drink for a woman, most of the ones he knew liked that too-sweet pink shit set your teeth on edge you tasted it. Not this one, though. Tougher than she looked. He was getting concerned, not worried, that he hadn't heard anything from Vince yet. He had Powers shadowing the guy and was waiting to hear from him also.

Diane Janzen accepted the drink and leaned back, crossing her legs, show-class legs, and she knew it—he could see that—sitting there in that tan one-piece dress that accented every line in her body. From a distance she seemed like some corn-fed Midwest girl, but up close where you could see the shark-gray eyes, you saw the body and the legs and her stance and knew this was a woman you had to reckon with. How many guys in her life had underestimated her and paid the price?

He was making sure of her. She had been a nice addition to this scheme, and was more reliable and less principled than her ex. Don Janzen would fuck this up, not because he wasn't smart, Janzen being one of the smartest operators Red knew of. No, that wasn't what would do him in. Guy wasn't *ruthless*. Sure, he was calculating and what was that other word, Maka something. Machiavellian, that's it. Janzen could think a thing through from every direction and come up with an idea. So he was worth something to Red because of that. Janzen's weakness was he thought he was smarter than everybody and he wasn't willing to do what had to be done. He could see it in him. He might nod his head when they talked of "fixing" the Springer problem, but watching him Red could see the guy was against it, not wanting anything to do with it.

The guy had another weakness, and it was sitting right in front of him with her legs crossed, sipping a Scotch and soda.

"So," he said, "tell me what you found out."

Diane set her drink on the glass-topped coffee table. It didn't make a sound when she sat it down, though he couldn't see her making any special effort to do so quietly. She said, "The title is in Jesse Robinson's name and his heirs get it if he dies."

"Who's his heirs?"

"I'm working on that," she said, but he thought he saw something in her eyes when she said it. That was Red's gift. He could read people. Which pissed him off at himself when he thought of Springer. She was good, very good, at hiding things, but there was just a momentary little thing going on with her he saw. He didn't know what it was, but he would figure it out.

"So, why does Robinson get the deed, and why doesn't he know about it?"

"The old man liked Jesse," she said. She leaned over and got her purse, giving him a little thigh shot when she did, Red wondering if she did that on purpose, then deciding this one did everything on purpose, but he didn't think it was sexual, more like she was distracting him. Besides, in this town there was more cooze than a guy could dick in a month. He could pick up the phone and get three like her. Maybe not like her. She was probably a wildcat in the rack. Something to think about, but she was also the kind would use her body like a credit card.

She got a pack of cigarettes out of her purse, held the cigarette in front of her, waiting. Red produced a lighter, flicked the flame to life, and held it out to her.

She cupped his hand in hers as she lighted it, then sat back again, and smiled at him. Oh yeah, she needed to be watched.

She said, "Jesse played major-league baseball for the Diamondbacks for two years. Before then, and one year after, he played minor-league baseball here in Vegas, and the owner of the Triple-A team, I think that's right, loved Jesse. They became friends. That was back when Jesse was lovable . . ." She blew a cloud of smoke, then continued. "Apparently, Jesse came back and played one last year of minor-league ball for the old guy. Jesse was finished in the major leagues, couldn't hit the curveball, but was still good enough to help the Vegas club win a league championship. The old man had never won one, and Jesse came back and had a great summer. The old man never forgot that. He paid Jesse a bonus and told him someday he would do something great for him but didn't tell him what it was."

"And what was that something great?" said Red, wondering how she knew this shit. "Cut to the fucking chase, huh?" Why did everybody he talked to lately want to be dramatic?

"Patience," she said, soothingly, brushing her hair back, exposing her throat. "The great thing was that the man is leaving the minor-league team and a parcel of land to Jesse when he dies. And he's dying. In fact, he's in a coma, and the word is he won't last more than a week or two."

"And the parcel of land is sitting right in the middle of the land we need."

"Right."

"And you say the old man is dying?"

She nodded. "He's comatose."

"So," he said, thinking the woman was well informed, "the old man dies, the land goes to Robinson, but he doesn't know it yet?" Or the guy knew it, just didn't realize how important it was. Or knew it and was in it with her. Something to think about. She nodded again. Red took a sip of his bourbon. He should lay off the stuff like his doctor said, what with his blood pressure—which made him think of that cocksucker from Aspen and how he'd like to turn Powers and Vince loose on him—but liked the way bourbon tasted and his medication kept it at manageable levels. Hell, a guy could watch everything he ate and drank and get hit by a bus. So, the whole thing was just a gamble, like everything else. "And if something happens to Robinson, then what? It goes to his heirs, but we don't know who that is? We got to buy this Robinson guy out, right?"

"The problem is, if we make an offer, Jesse will know something's up and he'll hang on."

"What's your solution?"

She raised an eyebrow. "I thought I was looking at the person who could provide the answer."

See, he was thinking, this was the difference between this broad and her ex. She'd go all the way. Wanted things. Liked power. Not that Don didn't like power, but to Don Janzen it was a game—the guy had a corporate mentality—a way to keep score and show everybody what a hotshot he was. This lady, though, she loved power for what she could do with it. She

liked having power *over* people, a wicked, nasty, controlling bitch, and she was doing it now, trying to
have power over him.

"You got no problem acing your ex?"

She sipped her drink. "None."

"So, after we solve Robinson's problem, what
about the heirs?"

"I'll take care of that."

He looked at her, sure now that she was holding
something back from him.

"I promise," she said, clicking her fingernails.
"Trust me."

Diane Janzen left and Red could smell her perfume in
the place. It was afterward, when she left, that Powers
showed up, a big smile on his Texas face.

"What?" said Red, irritated with the grinning. Why
did these stupid hicks grin at you? It was crazy. Now
this country asshole was pushing back the front of that
stupid shitkicker hat, like the one Harry Truman used
to wear, and said, "Listen, old hoss, sometimes you just
have to savor the moment. You know, pleasure yourself.
I'm having one of those moments."

"I got a fucking duodenal ulcer that is already
working itself into a red flame like lava, what with
the booze, and now you're giving me more shit to get
acidic over. I ain't got the patience to savor things,
you know? I just want to know what it is you're smiling like a jackass about."

"Found your car. That's the straight of that."

"Where is it?"

"Yeah," said Powers. "You got any that fancy cac-
tus juice? A nice tequila would work itself down my
throat real nice about now."

"Help yourself."

Powers walked over to the bar and poured himself

a double from the strange-looking bottle, round at the base with a long, slender neck. Took a sip, smiled, and looked at the light amber liquid. "That'll cut the dust and make you forget what you don't want to remember."

"How about it with the sagebrush bullshit? Damn. Will you quit fucking around and get to it? I was a younger guy when you came in."

"Well, here it is. It was sitting in the parking lot at Streamers."

"What?" Red felt his stomach churning. "So, go get it."

"This part's gonna take some reflection. Who you think's been hanging around Streamers?"

"What's that to you? I'm working for you now, that it? But what the hell, huh? If it'll get you to cut the bullshit, I'll sing you a fucking Cole Porter song. Janzen's there of course. Springer . . . Not that guy. Tell me it ain't him?"

"Yeah, I saw him driving it."

Red took his cigar and threw it across the room.

Red stood there for a minute, thinking about it. Springer again. How much more shit could this Aspen asshole stir? How much did the guy know? He was everywhere. Just about one more time the guy's name popped up and, deal or no deal, he was going to have him clipped. How many people was he going to have to ice to get this done? It was like a movie, one of those Tarantino things, where too much was going on to follow.

Thing is, he was beginning to think Springer liked it that way.

"Listen," said Red. "Take the extra key"—looking around for it now—"and go down there and drive it over here. Then, when that's done we'll—"

"Can't do that. He took off in it."

"Why didn't you stop him?"

"You told me to leave him alone, remember?"

This fucking cowboy.

Fucking Springer.

Right off, Sanborn Meeks knew this was trouble. He knew this cop. The foxy black detective from Metro who never let go. He'd run on to her a couple years ago when he was working for a local lawyer in a divorce case. She got on his case and stayed on it until she made a case for breaking and entering. He had to get the stuff on the guy's wife, didn't he? He got off when the assistant prosecuting attorney, a really dim broad who wanted to be important, lucky for him, filed the wrong complaint, but he made sure he steered clear of this lady cop since. Tara St. John. How could somebody looked so hot be so damned mean?

He saw her get out of her car, those great legs the first thing he saw, and then walk to his office and enter. This place needed a back door, that was all there was to it. She said she wanted to ask him some questions. He said, sure, but as much as he wanted to, he didn't know what he could help her with.

She asked about Springer and told him not to lie about it because she already ascertained that Meeks knew Springer. Well, that was good to know, because he was already forming the words "I don't know him" when she said that. She wasn't trying to trip him up, because it looked like she was in a hurry. Yeah, so he knew Springer, he told her.

She asked what Springer was using Meeks for, and he told her he was just a friend, which made her eyes sort of narrow, making her look even sexier and more scary at the same time.

"I don't have time for your bullshit, Sanborn. You're going to tell me what I want to know or I'm going to take you downtown and ruin your day."

"Why pick on me? Man, oh man, why can't you ease up a little? How come you always gotta come at me? I'm just trying to earn an honest living here." She made a face when he said the word "honest." "Okay. I know Springer. So what?"

"You think I'm bluffing, right?"

"No, I do not. I know how you are, and you scare me, so I don't want to get on your bad side." Man, he so didn't want to get on this woman's bad side.

"Then talk to me."

So he did. Leaving out as much as he could and still satisfy her, hoping all the while that Springer didn't find out. Springer wasn't mean, but he was a guy could make you uncomfortable.

Shit, those two should get married and make each other miserable. He'd bet their children would be born with a full set of teeth.

Right there'd be some divorce work he'd never want any part of.

Three o'clock in the morning they busted into his place and started waving guns in his face. Two of them. Hard-looking guys with guns. Vince was barely awake but saw the girl he picked up putting her clothes on and leaving. The two guys just looked at her and let her go.

"She let you in, didn't she?" Vince said.

"What can I say?" said the taller of the two. "This is Vegas. Chippies everywhere. You pay enough, they'll do anything you ask. Was it good?"

"What do you guys want?"

The other guy reached out and slapped him. Vince, who normally could've brushed that aside, wasn't awake yet and didn't get his guard up. Still, the guy was quick and had to be somebody who'd been in the ring at one time.

"Hey," said Vince. "What's that for?"

"You didn't answer the question."

"What?" The other guy swatted him again, but he was able to deflect it some and it bounced off the side of his head.

"I asked you, was it good?"

"Yeah, yeah," said Vince, looking at the guy that hit him. "It was good. It was good, okay? Shit."

"It was free, too," said the tall man. "Our employer paid her. A gift. You appreciate getting free things, don't you?"

"You gonna tell me what you want or—"

This time the guy didn't use his hand. He had one of those steel wands. When Vince put his guard up, the guy whacked him on the shoulder with the rod and it sent electric waves of pain down his arm, making his fingers tingle.

"Fuck!"

"I'll ask you again. You appreciate getting things, don't you?"

"Yes, yes." Yelling it. Surprised at how loud his voice was.

"Well, that's good. Because you see, the hooker, she's got an STD. That's a damned shame, isn't it? See if you can figure out which one she's got."

"Are you fucking kidding me? You got me a whore to give me a disease?"

"Maybe we have the antidote. Maybe not. Might help if you can get immediate help. Of course, that would require us to allow you to leave in time to get that help. All of which depends upon whether you're going to cooperate with us or not."

"What choice do I have?"

Tall guy shaking his head now. These assholes. "None."

Vince rubbed his shoulder, realizing he was naked; he brought the bedsheet up over his crotch. This was a terrible situation. He could feel his scrotum tightening up. Wanting to get up and wash himself. Scrub his cock with Lava and peroxide. VD. Holy shit. He'd gone down on the girl, too.

"So," said the tall man, "You going to cooperate or not?"

"Yeah, sure. What disease she got? She got AIDS?"

"Maybe not AIDS. You could be lucky. Maybe it's only herpes or something." Vince touching his mouth now, thinking about it. "First things first. Who was in on the armored truck robbery?"

"Man. What? I don't know what you're—" Then, seeing the other man raise the wand again, Vince said, "Wait, wait. Shit. I'm going to cooperate, just make him lay off with the stick, huh?" He reached beside him, and picking up a pillow he put it between him and the wand guy. "You want to know about the armored truck robbery? How do I know you're not the cops?"

"Like the police would hire a hooker and have someone come in at three in the morning? That what you think?"

"Who you working for?"

"Look at us, Vince. Don't we look serious? We've got guns, we're fully dressed, and we do this shit for a living. That means we ask the questions and don't answer any. You think you can remember that? Now, again, who went with you on the armored truck hit?"

He thought about it for a moment, then said, "A guy named Springer. Cole—" Couldn't get it out before the guy smacked him with the wand. Harder than the first time. Shit, it hurt. Now the mean guy pulling out a gun and ramming it against his face.

"Lie again. I fucking dare you to lie to me again."

Vince looked back and forth between the two men. Trying to think a way out of this. Give them bad information? What the hell did he care about Janzen? But he gives them Janzen, they visit him and don't kill him, or he denies it, then what? He could say it was the bitchy ex-wife. There was a thought. But again, the same problem. If he said Red Cavanaugh and Cavanaugh sent them, he was in worse trouble than ever, no shit. Who else? The wrong answer here was going to be trouble. He mentions Nicco, who had no connections to any of the others that he knew of. Chewy and Lunchbox? But if they went to those guys, what happened they said there wasn't any money to be had. Janzen had it. But again, the problem with Janzen, plus what would happen to the money then? At least, if he didn't give them Janzen, he still had a shot at a piece of it.

Or they might shoot him. He didn't have any doubts about that.

So he decided.

"I give you the people, you going to mention my name?"

"No, Vince. We're all friends here. We won't mess with you. We'll take it out of the other guys. Of course, you won't be stand-up then, and I'll lose respect for you, but my buddy here won't beat you into a raisin and I won't shoot your ugly face off, something like that. Sounds like a good deal to me. And it's the only one you're gonna get."

"How I know I can trust you?"

The tall guy spread his arms. "You don't. You live in Vegas, every once in a while you just gotta spin the wheel." The guy reached down and patted his cheek. "You know what I mean, Vince?"

So Vince told them. Nicco, Chewy, and Murphy and some guy named Lunchbox.

The tall guy said to the other guy, the one with the wand. "You recognize those names?"

"Yeah," said the man, whose voice sounded like he gargled sandpaper. "I know two of 'em. Don't know any Chewy, though."

Vince said, "He's a black guy. I didn't know him before."

The tall man said, "Well, that's helpful. There's only about ten thousand colored guys in this town, but probably not a lot of them go by Chewy. Where's the money?"

"I ain't got it." Putting his arms up quickly, but the guy didn't hit him.

"Who does?"

Now he had a problem. He'd already mentioned Springer, and they didn't like the answer, so he told them he wasn't sure. Hadn't seen them before. He was surprised when they accepted that answer.

The taller guy said, "Okay, Vince, we'll let you slide this time. And . . . oh, don't think we won't check this out. It doesn't check out, then we come back. We found you this time, right? Won't be hard to do it again. *Capisce?*"

"Yeah," said Vince, nodding his head repeatedly.

The two men started to leave. Vince said, "Hey, the clap thing. What'd she give me?"

The tall man looked at his partner, then back at Vince. He smiled and said, "I think she had a yeast infection. Just wash your joint off good and you'll be copacetic."

TWENTY-TWO

Sonny Parker called Springer and said he wanted to meet with him. Springer, thinking that was pretty interesting, agreed to meet at the driving range.

"Hard to bug a driving range," said Parker.

"Old habits?"

"You're saying something, right? You're always saying something. I know you like thinking you're clever the way you talk, but I'm telling myself it's just the way you are. But clever isn't always the way to go, is it?"

Springer told him he would meet him at the driving range, asking could he use Parker's clubs since he hadn't brought his along. Parker saying sure, but not to outdrive him. Springer saying, well, he'd do what he could. Parker saying, at least *you* didn't smart off again. Springer telling him he was good at taking verbal cues.

They met and Checkers was with him. Checkers smiled at him and stood back behind the driving range, at a nonlistening distance, and nodded at Springer. Good to know he hadn't pissed off the whole town.

Parker was wearing tailored white golf slacks, with a mint-colored polo shirt with the words "Palm Springs

CC" printed on it. He pulled out an Orlimar driver and loosened up.

"I've heard you can use the seven iron exclusively on the driving range and it'll groove your swing."

"Yeah?" said Parker limbering up with the driver across his shoulders and twisting his torso from side to side. "I heard that, too. But I only want to knock the shit out of the ball." He shrugged. "A character flaw, Cassie says. She's the type will come out here and spend thirty minutes warming up with her pitching wedge and putter after stretching for fifteen minutes. The dancer part, I guess. Me? I just want to hit. You a ball striker?"

"Maybe. I kind of like the short game, too. It's like this situation, I guess. You want to go for all of it, but maybe I'm already on the fringe and you're too far back to catch up."

Parker nodded and placed a ball with a red ring around it on the tee and took a couple of warm-up swings. "Yeah? And I've got it that you wouldn't come here unless you thought there was something in it for you." He put a hand to his head, like he was just realizing something. "What'm I saying? You're not a ball striker. You're a ballbuster. What makes you that way?"

Springer watching him, listening to what was not being said. "What is it you want to know, Sonny?"

Parker took a nice swing, Springer seeing the man knew what he was doing, sending the ball past the 200-yard marker then bouncing out to 220. Parker got another ball out of the bucket and looked up at Springer. "Will you tell me what I want to know?"

"Up to a point."

Parker hit another ball that sliced off to the right.

"I hate when that happens," said Parker. "What is that point?"

Springer shrugged.

"You mean," said Parker, continuing, "that you'll tell me what I want to know as long as it suits you, fits into what you want, and doesn't affect your leverage."

Springer squinted out across the fairway and said, "You know, if you'll bring your right hand over some more and keep your shoulders level, it'll straighten out that slice."

"So we're talking about my golf swing now. That it?"

"If you want."

Parker placed the clubhead on the ground. Looked back at Checkers, then at Springer. "Cassie says you can be trusted. Not that you're a Boy Scout or anything, just that you can be trusted. I agree with her up to a point. My take is you can be trusted if you've *decided* to be trusted. And I think you can be trusted to serve your own best interests. How'm I doing so far?"

"Not bad. So what are my best interests?"

Parker smiled. "I know Jesse Robinson is alive."

"That's good to know. I'd miss him."

"Not a big deal, huh? Even though I also know he's a close friend of yours. Something you don't mention the first day we met." He looked at Springer. "You should play poker. Professionally."

"Don't like to sit that long." Thinking how funny that was since he used to stand for hours when he was in the Secret Service.

"You don't even flinch when I mentioned Robinson. Hence, I'm saying you know where he is and have always known. Something happens in this town, I know it. Take that armored car job, for instance. I know who and I think I know why. I sent somebody around to ask about it. These are the kind of people that ask and people are glad to tell them anything they want to know. You hear what I'm saying to you? And here's something else. I think you have similar information. And I want to know, just between friends, how and why you think you know."

"And if I decide not to share my thoughts on it?"

Parker laughed to himself and looked side to side. He reached up and pulled on his nose. "It's not like that at all. You think I'm such a bad guy I do things that way? C'mon. I'm reformed." He shrugged and put his palms up. "I'm fucking Joe Citizen, for chrissake. Cassie's doing. Besides, it make any difference to you if I went that way?"

Springer shrugged again.

Parker turned his head a little, thinking about it, and said, "Yeah, it *would* make a difference if I muscled you." Pointing at Springer. "I think it would make you *more* resistant, wouldn't it? See, that's where Cavanaugh fucked up. He pushed with the shitkicker and you don't like it, so you pushed back. See, this is what I do. I size up people. Kept me healthy and thriving in this open-air shark tank for three decades. I know who to trust and who not to trust. I push you and you're going to bull up and irritate me as much as you can. That's what you do. It winds your clock. I don't know why it does, or why anybody would be like that, but it's what you are."

Springer looked out across the driving range. The sprinklers were making rainbows in the hard Nevada sunlight. "We've got reasons to help each other, Sonny."

"Ya think?"

Springer nodded. "Otherwise you wouldn't be here. I know you won't help because you've suddenly become a philanthropist, and you know I won't help without cause because I've got people to protect."

Parker put a fist on his hip and looked at Springer, shaking his head. "Figured it went that way. Hero complex." Pointing at him with the driver. "See, that's where you're always gonna have problems. You're part con man but got this streak of—what do we say here? You got this streak of gallantry going. You feed that, and it might not go so good for you in this town. You can't think about other people when you jump into something like this, trying to be a savior. For business ventures you've got to get that stuff right out of your head."

"And this is business?"

Parker tamped the clubhead on the ground. "You like to come on like you don't know things, don't you?" Shaking his head, amused. "Okay, that's the way you want to go. You and me, let's say, have been on both sides of . . . well, both sides of these things. It's to our mutual, I don't know, benefit, I'd say, if we pool resources." He paused to let Springer think about it before he said, "You. You're not saying anything."

"You wouldn't ask to meet me if you didn't need me more than I need you," said Springer. "This is your town. You had an advantage, you would just go on without me. So I've got something you want."

"You're a bold son of a bitch, I'll give you that. A little condescending, that the right word?"

"It is. But am I right?"

Parker pointed the grip end of his club at him. "In the old days I coulda got what I wanted out of you."

"It were the old days, I'd have left town when you said you wanted to see me."

Parker lowered his head slightly, looking up at Springer, saying, "Bullshit. You woulda had to prove you're not scared. That's how it is with you."

"We going to continue talking in code or try to do this without it?"

"You going to tell me everything you know?"

"Are you?"

"I asked you first."

"Then no."

"But you expect me to tell you everything?"

"Sure."

"You think funny."

"I've heard."

"What makes you think you can withhold stuff and expect me to open up?"

"Seem's a little one-sided to me, too." He reached up and wiped a small bead of sweat from his neck and wiped his hand on his shorts. "Look at it this way. If you were protecting Cassie and something you might say could adversely affect her, would you tell it?"

"Some days, maybe," Parker said, smiling. "But no."

"And even though you might be withholding things that might harm her, would you still be willing to tell everything else?"

Parker shrugged, looking at Springer. "Go on."

"Well, that's my situation. I'm willing to tell you everything as long as I don't have to tell anything that might bring harm to someone I care about. That make sense?"

"It's starting to. But I gotta admit you're the only guy I've ever met I could say that to. Not that I don't know guys more trustworthy than you, but getting to know you, things you say have a different perspective than if someone else said it. Knowing you better puts things you say in context." He puffed the cigar and set it down in an oversized ashtray. "I can't even believe I'm talking like this, let alone talking to an ex-fed."

"Well, you're the resident capo, so you're allowed."

"I am that. Tell me. You're not going to turn out to be some kind of a do-gooder, are you?"

"Not so you'd notice."

He pointed his club at Checkers. "You see my man,

Checkers, over there? He thinks you're okay. Cassie thinks you're okay. That's the two people I trust most in the world. First day I met you, you could've been a real asshole with Checkers, but you allowed him his dignity. You know about respect. I know that's used so much in the movies that it sounds clichéd but I still hold with it." Then, smiling, he said, "*Capisce*?"

Springer smiled at him and nodded. "*Capisce,* huh?"

"Yeah. What the hell, huh? Gotta have some fun. No use being the resident capo you don't get to haul out the old stuff, right?" He took a step toward Springer, put the clubhead on the ground, and cupped his hands on the top of the grip. "You don't like Cavanaugh much, do you?" Springer cocked his head to one side, admitting it. "Yeah, well, I don't either. I heard about you parking his car in the fountain years ago. Now I hear another car's been stolen. Yesterday, in fact. Ironically, and I say this with the best of connotations, it seems it's Cavanaugh's car again. Now, what're the odds you're in town and that happens again? Most guys in town, especially people in the life, know better than to do that. So, it's either somebody stole it got no brains or got king-size balls and don't care if it pisses off Red. Or maybe, someone did it who *prefers* it pisses him off. You got connections with the Janzens and I want to know, that is, if possible, I would *appreciate* knowing what you think of them."

Springer liking this tough guy with the smart wife. "Don? He's smart. Wants his way. Will do about anything to get his way."

"Is he smart enough not to fuck me in the ass?"

"Yeah. He wouldn't do that. Not unless he was pushed. Or he thought he could get away with it. Or . . . he didn't have any other options."

"Is he dangerous?"

"He'd like to be a tough guy. He doesn't scare very easily. I don't know, pushed hard enough, maybe. Diane's the dangerous one."

Parker leaned back from the club and screwed up the corner of his mouth in a wry half smile. "Yeah, that's what I figure."

"The difference between them is she is more calculating and crafty than Don, and she's got more weapons."

"She ever turn them on you?"

"Sure."

"I think Janzen set up his own robbery."

"Why do you think that?" said Springer.

Parker was shaking his head. "No. Not like that. You're cute, but I'm not going for it. You first. You gotta give me something."

"Okay. But it's not much. Somebody thought they were killing Jesse Robinson; instead, they killed a guy named Clarence Tangent. Street name was Styles."

"Yeah, I knew that already, too." He turned and spoke to Checkers. "Checkers. You mind going down to the clubhouse and get us a couple beers? Get one for yourself, you want. Tell them to put it on my tab." He looked at Springer. "Heineken okay with you?"

"Sure."

Checkers left to get the beer.

"You know what's going on with me and the Janzens?" asked Parker.

"I've kind of pieced it together. You have some deal going, land or something, I'd say. Has something to do with forcing Jesse Robinson out of business a few years back and taking it over."

"That last part I didn't know about."

Springer related the pressures brought to bear on Jesse until he lost his business. Parker asked where this place was Robinson had owned, and Springer told him. Parker saying how that explained a lot of things. What things, Springer asked him. Parker told him there was a deal in the works and Jesse's old place was part of it, but there was a lot next to it owned by old man Cabot, owned a minor-league team.

"I know Cabot," said Parker. "An oddball old guy. Likes doing crazy shit to amuse himself. Reminds me of somebody, but, hey, takes all kinds, right? He likes that kid, Robinson. You know, I've been negotiating with that old fart for that section of land for years, but he keeps smiling and telling me that it'll only be available for sale upon his death and I'll have to talk to the new owner. And him lying there in bed dying of cancer, smiling at me."

"Who's the new owner?"

"He won't say and now he can't."

"What do you want to bet it's Jesse Robinson?"

"Why do you say that?"

"It's the only thing that makes sense. Jesse gets run out of business, the Janzens take over his place. There's a deal going down, an important one, or it doesn't attract you and Red Cavanaugh. I come to town and I'm threatened by the police—"

"Sullivan and Madison, right?"

"Yeah."

"They're on Cavanaugh's payroll. Nothing big. But they think they're rogues and nobody knows it. Too stupid to be subtle or to know everybody knows. I got people downtown can close them out whenever I say, just nobody cares enough to do anything about it. They give Red inside stuff and once in a while they pressure people to move on down the road. Good to know who they are and leave them in place since they leave a trail. They're morons. Still, they've got badges. But go ahead."

Springer nodded. "So, a couple of nights later, Vince

and a couple of locals threaten me, too, and then that big cowboy bounces me around."

"Why you hit him, huh?"

"Well, it was one reason."

"That was something. Then the lady cop, she gets you off. Man, there's a woman should be making movies, not carrying a gun. You just walk up and hit a guy. That the way you do things?"

"He's the type needs to be hit once in a while. You don't, it's like the bully in the schoolyard. He comes by every day asking for your lunch money and then he keeps asking for more. I've got no time for him and had to let him know how things were going to be. His name's Powers, and he's there with Cavanaugh at your place after telling me somebody doesn't want me in town. Now, Cavanaugh has reason to want me out of town, but he's not stupid, so suddenly the pressure stops. No more Powers, no more get out of Dodge by sundown. So, why take so many runs at me and then nothing?"

Parker was nodding. "They got a reason not to attract attention."

"Then there's the armored truck thing. Only I don't think they got any money."

Parker narrowed his eyes, "Why do you say that?"

Springer nodded at Checkers, who was returning with two green bottles. Checkers handed the beer to the pair, then backed away again. Springer took a swallow, which felt good in this heat, and then he said, "Because there wasn't any money to steal."

"What's that mean?"

"Uh-uh." Shaking his head now. "Your turn. I want to know how this deal is working, and is there any way to force the others out of it?"

"You want too much."

"Then I'm through. What I've got, you're going to want to hear. I promise."

"You like being circumspect, that it?"

"Big vocabulary for a resident capo."

"How good is what you got?" Parker asked.

"So good it'll knock you out. It involves Vince."

Parker leaned his head forward. He had his attention. "So, give it."

Springer looked off toward the clubhouse and shook his head.

Parker put his hands up, "Okay, okay. You're a pain in the ass, you know it?" Then he told Springer the land deal. The way it went was like this. There were four of them. Three big owners and a silent partner with a sliver of the deal, maybe providing protection. You know, making sure no one muscles in. Cavanaugh could do that. Parker knew the silent partner was Cavanaugh, who was always in the shit with the Gaming Commission and couldn't buy anything except through a proxy. Don Janzen had forty-eight percent, Diane had forty-eight percent, Parker had three percent, and Cavanaugh had one percent that couldn't be talked about, got it through a proxy, which Springer already knew about, except Cavanaugh's part. If Don Janzen came up with enough money, the contract stated he could buy out the others. Diane had the same deal, as it was part of the divorce settlement.

"Don hadn't figured on the divorce," said Parker.

"Don have enough money to buy everyone out?"

"No, he's already borrowed against the casino, so he can't scratch up enough on a second to make the nut."

"There's millions in his vault all the time."

"The law says he's got to keep a certain amount of cash on hand to cover bets. He can't use that money."

"What if," said Springer, pulling on an earlobe and warming to this thing. "What if he could collect the insurance money on the robbery? Would that be enough?"

"Again, he would have to put it right back in the vault to cover the house bets."

"How about this, then? What if he staged the armored car hit, keeps the money himself, and collects the insurance money."

Parker pointed at him. "You got a twisted way of thinking, you know? There's no way he could account for the cash. Where would he put it?"

"Cavanaugh launders it for him."

"That's not bad." Parker put a hand to his chin, one finger touching the corner of his mouth. "He'd have to cut Cavanaugh in on the deal."

"Maybe. Something Don would factor in. But maybe not if it was a cash deal under the table. Cavanaugh can't own anything in Vegas that deals with gambling, right, so maybe Don gives him so much cash and a few points on the venture, all off the books. Don gets what he wants, and Cavanaugh gets a proxy."

"It could work, but it's a long shot. I mean, the risk; it's long odds you could pull it off. Insurance investigators, the Gaming Commission, the FBI." Counting them off on his fingers. "A guy would have to have a pair like Godzilla or just be nuts."

"Don loves to gamble. Especially if the gamble's worth the risk to him. Is it?"

Parker reached up and scratched the side of his face. "Maybe. Yeah, it probably is." Thinking again now, he began shaking his head, agitatedly. "But forget about it. Nobody would have the nuts to pull something like that off. Not Janzen, not even Cavanaugh. Where you get ideas like that, anyway? Reading comic books?"

Then Springer told him. He said, "I've got the bags from the armored car."

"Are you fucking crazy?" Sonny looking around now. "You got what? Are you some sort of mental defective? What's that mean, you got the bags?"

Springer reached out and Parker handed him the club. Springer took a stance and said, "Even better than that. It was Vince pulled the job."

Parker started smiling like he wasn't going to stop. "Yeah, I knew that already, just wanted to hear you say it, see if you were going to shoot me straight. So," he said, "what do we do with this?"

Springer took a swing and the ball sailed down the middle of the course. He looked up and said, "Funny you should ask."

TWENTY-THREE

First it's one Janzen, then the other. Getting it from both of them. This extra-deadly older girl bitching him out. How could you allow Springer to do that, calling him Cole, she asked him, and he said, who knew how the guy did anything, her forgetting all about the afternoon in the sack. She even gives him a bag of blow and a tool to snort it. Vince didn't understand it. Most chicks he hosed were nicer after. On his side. Not this one. It was like she thought she had hosed *him*, been on *top*, you know, not the other way around.

In the old Rat Pack movies, the ones Vince liked, the chicks were happy just to hang around with the Chairman of the Board. Slap her around, Frank wanted. And if he banged her . . . well, she was his from that moment. That happen anymore? Who knew?

"Well, I don't wish to see you around here again," she said. "So I'm going to ask that you stay away unless I call for you."

"You're kidding me, right?" came out of his mouth before he could think of something else to say.

She laughed at him. "It would be helpful if you

were a little more perceptive. You don't see that I can't have you around? Vince, darling, Springer knows. He knows you robbed Streamers. And he's smart. Smarter than anyone you know. And too much of a con artist to let it go. There's no telling what he's going to do with that. And don't get any notions about going after him. He'll eat you alive. I'm part owner of Streamers. I can't be seen with the person that robbed my own place. I don't want the police to connect you with me, and I will especially stipulate that Cole doesn't know about you and me. Does that register with you?"

"Yeah, well, it was him took the money." He snapped his fingers. "Hey, that could be some kind of loophole, you know?"

She closed her eyes. Her mouth was open and her straight white teeth were set in a line. She opened her eyes. "Vince, don't start thinking of a way out of this. You've done enough."

"Listen, baby, we can make this work," he said.

She crossed her arms on her chest and looked at him. "Are you going to make me call security? The police?"

"Why you being this way? There's no—"

"Get . . . out." Teeth clenched. "Now."

So he left. How you figure somebody like that? One minute she's all claws and heavy breathing, the next she's telling him not to ever come back. Fucking women. Who needed them? Plenty of them around.

Maybe not like that one, though.

Probably a good thing, he decided.

Sanborn Meeks had been drinking. Springer saw it right off when Meeks showed up, all florid-faced and rubbing his jaw intermittently. Springer was in a new room at the Crest, a motel off the Strip, after moving out of Streamers. Keep a lower profile. He also rented a room with a view of Streamers for observation purposes, putting Sanborn in the room with "enough surveillance shit to start a porno flick." Sanborn's words.

Vince and Nicco would be after Springer now, mad enough maybe to start pulling triggers. Nicco looked the type, and Cavanaugh was always a worry, so he'd picked this place. If he'd guessed right, Don Janzen would know soon enough that Springer picked the robbers clean. That was good and worked to Springer's advantage.

That is, if nobody killed him first, which wouldn't be much fun and would infringe upon his retirement plans.

Whoever killed Styles thinking it was Jesse Robinson had beaten him to death. That suggested Vince. He was a boxer, but for the most part Springer had only heard the guy talk tough and act stupid. Whoever it was, and Vince was a possibility, enjoyed doing it. Or maybe wanted to make a point. Styles was badly mauled and beaten. Maybe they knew it wasn't Jesse and wanted to send a message. But why choose Vince to do it? He was a lot of things, but Springer wasn't ready to peg him as a killer. It just didn't add up. But they'd used him to rob the armored truck. What was the difference?

The difference was that Don, or whoever, wanted somebody dumb to pull the robbery. Did he want a pawn? Someone he could give up who wouldn't know what to do about the fact there was no money in the bags? Sure, Vince could say Don put him up to it, but Springer knew Don had already considered that angle and would have taken steps to insulate himself from Vince. Why steal from myself is what he'd say. Where's the money if I took it? Springer also would bet that only Vince knew of Don's part in this scam.

And Don would have the money in a place they couldn't find it. He'd have that factored into the scheme. However, Don wouldn't have factored in Springer following Vince to the getaway car and ripping him off.

Who gained from Jesse dying? Jesse didn't know about the land deal, at least he hadn't mentioned it. Maybe they could've bought him out. Here's x amount of dollars, now get lost. Why didn't they try that? Why kill him?

Because there was some reason Jesse couldn't be alive or something Jesse knew that he didn't know he knew. It was, like Sonny Parker said, "crazy thinking." But the whole setup was convoluted.

Maybe Don would benefit and hire the killing done. Vince was hanging around Don a lot. But, for all his faults, Springer didn't see Don as a killer. Cavanaugh? Now there's a candidate. And Vince had connections with Cavanaugh, too. Powers? For all Springer knew, Powers wasn't even in town at that time. Maybe he'd taken Springer's advice and left town. He smiled, realizing that wasn't a possibility. Powers wasn't going to be frightened off. Even if he wasn't as big as a refrigerator, the cowboy wasn't going to pay any heed to Springer's warning.

Jesse had blackmailed the Janzens at one point. But he stopped. Why did he stop? Because he didn't like the idea of being a blackmailer is what Jesse told him, and Springer believed him. But then Springer had another thought and asked him if he was sleeping with Diane again when he caught up with him at Jesse's apartment.

"Man," Jesse said, "where's your head at?"

"You going to answer the question?"

"What business is it of yours?"

"Aw, no. You did sleep with her."

"What if I did? It don't hurt nothing."

"That's well thought out. You ever think that could be why somebody wants you dead? All the talk about revenge and getting forced out of business before. That's all out the window, she lets you get under the sheets. You've got to quit taking intelligence-reducing pills, Jesse."

"You're jealous."

Springer looked at him, not believing any of this. Sometimes you just had to let people work things out. Some of it long-standing and without comprehensible foundation. He let out a breath and sat down.

Jesse said, "That's right." Animated now, stalking up and down, his head bobbing. "You're ate up because I was her man. Took her away from you, years ago."

"If that makes you feel better." Springer wondering why the conversation was taking this side road.

"You don't know shit about being black, Springs."

"So," Springer said. "What is it? Being white invalidates my viewpoint?"

"Don't start that patronizing shit. You always thinking you smarter than everyone."

"In this case, it isn't all that hard."

"Well, fuck you, man."

"Why the heat, Jesse? Because I ask you questions about a woman? What are you going to do? Yell at me some more? I don't see how this is productive."

Jesse sat down, too. "No," he said. "No, it's not."

"I want to know what things you talked about. What things she asked you."

"You know, just things. What you whiteys call 'pillow talk.'"

"Whiteys? How about it on the race issue, Jesse? Give it a rest. What do you call it?"

"We call it, I got things to do, bitch." Jesse smiling now.

"And they say chivalry is dead."

Jesse laughed. "Okay, we talked about Jesse Jr. How was he doing? Things like that."

"You bring it up? Or her?"

He thought about it for a moment. "Me, I guess."

"How is he doing?"

"She said fine. Got himself adopted by some nice folks in Atlantic City. Good family. Good schools."

"Didn't you have some trouble in Atlantic City a few years back?"

"Yeah. Hit some punk-ass dealer was dealing cards off the bottom. They locked me up, said I couldn't come back to that town. Ever. I got probation, but if I go back there they're going to activate the sentencing. That's one town I'm never going back to."

Springer filed that away—the fact that she placed Jesse Jr. in Atlantic city where Jesse Sr. wasn't allowed to go, then said, "She ask you about a guy named Cabot?"

"Mr. Cabot? That's funny, because she did. We talked about him a lot. I told her I liked Mr. Cabot. Still visit him from time to time. He was good to me. She thought that was nice, telling me it was good to see that kind of friendship between an African American and an old white guy."

"She called you African American?"

"Yeah, she talks like that. A way for her to let me know what my place was. I say anything about it, she would act all hurt like I didn't understand, telling me she had my baby, didn't she? What kind of prejudiced person would have a black man's baby? That's how she phrased it. Not, I had your son, Jesse. No, it was a black man's baby."

"Well, you know how us whitey's are."

"Okay, I was out of line a few minutes ago." He pursed his lips. "Maybe about the other things, too.

But you a probing mother-fucker. You oughta give some thought about your diplomatic stance."

Springer shrugged, thinking some more. Things could get complicated at this point. At present, he didn't know who had killed Styles or who was conning whom but was sure it was going on. However, it could be so intricate a web of deceit he might never be able to untangle it until Jesse was dead. And he was sure on that point. For some reason, Jesse had to die for someone else to benefit or even revenge.

Springer said, "Right now, I'm thinking Diane may have come on to you"—he raised his hands to ward off another tirade from Jesse—"in order to get you off her back and keep you from blackmailing them again. I know it sounds far out, but there is some reason these people are trying to keep from calling attention to themselves."

Springer had decided to trust Parker. That much was done. One alliance. He didn't know yet whether he could implicitly trust Jesse. Springer trusted Jesse's friendship. However, there was something going on with Jesse and Diane. And Diane liked intrigue. Always did. Diane looked innocent, that heart-shaped farmer's-daughter face hiding the manipulative nymph within. It had always worked to her advantage and she would rely on it.

Then there was the problem of Tara St. John. She was able, sharp, and ambitious. She suspected much and knew things she wasn't saying. He didn't blame her; he was doing the same and would do so in her shoes. But she was a wild card here, the one person who could connect the dots and blow things up in his face.

Follow the money. Always.

He looked up at Jesse and said, "Jesse. Don't get

touchy again. But when's the last time you saw Jesse Jr.?"

Tara St. John found what she was looking for. What Springer had said about the arresting officers in Jesse Robinson's arrest in 2001. He knew their names. She did, too. Officers Madison and Sullivan. What she was doing would get her busted down to water-waste patrol if she was caught skipping procedural steps.

The flip side was that if she was right and she could trust Springer, then she would make huge strides in her career and Madison and Sullivan would have to turn in their badges. What was wrong with a girl thinking about her career? Nothing she could see.

Sanborn Meeks had given her information she could use. Some of it was bullshit, of course, Sanborn being a bit of a lowlife, but loyal, in some strange recess of his mind, to Cole Springer, so the information had more or less dribbled out. Springer had that going for him. People wanted to like him. Wanted to help him.

The state had a witness, Rusty McFarland, in a safe house off the strip. Rusty had taken two falls on federal counts. The third would send him inside for all day long. Rusty knew that, so he was willing to give up some big shots the state guys wanted, and they were basically hiding him out from the feds, who likewise coveted Rusty's testimony.

Rusty was a chain-smoker with emphysema and had been a mob button man back in the old days. Carried a straight razor and a .22 derringer. They called him Rusty Derringer because of it. Rusty's way was to put one in the base of the skull from behind and make sure with the razor. A nasty man, Rusty didn't want to spend his remaining years in the lockup breathing stale prison air.

"They told me, ya see, I turn these guys, the worse I get is the federal prison hospital in Springfield, Missouri," Rusty was telling Tara. His voice rasped like he'd had his throat cut. "That's where they kept Gotti 'til he kicked. Cancer. The don got cancer. Fucking crazy world, isn't it? One day you're wearing suits cost as much as a used car, next day you're in prison issue counting the hours until your next hit of morphine."

"Rusty," said Tara, "you know Red Cavanaugh, right?"

"Ol' Red? Yeah? He's my people, you know. He's a Scot. Maybe some black Irish in there, but the bastard's name is Cavanaugh and his hair is red as a sheepherder's knees."

"You worked for him."

"Yeah, I did some stuff for him."

"Wet work?"

Rusty sat back on his bench. "You're a good-lookin' girl. Black, aintcha?" She could smell his tobacco breath on her face and tried not to grimace. "But there's some white in you, too. Am I right?"

"What kind of work did you do for Red Cavanaugh?"

"I ain't giving up Red. He's not who I agreed about, you know. Red was good to me. I may rat out those two cocksuckers tried to have me iced, but Red always treated me right."

She shook her head. "I'm not after Red. I'm after a couple of police officers."

"You internal affairs?"

"No. I'm homicide."

He started coughing. A liquid hacking cough. This went on for several moments. Finally, he gained control. He reached up with thumb and forefinger and wiped the tears from his eyes. "Fucking cigarettes'll kill you," he said, shaking another Camel from the crumpled pack and lighting it. "You're not internal affairs, what's your interest? This gonna help me any?"

"I'm wanting to close out two police officers. Sullivan and Madison."

"Sullivan and Madison? Yeah, I know those two shitheads. Don't like 'em either."

"So, you'll tell me what I want to know?"

"Anything. Just promise me those two assholes go inside. All I want."

"Do they work for Red Cavanaugh?"

He leaned forward. "You're not going to say nothing to Red about this?"

"He can't get you here."

"I don't give a shit about that. He don't scare me. I'm dying and I ain't no rat. I'm stand-up, 'cept for these two bottom-feeders tried to cash me out. Red never done me wrong and I won't do him wrong, neither. I tell you things, you gotta promise you won't use it against him."

Tara found herself nodding. Honor among thugs. It was something, wasn't it?

TWENTY-FOUR

Follow the money.

Or, in this case, follow the people who want the money, Springer was thinking. A lot of people wanted the money. Don and Diane Janzen, Red Cavanaugh, Vince and Nicco, and even Sonny Parker, though Sonny seemed to want, more than anything at this time, to burn someone, anyone, for his wife's sake. That probably meant Vince.

Sanborn Meeks was coming in handy after all. Never expected it, but Sanborn knew how to hook up a phone bendix and had a mini-camera, one of those so small it fit in your hand and a surveillance system setup. Those things were going to come in handy. Springer didn't want to know where he got them or what he had done with them before now.

Sanborn put a bendix line and wiretapped Don and Diane Janzen's phones. The way the bendix worked was once Sanborn had spliced into the phone lines, he and Springer could monitor conversations and even make calls from the Janzen's phone numbers via a remote line Meeks had rigged up in the hotel across the street from Streamers.

Springer asked him how he was able to get that done.

"Bribed a guy I know works inside there. One of the janitors. You owe me five bills."

"Pretty steep."

"In Vegas? Guy could lose his job. That's bargain basement for this town."

"The phone thing. That's illegal, isn't it?"

"Yeah. Beautiful isn't it?"

Springer looked at him. "You sure you're not a crook?"

If there was no money or little money in the other two bags Springer left with Vince, then Vince would by now be pissed off and going to Don Janzen. That is, if Janzen had anything to do with it. Vince would be pissed. Sure. But probably wouldn't know what to do about it.

Nicco, on the other hand, would likewise be upset but know what to do. Nicco would think things out and figure out how to use it to his advantage. Unless Springer missed his guess, Nicco was a career criminal. He wasn't upset when Springer shot his fat buddy, and unlike Vince, with his meaningless threats, Nicco would forego revenge in order to make a buck. Vince would focus on Springer, whereas Nicco would be thinking about where the money went and how to get his hands on it.

The more Springer thought about it, the more he liked the insurance angle. There were other possibilities, but it was the only one that fit so neatly. The adjusters would not know Don kept the money, if he did, and they'd stall as long as they could, but eventually they'd pay off, and even if he didn't recoup the whole nut, it would be a pile of bucks. If Don kept the money, then he could add it to his stash and greatly enhance his buying power, if that's what he

wanted to do, letting one of Cavanaugh's contacts
launder the money. Also, he would not have to rely
on other investors. If the deal Sonny Parker told him
about held, with Don and Diane holding 48 percent,
then Don, with a windfall of cash, could conceivably
buy a controlling interest and then even keep Parker
and Red Cavanaugh at bay.

Thing is, it seemed curious to Springer that a guy
could have millions in the bank and want more and
even be willing to risk it all. It was foreign to the way
Springer looked at things.

So there he sat, looking through a telescope and listening to phone calls come in and go out from Don
Janzen and Diane Janzen's office phones. Only problem with the setup was Springer and Meeks couldn't
listen to both phones simultaneously. They had to flip
a switch and choose between the two. Not much had
come in so far that would be any help.

When he was in the Service he had been called in and
told to "quit making decisions on the fly." In other
words, quit improvising. His position was that when a
situation was fluid, then you acted accordingly. The
position of his superiors was that he abandoned the set
plan too often and was capricious in doing so. Wasn't a
team player. But he liked working like that. Trusted his
instincts. It had served him well in Iraq and since.

Which is why, when he saw the dark blue Monte
Carlo pull into the parking lot and two guys get out—
one dark guy and a heavy-set guy limping—he decided to make one of those off-the-cuff decisions.

"I'm going down there," said Springer.

"I'll go with you."

Springer looked at him. "You monitor the phones."

"What if you run into some rough stuff?"

"If you're here, I won't have to watch out for you."

Which is how he ended up outside Don Janzen's

office and, despite Janzen's secretary's protest, was about to open the door.

The guy, Janzen, wasn't glad to see them but didn't look scared or nothing. Nicco thinking the guy was cool, not the type to react too quickly. Looking up at them like they were there after a job, asking what they wanted. Not looking like Nicco pictured him. Guy was wearing a polo shirt and shorts. Big window behind the desk where the guy could look down on the casino. A cool office. Handsome, clean-cut, looked like he worked out, you know? Was expecting some fat guy with a cigar and a sharkskin suit in his mind. Somebody Nicco could scare.

Not this guy.

Nicco came right out and said what he wanted. The money. All of it. The guy saying he was at a loss here about what he was speaking about. Nicco fishing a little bit now, telling the man, c'mon you know what I'm talking about. Not wanting to say "the money from the truck we robbed" because all these Vegas guys taped everything.

"Turn off the camera," he said to the guy.

That's when the door opened and the smart-ass who'd ripped them off came through the door, saying, in that tone he had, like he knew something you didn't, "Am I interrupting?" Then showing them his gun. Not a big one, but he remembered the guy knew what to do with it, not looking like he was trying to be tough, more like he was showing them the same stuff could happen all over again.

"I'm glad you're here," Janzen said.

"First time for everything," Springer said, not taking his eyes off Nicco.

"These guys are muscling me," said Janzen. "You make them leave and I'll make it worth your while."

Springer looked at Nicco and said, "Why do something like that?"

"Like what?" said Nicco.

"Try to intimidate a guy like Don here? Are you socially retarded?"

Nicco, sizing up the situation, deciding not to let the guy get to him, seeing he was trying to, shook a Marlboro out of a hard pack and said, "You can put the gun away. No need. No need to be uncivil, either. We're just talking here."

"So, what're we talking about?"

"Why you wanta know?"

"Naturally nosey, I guess." Then, looking at Lunchbox, who was shifting back and forth, the wound still bothering him, the Springer guy said, "That hurt much? Looks like it hurts."

"Fuck you."

"I'd say it was the other way around."

Nicco said, "How come every time I see you, you got a gun?"

"I put it away, I'm afraid you'll be unfriendly."

Nicco pointed at his chest with the back of his wrist toward Springer then put his arms out. "Who? Me? Why would I do that?"

Springer smiled. "Yeah, you're right. You're not the type to do anything straight at a guy. You're more a back shooter, aren't you? I mean, I heard all your stupid threats in the car the other day. Tiresome's what that is."

Now the guy *was* getting to him. Didn't want him to, but the guy was laying up a big debt. "Why you busting my balls? That why you come here?" He pursed his lips, looking to Lunchbox and then back at the smart-ass. "I gotta tell you. I really do. This isn't a smart move on your part. No, it isn't."

"Cause you're such a tough guy, right?"

"You're about one step from fucking with me, and that's not gonna work."

"One step? I've been doing it since the first time I laid eyes on you. When are you going to catch on?"

"Put the gun down and we'll see what's what."

"Are you kidding me? Nicco, look close. I'm bigger, faster, and in far better shape than you. Even if Fatty helps you, I'm going to wear you down, and then I'm going to drop-kick you around the room. I mean, thanks for the offer, but some other time, huh?"

"Why're you acting like this?"

"Because I know you're not used to it." He looked at Janzen. "That camera on?"

Janzen shook his head and said no.

"Well, turn if off anyway," said Springer, smiling now. Nicco seeing the guy didn't trust Janzen. Now wondering how the hell he showed up like this or even why. The guy just pops in and out, like the day he took the armored truck bags off Vince, in his mind blaming Vince since he knew the guy and let the black guy in on the deal.

Janzen looked at the wiseass, smiled, reached into his desk and did something. "There."

Springer nodded at the window wall that looked out on the casino floor. "That, too."

"Why are you so mistrustful?"

"History," said Springer. Nicco not knowing what that meant but getting the feeling he was in the middle of something that wasn't all about the money. Something between these guys. Talking to him and Lunchbox like he did showing he wasn't afraid. Making jokes. Now watching the guy move closer to Lunchbox. What was he doing? Watching Lunchbox's eyes, Nicco could see the fat ass was gonna make a move.

Shit. Nicco getting ready but thinking Springer was up to something.

Springer said, "You two think Don here has money, don't you?" He moved closer to Lunchbox.

"The fuck's it to you?" Watching Lunchbox edge toward the guy.

"Because Don doesn't have the money." Closer to Lunchbox now. Almost there.

"What's that mean?"

"It means you and double-ugly here are humping your own legs. Don's got nothing for you."

"Well," said Nicco, opening his arms, trying to distract the guy while Lunchbox made his move. "Then, if we're in the wrong place, let me apologize from the—"

Right then Lunchbox made a grab at Springer, but the guy was too quick. He made a quick step away from Lunchbox, who was already hurting from the bullet wound, and the wiseass cracked Lunchbox on the back of the ear with the gun. Nicco made a step, but thought better of it. Guy was fast. Always another time.

Lunchbox staggered off and sat in a chair, holding the back of his head, yelping when he sat down too hard and the ass wound bit him. Lunchbox said, "Why you always picking on me?"

"Because you're stupid and keep doing stupid things. Like being here when I don't want you here. You want some of the money, I can give you some. Not because you scare me, because we can all see you're pathetic. But it's better than worrying about you two clowns dogging me and me having to shoot you or slap you around some more."

This guy was really pissing Nicco off, but what could you do, huh? Guy had a gun.

Springer said, "You want to know my deal or not?"

"Yeah, sure. Where you stayin'?"

The guy really laughing now. Even when he wasn't saying anything this guy could piss you off. "That's really cute, Nicco. Just like that, huh? I'm going to tell you where I'm staying like we're cousins from Iowa or something. I may just hang around with you just to see what you'll say next. Hey, did you ever sit in the corner of the classroom with that dunce cap on when you were a kid?"

"You better fucking shut up. You know? I'm getting tired of this shit."

"I don't care. You don't seem to be able to understand that. I want you out of here." He pointed the gun in Nicco's direction.

Nicco had already seen him shoot Lunchbox and didn't need convincing. "Okay." Nicco's head bobbing. "Okay. We'll go." Pointing at Springer now. "But this ain't the end of it. Uh-uh. Not by a long ways, cocksucker. We'll see each other again."

"I can't think of anything to say to that, what with you being such a tough guy."

Nicco shaking his head. "This is bullshit. You mentioned money."

"If you're interested, I'll give you some of it. Thing is, I don't like Vince very much. You either, when I think about it, but mostly it's Vince I don't like. Think about how I knew about the hit on the armored truck."

Yeah, thought Nicco. That explained a lot. That fucking palooka, Vince, with his way of talking like you were watching a bad impersonation and spreading the word about the hit to anybody who walked off the street. And because of Vince being a dumb ass, he had to put up with this guy's shit. Now the guy was talking again.

"Thing is, Don here and I are in on this thing together. We just used you guys."

"What?" said the Janzen guy, rising up in his seat.

"It's okay, Don," said Springer, motioning at him with his free hand. "There's nothing they can do with it. You did turn off the camera and the monitor, right? I mean if you didn't, then you've got trouble."

Janzen nodding his head now. "Yes, I turned it off." Nicco seeing the guy was glad he did, too. What was this guy's angle? Man was fucking with everybody in the room, even the casino guy. Deciding he needed not take this Springer too light.

Springer continued. "Now, thing is, we don't want to give Vince his split. I've decided to give you all his part and blow him off."

"How much is that?"

"Fifty grand."

Lunchbox said, "Fifty?"

Springer nodded.

"There must've been a couple of million somewhere," said Nicco.

"Doesn't matter if there's a billion and a lifetime pass to Disney World, you only get fifty and I'm not shooting you in your face. I don't know if you're going to get a better deal today. I don't have to give you anything."

"So when are you gonna give it to us?"

"I'll get hold of you."

"How you gonna do that? You don't know where we're staying or nothing."

"Nicco, look at the situation. I know everything about you. Found you here didn't I? Think that's a coincidence?"

Outside, Lunchbox was groaning about the lump on his head and his ass hurting.

"Quit crying," Nicco told him.

"Guy got lucky," said Lunchbox. "I almost got him. Then we'd see if he liked to talk that shit."

Nicco told him. "You don't get it, do you? He was sending you a message. He let you get close so he could show us what he could do. Did it intentionally. And you, ya dumb fuck, what were you going to do, you get hold of him and him with a gun? Huh? Get shot again? Once in a while, it'll be okay if you don't fuck up. What've you got so far for it? Shot in the ass and hit on the head, that's what. Am I right? When you gonna learn?"

And, Nicco was thinking, maybe Springer was telling them no matter how close they got, touch him. But Nicco was gonna prove that wrong. That man just rattled the wrong cage.

After the two thugs left, Don Janzen stood up and walked over to the bar, saying, "So, what was that about?"

Springer walked to Janzen's bar, like he was at home, flipped a rocks glass up into his hand and selected a bottle of Glenlivet, pouring himself a couple of fingers. Took a short sip, smiled, and said, "Why, Donald. Whatever are you talking about? I was hoping you'd tell me."

"So, it's going to be like that." Don nodding his head. "Do you really have my money?"

Springer took another short sip, letting the Scotch roll around his tongue and gums, feeling the warmth and smoothness of the malt. He held the glass up and looked at the amber liquid. "Now, that's the way all Scotch should be. Smooth, subtle, yet some heart to it."

"You stole my money. I don't know how you did it or what those two had to do with it, but you need to

return it. Give it back and I'll forget the whole thing
and won't call the police."

"Okay," said Springer, walking back toward the
desk. "I like that. You don't have one rock in your
pocket, so you bluff. I'm not from Vegas, Don, and
that stuff's not really working for you here." Pointing
at the phone now. "So, go ahead. Call the police. I
think it's a heck of an idea."

Don set his hands drink down, looking off toward
the drawn curtains now. "What's going on? Why'd
you tell them you've got the money?"

"Because, if I hadn't, at some point they find you
and force you to tell them where you put it. There's
no way around that. Be harder to do it, they think I'm
with you."

"Why would you think that?"

"That's what those guys do. You should know better. You're a smart guy, but smart doesn't work with
these guys. All they know is you've got something
they want, and eventually they'll get around to getting
it. They don't have much imagination either, so it'll be
what you think they'd come up with."

"Why tell them we're in this together?"

"Keeps you honest. You need me. Without me
they'll eat you alive. Now you need to keep me happy
and healthy. I don't think you're a killer, Don, but
somebody around here is. You've got yourself in a
mess, and there's no way out except through me."

"Say that's true. Why help me out?"

"I've got my reasons."

"I don't have any problems." Don's pride at war
with his intellect, Springer was thinking.

"Good to know. Keep thinking that. Thinking that
way is going to get you killed or in jail. Maybe, at
best, they'll just send you to ER for a few days. Break
a few fingers, maybe your elbow. I knew of some

guys, about like those two, wired a guy's nuts to a door and kept slamming it until he'd write them a check for $5,000. Five grand. A check, if you can imagine that? I wonder how they thought they were going to cash it. And the worst part? They had the wrong guy." He took another sip of the Scotch, set the glass down. "These aren't honor students you're dealing with. Way I see it, and I'm not kidding, these guys aren't screwing around and they'll be back to ask again. You're a fixed target, easy to find, and you've got a deal going which is going to cause you to stay put. I've more or less figured out you sent Vince and that oversized cowboy to see me. Or, at least, you knew about it."

"Why are you doing this?"

"Because you don't know me anymore. You used to, but now you don't."

"You're fishing."

"Yeah. You're right about one thing. I've got your money. But only a small percentage."

"What does that mean?"

"Vince probably told you. He had to. He's stupid enough to run right in here and tell you everything." Springer looked off toward a painting on Janzen's wall. "Maybe what he did, he told you he didn't get anything, and you told him there was money in one of the bags and he was surprised by that. A payoff. That close?"

Springer watched him. Don wasn't dumb. Don was cool, but Don was screwed here, and Springer knew he would be thinking of ways out of this without tipping his hand. Gambling was Don's world, not Springer's. Springer was a risk taker, sure, but that wasn't the same thing. It was the difference between bluffing on your hole card and deciding you could back down a bigger man by your attitude. The first one you had no recourse; they called you and you might lose a few bucks. The second one might require you weren't bluffing and could cost you more than you had to give up. You had to be able to back the stance.

Don couldn't back this play. But whether due to his pride or stubbornness or to thinking he was slick enough to slip out of this, Don was holding out. Buying time so he could think, probably. Don was the type who always thought there was a way out. It was the brick clever people carried.

"You know," said Don. "You've always been a pain in the ass."

"Talking about me isn't going to help your situation. Decide."

"Decide what?"

"To trust me."

"Why the hell would I do that?"

"Because you have no choice. It's me or the sharks. Doesn't seem all that difficult to comprehend. I can understand you'd think I'm playing you, and I could do that. I've done it before and I like it. I even prefer it. But I wanted to do that, all I'd have to do is turn you over to the police, let them go through your life or even just go to Red Cavanaugh."

"Or," Don said, "I can turn you over to the police."

Springer blew some air between his lips. "I always thought you were smart, but maybe you were just sneaky. I mean, I'm pretty sure I'm talking to you in plain English because I recognize my voice telling you. You are listening, aren't you?"

"Get the hell out of here."

Springer put up a hand, cocked his head to one side, and shrugged. "Okay." He turned to walk out. This was the part that was dicey, because Don might decide to get ballsy, because of his pride and their shared dramas, and risk the bad guys and the police just so he wouldn't have to allow Springer to help him. Also, and this was the really scary part, Springer could've miscalculated Don's part in the robbery. Don might actually not know who robbed the armored truck, but with Nicco and Lunchbox showing up he was pretty sure that wasn't a possibility. Springer had his hand on the doorknob when Don said: "All right. Okay. Turn around. I'll listen to what you have to say."

Springer turned around. He nodded and walked over and sat down again.

"Now what?"

Springer said, "I've already talked to Sonny Parker. I'm going to talk to you again and then the three of us will get together. We'll get you out of this, but you have to do what we say."

"You talked to Sonny? Shit." Don was rolling a pen in his fingers, pointing it now and saying, "You're a real son of a bitch, you know it?"

"Since I've been in town, everybody talks dirty like that to me."

"With a little reflection, I'm sure you can figure why that is."

The fat guy, Lunchbox, was easy enough to find, living in some shit-hole apartment that rented by the week, clothes scattered around a place smelled like dirty underwear. The other two, Nicco and Chewy, were going to be tougher. So he started with Lunchbox. Powers just walked in on the guy, pretty as you please, the lard ass feeding his face, what else? Eating some kind of pasta dish, lotsa tomatoes and meat, washing it down with beer. Real healthy. But a guy's last meal and all, huh?

Lunchbox glanced up at him, not looking surprised or scared, his mouth full of reddish-brown crap, asking what do you want? Powers seeing half-chewed food in his mouth and on his lower lip.

"Where can I find Nicco?"

"I don't know nobody named that. Get the fuck outta here. Can't you see I'm eating?"

"Don't you clean up after yourself? I wouldn't keep a horse in a barn looked like this. Place smells like a monkey cage."

"That's supposed to be funny, right?" Kept right on eating.

"Pay attention. I want to talk to Nicco."

"Clean your ears out. I don't know him."

"Why do you feel like you have to lie to me?" said Powers. "That kind of offends me, ol' pard."

Guy looked up at him, wiping his hands on his shirt. "Like I give a shit what offends you? How'd you get in here?"

"Door was unlocked. Figured you for the hospitable type."

"Well, I ain't. So, get the hell outta here 'fore I throw your ass out."

"All my life I hear how fat people were jolly, and then I meet you. Hell, you don't look like you can even get up outta that chair, never mind throwing me out. Now, I'm getting tired of trying to be nice to you, partner. I want to know how to find your buddy, Nicco, and the colored guy, whatsisname, Chewy or something." He pulled out the six-shooter and cocked the hammer. "You don't tell me what I want to know, then I'll just have to ask somebody else."

That got the man's attention. But he still wasn't scared, saying, "I had guns pointed at me before. This ain't original."

Powers pulled the trigger and the impact of the bullet

upended Lunchbox, blowing him backward out of his chair.

"Yeah," said Powers, his ears ringing. "But you ain't never been shot. There's a helluva difference. You see that now, right?"

TWENTY-FIVE

They say that Lady Luck knows no master, that she smiles on whomever she pleases. Today she was laughing out loud is what Springer was thinking. He got back to the hotel room after talking to Janzen, and Sanborn said, "You won't freaking believe this when I tell you."

Sanborn was smoking cigarettes in the no-smoking room. Smoke alarms were lying on one of the beds. When Springer asked what they were doing on the bed, Sanborn told him they kept going off, so he'd taken the batteries out so he could smoke. This was the way Sanborn did things.

"So what is it I'm not going to believe?"

"Nicco called Diane Janzen." Sanborn was nodding his head. "That's right. I figure you're in Don's office, so I switch over to Diane's phone and Nicco calls her. No shit."

"What was said?"

"Not much. Mostly her cussing at him and telling him he wasn't supposed to contact her and she thought he understood that. She was pretty short with him."

"I'll bet Nicco liked that."

Sanborn snorted. "Yeah. Nicco said he remembered

that but something had come up and he didn't have a 'fucking history with taking shit off women.' Diane said, 'That's unfortunate,' and hung up."

"That's it."

"All I got."

"Well, it's something. I just don't know what." Springer chewed on it. Nicco and Diane? Why? It didn't add up. Or did it? Was Diane in on the bank job with Don? What was her part in all of this? Could it be possible that Diane and Don's divorce was a sham? Maybe they were setting up the other principals, pretending to be mad at each other and then scooping up all the goodies. Possible. But when Springer brought up the idea to Sonny Parker, Parker didn't like it.

"No," Parker said. "That's not right. I don't see that at all. Not that they're not capable of something like that, but . . . no. Doesn't work. I really believe the only thing Diane wants from Don is his sack over a low flame. That woman truly dislikes him. If she don't"—he held up a finger—"and I'm not always right"—smiling now, saying—"but seldom wrong, then she needs to be in Hollywood instead of running a casino in Vegas because she puts that blonde with the funny nose, Meryl Streep, to shame for showing extreme dislike."

Parker was saying this, sitting on the back patio of his house at one of those huge beach-umbrella tables, sipping the mint juleps Cassie made them, Parker wearing shorts and a tank top that said "Harrah's" on it. Just a guy at home, taking it easy. You'd never see him as a guy who at one time could make one phone call and bring down the house on someone's life.

Parker was smoking a cigar and offered one to Springer, but it was too hot for that, so Springer stayed with his julep, which was sort of interesting, but the sugar got to him on the first couple of sips. After the bourbon kicked in they were usually okay. He'd prefer they just poured the bourbon in the glass with the mint leaves and ice.

Parker blew a thick cloud of blue smoke and said, "Something's up, isn't it?"

Springer nodded his head slowly. "I think it's safe to say that."

"Am I getting played?"

"I don't know. Maybe. I can't tell yet."

"Damn shame." He gestured at Springer with his cigar. He had one leg over the arm of his lounge chair. The sun striking the pool was hard to look at, and the heat shimmers made the Vegas skyline waver. "You see, before we had computers and college boys who wanted to be tough guys, you could trust guys. Even bad guys. Because if you couldn't trust them, or even if you *thought* you couldn't trust 'em, they knew better. Because the minute it looked bad, you just took care of it."

"You mean killed them."

"You said that, not me."

"Well, even if things were that way, you wouldn't know who to kill in this situation."

"See, that's the beauty of it. You start with one, send a message to the rest. They didn't straighten up, then you did another one. It's like paddling a kid. Once is about all it takes and they look at you differently."

"Well, that's not what we're doing here."

Parker was sitting up now, both feet on the floor. "I've gotta have somebody for Cassie's little brother. I know the brother's a lowlife—" He paused and looked toward the house. "It doesn't matter. Somebody's gotta take the weight for that."

"They have to die?"

"Not necessarily. You getting hesitant? I checked you out. You were in a war. You shot people."

"That's just an ugly rumor."

"Okay," said Parker. "Nobody has to get whacked." He stopped, then said, "Nobody says 'whacked' much anymore, do they?"

"I can't believe I'm talking about this," Springer said, making a face when a lump of sugar hit the back of his mouth.

"It's the sugar," said Parker. "Settles to the bottom of the glass. I tell her, Cassie, what the fuck, stir it up and dissolve the shit, but she's from the South, you know, and says that's part of it, like who in the hell is sitting out on the gallery of an antebellum mansion thinking I'm hoping there's a big sugar hit at the bottom of this."

"So what if this person, or persons, whoever, goes to jail or is placed in a situation where they're no longer able to function?"

"Meaning?"

"As opposed to killing them."

"Now, who mentioned killing? That's a bad word. I thought we resolved that issue."

Springer put his glass down. Parker said, "You want another?"

"No. I feel cavities forming."

Parker leaned over, elbows on the table, his face in one hand. Thinking about it now. Springer sat quietly, stoically, like he had to in the service. Giving Parker the impassive face, the one didn't tell the other person anything. Funny the way people would tell you things when he did that, finding it more a device than something he did naturally. It worked well in the public sector also. After thirty seconds, Parker said, "Okay.

Here's the deal. We got Don by the short hairs. He's pretty much gotta do what we want." Springer not sure on that point, knowing Don always wanted to do things his way. "His only alternative is the cops finding out about his part and Cavanaugh distancing himself. Don's sitting on top of a pile of cash, waiting to leverage a deal. There's Cavanaugh in the shadows with his bunch of wannabe hoods. I don't like Vince any more than you do. I'm choosing him to be the guy that takes the fall for my shit-for-brains brother-in-law. You like the sound of that?"

"So far. You know a guy named Nicco?"

"Yeah." He sat up. "I do."

"What do you think of him?"

"He's a thug. He's been around, done some dirty stuff. Guys use him because he gets things done. How's he involved in this?"

Springer told him. Then he added, "He made a call to Diane Janzen after I braced him and Fatty."

"You're fucking kidding, right?"

Springer shook his head.

"I don't see how that fits, but it's gotta fit somewhere. You're telling me somebody thought they killed Jesse Robinson and it's one of these people."

Springer nodded again. "I don't know how it could be any other way."

"Vince is in on this, and so is Lunchbox? Know of him, too. He's nothing. All breath and big underwear. You shot him in the ass?"

"I may have hit him on the side of the head or something, too."

Parker shook his head. "You think you could maybe complicate this up some more?"

"I want to feed Nicco and Vince to Tara St. John. She needs something out of this. Otherwise she may choose me. You get the satisfaction of seeing Vince go to jail, you can sit right there and watch her cuff him, and I get Red and whoever is trying to kill Jesse."

Parker looked at him, deadpan, and said, "Anything else?"

"Any loose money."

"Loose money?"

Springer nodded. "Yeah. Any money not yours that's not accounted for, I get to keep."

"Hell, I don't care. Knock yourself out. How much money we talking about?"

"Penny-ante." He held up a hand and put his thumb and forefinger close together.

"Sure, I believe you. That leaves the ex-wife, Diane. What about her?"

Yeah, Springer thought, what about her?

"And what about Don Janzen?"

"I don't know yet. We use him; I'm thinking maybe just let him go on with his life. He might still be able to work with you. Right now"—looking at his watch—"he's waiting to meet with us."

Parker said, "Why use him? He's dishonest." Springer leaned back, lifted his chin. Parker said, "Hey, don't look at me like that. Everything's not funny."

"Maybe, but a lot of things are."

Diane Janzen looked at the casino camera and called down to her floor boss, telling him to keep an eye on the man at hundred-dollar black jack table number two. "I think he's counting cards."

She hung up and lit a cigarette, one that Don had left in her office. She hadn't smoked one in years. She inhaled the smoke and it felt like the first time.

She was running out of options. Vince and that thug weren't going to be able to do what she wanted, now that Springer was involving himself. She would just have to accept the fact that she had to go another direction.

A woman had to do what she had to do, didn't she?

Springer hung up the phone, turned to Sonny Parker, and said, "Okay, Nicco's hooked."

They were at Don Janzen's downtown office. Not at Streamers, Springer had told him. Janzen asked him why not, and Springer told him because of his ex-wife. Janzen wondering about that and asking if Springer didn't think she could be trusted. Springer just looked at him and Don said, "Oh."

Don opened a bottle of Johnny Walker Black and poured a glass for Parker. Springer declined.

"I don't get it," said Don Janzen, setting the whiskey bottle down. "Nicco shows up and you give him the money, then what?"

"You don't have to know, Don. You just have to stay out of jail. See how this works out for you and me?" He stopped for a minute. "Well, for me. Now for your part. You're going to call Vince and tell him you know something's up and you're taking steps."

"What difference will that make, besides making him want to come over and beat the shit out of me?"

"I want him worried and thinking about things."

"Why does he care what I tell him?"

"Because you sent him to rob the armored truck. Because Vince knows you have the money. How many times we have to go over this? You have no plausible deniability or any other kind. Doesn't matter even if you did. I'm not going to turn you in as long as you go along, so don't pretend with me. You're in and that's it."

Sonny Parker said, "And you think Vince will tell Red Cavanaugh?"

"No. But he'll tell somebody. I think he's scared to tell Cavanaugh. And just as scared not to."

"Or neither of those things could happen," said Parker. "Cavanaugh could send the cowboy after you."

"Yeah," said Springer. "But I have to know who to be afraid of, and this could smoke them out."

"So," said Don, "I'm betting my life on something you may or may not be sure of."

"Think of the alternative. You could be talking to Tara St. John, who would rather send you to jail than take a vacation. Maybe you could charm her up like you did before. That sound good to you?"

"What do you think? The woman's a pit bull." Smiling, a smirk actually, was what Springer was thinking, becoming the old Don Janzen from high school now, saying, "But she's a tiger in the sack, isn't she?"

"You know, Don," said Springer. "Ever since I hit town I've been coming up with reasons not to punch you in your head. Saying things about her isn't helping your case any."

"Kind of touchy about her, aren't you? You think you're scaring me?"

"I'm not asking you to be scared, I'm asking you to be smart. Be smart, Don. You can do it if you'll think about it."

Parker said, "I hadn't seen this happening, I wouldn't believe it. How old are you guys? How about it with the schoolyard bullshit? That okay with everybody?"

Springer looked at Don some more, smiled, and nodded at Parker. Parker said, "I'm going to have to agree with Don on this lady cop. She's a hard case. Even when she first started at Metro, people walked around her. Like she's always got something to prove."

"There's nothing she can charge you with even if

she wanted to and she doesn't want to. She gets Nicco and Cavanaugh and whoever killed Styles. That will placate her."

"What about me?" Don said. "She'd like to throw me in jail."

"A risk I'm willing to take," said Springer. Smiling big when he said it.

Parker and Springer left Don and walked to the parking lot. They had traveled together.

Sonny Parker said, "You think Don will do what we say?"

Springer shook his head. "No. But if I'm right, it won't make any difference."

After getting things set with Parker and Janzen, Springer returned to Jesse and told him, "I've got a lot of it figured out. What I don't know, or didn't know, was the connection Diane Janzen has. Why do I feel like she promised you something?"

Jesse shaking his head, saying, "Everything's not a conspiracy. You got your head full of not liking Diane J."

"What was it? Money? Revenge on Don? Or maybe you and she ride off into the sunset."

"How you like it, I hit you in your head?"

"I wouldn't. Unless you're hiring it done, I wouldn't dwell on it much."

"I love you, Springs, but lately you been pissing me off."

"Pretty much the standard reaction. You want to take your shot so I can rush you to the emergency room or shut up and start talking to me?"

"Why you think that woman messing with my head?"

"Because that's what she does. It's what she's always done. You know that."

"And you're immune, right?"

"Didn't say that. But we're in Vegas, so I'll bet if you don't pull away from her, not only will you not get whatever she promised, you may get put in jail or worse."

"What would be worse?"

"Think about it. Somebody tried to kill you once. What makes you think it can't happen again?"

Jesse looked down at the floor for a long moment, working the corner of his mouth. "Okay, she says she can make me rich I go along."

"Go along with what?"

"Says she's got a deal with me. Something with Jesse Jr."

"She say what it was?"

He shook his head.

Springer said, "You fell for that?" Jesse giving him a look now, Springer saying, "Okay, I take it back. She didn't tell you, so what did she say?"

"Said she couldn't tell me, 'cause if she did, I'd cut her out of the deal."

Springer had to think about that one. Could be. "That's a possibility, I guess, but it doesn't fit everything else. I think she's right in telling you she thinks you'd cut her out. I'm going to ask you something and I'm not trying to get you upset with me."

"So ask."

"The last time you saw Jesse Jr. he was five, right?"

Jesse nodded.

"It fits."

"What fits?"

"I'm still thinking on it."

"You always thinking. You think too much. Don't do that shit. You gotta say."

Springer telling him that maybe Diane had a _____ for keeping Jesse Jr. away from him. The stor___

Jesse Jr. being in Atlantic City and Jesse not being allowed there setting off alarms for Springer. Jesse asking, How come's that? Springer telling him, you can't go there and your son being there where you can't see him is too perfect. Jesse not understanding why that was so perfect, and Springer saying now, because Jesse Jr. has to be out of town for this to work. Springer didn't say he hadn't figured out why the kid had to be out of town.

"When's the last time you had sex with Diane?" Springer asked Jesse.

"What's that got to do with anything?"

"Maybe nothing.

"You getting jealous again?"

"Thought I could hide it, but you're too smart for me. I came all the way out here to Vegas, set up this incredible scam where I get the shit beat out of me, threatened by thugs, and trick Vince into robbing an armored car because I'm jealous and can't live without her."

Jesse said, "Does seem kind of stupid."

"It's real stupid."

"I ask you to affirm that?"

"When was it? Did she jump you before they killed Styles? Or after?"

Jesse chewed his lip. Shrugged. "Before."

It was like he thought. Springer said, "Was it any good?"

Jesse shaking his head, "Aw, hell, Springs. It's all good. You know that."

Springer smiled. Jesse, too. It was getting better.

This thing could work yet.

TWENTY-SIX

Springer left Jesse, pretty sure he was on board, but there were no guarantees when Diane Janzen was involved. Her powers were at their height, and she always could turn a guy inside out and leave him wondering at what point she had left him grabbing air. How many balls did she have in the air, Springer amused by the unintended pun in his head.

Time to visit Nicco and tempt him to do what Springer had in mind. The dangling carrot was money, and the motivation was Nicco's greed, which is all those guys cared about anyway. Nicco could be fuming about the way Springer fleeced them, but all that would be forgotten once he heard how he was going to come out with a large amount of cash in his pocket. That's the way most recidivist career criminals thought, and he doubted Nicco was any different. The lure of the money would outweigh any animosity he had for Springer.

And even if it didn't, and Nicco ended up behind bars, it would be years before he would be able to get back at Springer.

He didn't know where Nicco was located but did know where to find Lunchbox through Sanborn's contacts. So, roust Fatty and get what he needed. He just was hoping Nicco didn't realize Springer needed Nicco as badly as Nicco wanted the money. If Nicco turned out to be less than greedy, Springer might come up with an empty sack and maybe some jail time. Think happy thoughts, that's the key. Nicco would have to be thinking five moves ahead to see what was going down, and he doubted Nicco thought past his next cigarette.

Looking around the fat guy's apartment, Powers found what he wanted. Nicco's phone number and address. And just like the fat guy, Nicco didn't bother to lock his door. What was with these owl hoots who were dumber than a wood post? Powers walked right in and said to the guy, "Boss says I have to do this with you."

"The fuck're you anyway?"

"I'm the guy they send around to straighten shit out. Stuff you and the Dalton gang bow-dicked."

"Who's your boss and why's he sending a shit-kicker like you around?"

Powers pushed back the front of his Stetson. "Maybe it's Italian appreciation week."

"Glad they could send a comedian. I'm not Italian," said Nicco. "I get that all the time, but I'm mostly Greek. May be some Italian in there, I don't know. I'm not into that genealogy stuff. What I am into is asking you why you got the balls to come around here busting mine?"

"We're on the same cattle drive, hoss."

"You gonna get to it? Who you working for?"

"Somebody you should pay attention to."

"Yeah? Who talks like you? Maybe you're a cop. They do shit like this, thinking they're clever and you're dumb. What about that? And if you're not, how about proving it without all the Roy Rogers back-in-the-saddle bullshit."

"That was Gene Autry."

Nicco opened his arms, palms up.

Powers said, "It was Gene Autry sang 'Back in the Saddle Again,' not Roy."

Nicco leaned back in his chair, placing a foot on a knee and looking off to the side. "Well, 'Yippee-ki-yay, motherfucker.' That's Bruce Willis. Now, I got things to do, so if you'll, you know, saddle up and hit the fucking trail, you hear what I'm saying to you?" He took a drag off his cigarette and continued looking away from Powers.

Powers rubbed a hand across his face, thinking this was just part of the job and he would do what he'd come to do. "What have you been up to with Vince?"

Nicco looked back at him like he didn't know he was there. "You still here? Was there something in my demeanor giving you the idea I want to talk to you?"

"Where's your buddy, the fat guy?"

Nicco laughing now. "What is it with you? We know each other?" Sucking in his lower lip now, getting pissed off. "Listen, Cowboy, why don't you just head for the old roundup before I start to get tired of seeing your fucking goat-roper face and rearrange it. You savvy that, kemosabe?"

"You want to know about that fat partner of yours or not?"

"Lunchbox?"

Powers nodded.

Nicco shrugged. "Fuck you."

"We're not getting along here, pard. And that's not good."

"Here's a news flash for you, Duke. I don't care if I get along with you, and when you're gone, I won't miss you." Nicco standing now. "And you're gonna get gone, you can count on it."

"Well, I was hoping you'd be willing to help me

out, but since you're not . . ." Powers pulled out the weapon, a .357 Magnum wheel gun. Nicco getting interested.

"You're gonna shoot me I don't tell you where Lunchbox is. That's the way it is?"

"Lunchbox. That's who we're talking about," said Powers. "He ain't around anymore. I don't know what happened to him, as he was in perfect health five minutes before the last I saw of him."

Nicco said, "That's supposed to scare me, right?"

"Red wants to know what's going down with Vince and the other idiots."

"I don't know what you're talking about. As for Lunchbox, he's already been shot once this week, so it don't matter it happens again. You're gonna shoot, then shoot, ya hick-looking no-fucking-brains-having cowboy asshole. I had guns pointed at me before, so this ain't original. I don't know why I gotta listen to a whole bunch of stupid cowboy talk if you're gonna do that. So, shoot me." Spreading his arms now. "Just shut up while you do it. And you can tell that bitch, Diane, I hope that gash under her nose heals up."

The part about Diane Janzen was interesting. Red might be interested in that also. He said, "So, you're gonna make me shoot you, that's the way it's going to be?"

Nicco smirking at him now. "No, I said you can shoot me if it'll stop the prairie dog bullshit coming out your hole. Anything's gotta be better than that. You the cure for insomnia? But if you shoot me, you ain't gonna be rich." He laughed to himself. "Yeah, that's right. I die, some information you'll like dies with me. You'll just stay some poor cowboy dicking farm animals on the weekend."

"What're you talking about?"

"I know where there's a shitload of money and

maybe I can get my hands on it. With Lunchbox gone I could use some help."

"You ain't got no money."

"See, you don't listen. Never said I have it. I said I know where some is. Never said I didn't know how to get it. What do you say, Roy? You interested?"

Springer was surprised when he saw the big Chevy pickup. Springer was within a block of Lunchbox's place when he saw the big Chevy rolling out of the parking lot, Springer pretty sure Powers didn't recognize him, since Springer had borrowed Sanborn's Infiniti SUV over Sanborn's protests.

"Why you gotta drive my car?" said Sanborn Meeks.

"They know the rental."

"So, drive the Benz."

"Can't do that either. It's stolen, and I've got other plans for it anyway." Looking at Sanborn's SUV now, saying, "And that's a car? I can't tell what it is for sure, looking at it. What kind of vehicle is this for a serious danger-loving private dick like yourself? It looks like a sandwich." Turning his head to one side, then the other, looking at it, having fun with Sanborn. "Not a sandwich I'd eat, though."

"Don't drive it, it's so ugly, then. Always gotta make a remark."

Rubbing his face with a hand so Sanborn couldn't see him smiling. "I said it looks weird. I didn't say ugly. C'mon." Springer held out his hand, palm up, and worked his fingers. Sanborn made a face, reached in his pocket, and handed Springer the keys.

"There," Sanborn said. "Be careful with it."

"Treat it like my own."

"I see how you treat things. And put some gas in it, okay?"

So when Springer saw Cody Powers pulling away from Lunchbox's apartment parking lot, Springer was sure he wasn't recognized. He decided to follow Powers. Powers didn't go very far, about seven or eight blocks, and stopped at another apartment complex. Springer made a note of the address and drove back to Lunchbox's place.

Springer arrived at Lunchbox's place, and rang the bell. No answer. Car was out front. Powers obviously there to see Lunchbox. He rang the bell again. Same result. Quiet here. Lunchbox's place was at the edge of town in an apartment complex built during the Nixon years. Springer walked back to his car, thought about it and then walked back and rang the bell again.

Still no answer.

Something was wrong.

He gave it some more thought and looked at the door. Two locks. One on the knob and a deadbolt. If Lunchbox was the type didn't lock the deadbolt, he could maybe get inside and look around. He turned the knob and the door opened, wasn't locked. The deadbolt either.

What he found was Lunchbox behind an overturned chair. Shot through the chest. Body was warm but no pulse, and there was a funny look on his face. Like he was thinking about something. The last thought the guy would ever have.

Powers. Had to be. And Powers meant Cavanaugh. Why kill Lunchbox?

Drawers out and things overturned. Powers was looking for something. What? Or maybe just making sure Lunchbox didn't have anything Cavanaugh didn't want him to have. Or make it look like a robbery. Springer's hand on the doorknob. He'd have to wipe it down. Not touch anything but give Tara St. John a call. What would she say? Why are you the one who found the body? Why were you there? Why are you always there? How do you know Lunchbox, a known criminal? Yeah, she liked questions, and she'd have some. More sitting around Metro while the window was closing on what Springer needed to get done.

This changed things for Springer. If this was a cleanup hit, then Nicco and Chewy and Vince would be in line also. Cover up the robbery. Why? How did Cavanaugh know about it? Who was connected here? If someone was covering the trail, that could mean Jesse was on the list.

He wiped down the doorknob and found a phone booth, which were getting harder to find, not wanting to use his cell phone and have that on record, dialed Metro and asked for Detective St. John. They asked who it was and he said one of her snitches. She has snitches? is what the dispatcher asked, Who knew? Just like the movies, huh?

Detective St. John came on the line and identified herself. Asked who was calling. Springer told her she might want to drive over to 1755 Madison, Apartment B, and see what was going on there. She asked why she would want to do that, and Springer told her there was a possibility a crime had been committed there. She wanted to know why he thought that, and he said because a red pickup was in the vicinity being driven by a big cowboy-looking guy with a bruised jaw.

"Is that you, Cole?"

He moved the phone to his other ear. "Who? You need to go over there and check it out."

"What am I going to find?"

"I don't know. Maybe a dead thug."

The line was quiet for a long moment. "Listen, Cole, there is too much going on here for you to play games. What did you see?"

She was recording the conversation. He'd bet on it. "That's all I have for you," he said, then, "I know a guy named Cole, though. Is he a good-looking guy with an affinity for strong women?"

Metro Detective Tara St. John was going to quote chapter and verse of the criminal code, but he hung up. Cole Springer. She didn't know what to make of him. Was he a clown or was he involved in this in some way. But why call her? No, he wasn't a criminal, she decided. But he did come right up to the margin of criminal activity without crossing over.

Tara left the building, got in her car, and drove to 1755 Madison. She called in her location and got out of the car. As she was getting out, an SUV pulled up. One of those expensive Japanese models with tinted windows so you couldn't see inside. She drew her weapon and was keeping it ready when the SUV stopped and Cole Springer got out.

"Wow. Is this a coincidence or what?"

She was thinking, just one shot, all I want.

"The fat guy took it like a man," said Powers. "And Nicco didn't know much but was cooperative, so I didn't have to plug him." But not telling the man everything. Some of it was to Powers's advantage.

"He know anything about Vince and what was going down?"

"He didn't know anything about Vince but did say he knew something about your little filly."

"What're you talking about?"

"Nicco mentioned Diane Janzen."

Red Cavanaugh thought about that. It was like he thought. This woman had a lot of oars in the water for such a little girl. What was her angle?

"What'd he say about her?"

"Said to tell her, hoped the gash under her nose healed up."

"So, he knows her?"

"Sure sounded like it."

"You ask him about her?"

"Didn't want to give him any extra information."

"What about Chewy?"

"Didn't find him yet," Powers said. "What about the kid with the mouth, Vince?"

"I still need him. For now. I'm thinking they pulled the armored car job. Pretty stupid, but they got it done somehow. Makes me think somebody else planned it if they did. They did it, then I want a cut and also want to know why Vince didn't say nothing about it. I don't trust him."

"Well, just let me know when you don't want him around anymore. There's a city boy rubs me the wrong way. And I don't understand it. If he went into business for himself without telling you, why are you letting that go?"

Cavanaugh looked at him. "I don't want him shot. Vince is known around town, and this isn't a good time. Nicco and Lunchbox, they're hired bullshit. Nobody cares. Not even the cops. And as far as it goes, you don't want to go around with Vince, even if he is a dumb shit. The kid can box. I mean he's good at it. You're a big guy, but he's twenty years younger and he'll wear you down and cut you up."

"Maybe I don't fight fair."

"Probably the best way with him. But just take it easy for now, okay?"

"I gun Springer?"

"No. He's too close to that colored cop. St. John. We have to walk around him for a while yet."

"How about if I saw him after Lunchbox?"

"You saw Springer after you left Lunchbox?" Powers

could see Cavanaugh didn't like that. Shaking his head. He brushed at an ear like there was a fly on it.

Powers said, "He followed me but I lost him." A lie. The guy followed him to Nicco's, but Powers didn't care. For one thing, it affirmed what Nicco told him about the money.

Cavanaugh said, "Damn. That cocksucker gets on my nerves, what with being everywhere and stealing my fucking car."

"So what do you want to do with him?"

"I don't know. May have to have him popped." He clenched and unclenched a fist. "It's just not a good time. It's one thing to get rid of Nicco and Lunchbox and the colored guy, but something else to do Springer right now."

"I gotta find the spook," said Powers, chewing a toothpick. "What'd you say his name was again?"

"Chewy. But I've got people on it. They'll find him."

"Well, let me know. And I need another gun. Had to ditch the Smith."

"What fucking century is this? I hate having to do business this way."

"Yeah, breaks my heart, too. What do you want to do about Springer?"

Cavanaugh chewed a thumbnail and said, "If things get where I got no choice, he's gotta go. But don't go in there guns blazing like it was the Wild West, for chrissake. Try subtle. It'll open up a whole new world for you."

"You're the ramrod," said Powers.

Cavanaugh made a face. "Diane Janzen, huh?"

"That's what the guy said. But he's just Greek to me."

TWENTY-SEVEN

Springer could see right off she wasn't glad to see him there. Women were interesting if you paid attention long enough.

"You're in a lot of trouble," Tara St. John said, securing her weapon on a hip holster.

"It would've been better I called you from inside on his phone so you'd have a record of my call? That way you could've put me down as a suspect, right? I like it. Funny I didn't think of it. Or—"

"Listen, Cole—"

"Or," he said, ignoring her, "I could have walked away and not called you, which I thought about. Which do you like better?"

"Why do you feel like you can't trust me?"

"Because I know how it works and I know how you are."

"Really? And just how am I?"

He shook his head. "Later maybe. Over wine and dinner. I'm more effective that way."

She looked at him for a minute, started to say something, changed her mind. He could see it and turned to walk toward the apartment. He followed her, but she turned around and said, "What do you think you're doing?"

"Backing you up."

"You're staying outside."

"You had to call in your location, I know that much. Isn't it procedure during a possible felony shooting to request backup? But," he hesitated a little, looking around, "I don't see any units pulling up? Why is that, Tara? Why are you doing this solo? Interesting a by-the-book type would do that."

"This is Metro business."

"It all comes back to what I said before. The way you are. You're not going to let anything stop you from tying this up and turning the key on somebody."

"Maybe even you," she said. "Wait outside."

She entered the apartment with her weapon drawn. Springer waited. Fifteen minutes later she came back outside.

"You take anything out of there?" she asked.

He smiled at the attempt—she was clever, for sure—and shook his head. "This the part where I break down and confess?"

"How about a simple no for an answer?"

"You're mad now because you couldn't trick me into saying I was in his place? I didn't kill him."

"How do you know he's dead?" she said.

"I'm a good guesser. And maybe I went inside before you came." She was giving him a look, so he said, "Maybe not, too. You won't find my prints on anything."

She put away her gun, took in a breath, and let it out. "All right, Cole," she said. "I give up. We'll try it your way. I don't like it, but I don't want to wait to find things out. Anything you can tell me will be off the record. I know you didn't do it."

He looked at her. "You have to go out to dinner

with me when this is all over. I need something for being your informant."

She put a fist on her hip. "I don't believe this. Do you always blackmail women into dating you?"

"Only the really exceptional ones." Shaking her head. He said, "C'mon, you know you want to."

"What do I get out of all this?"

"The fact that I saw Powers in the neighborhood just before I called."

"You were in the neighborhood also."

He nodded. "You figured it out and you didn't even have to beat it out of me. Top-notch police work, that's what it is."

"What is it you want from me?"

"I may need legal cover for someone."

"Who? Jesse Robinson?"

"And Sonny Parker."

"Sonny Parker?"

"I'll throw in Don Janzen. That make it better?"

Stern now. Jaw set, her eyes hot. Sometimes you go too far but that's okay, too. "Quit riding me about Don. What about you and his ex?"

"What about it?"

"I'm not going to promise not to arrest anyone."

"That's a shame. And here I was, willing to give you the people robbed the armored truck."

She said, "You *what*?"

"I were you, I'd decide something."

She was nodding now. "Okay," she said. "I'll see what I can do for Jesse and Parker. No promises on Janzen."

"And dinner."

She nodded. She was chewing her lower lip, which cause her chin to dimple. She even had a pretty chin.

"There. How hard was that?"

"Anything else?"

"Yeah, you've got to trust me on this one. I think I can deliver the bad guys."

"You *think* you can?"

"Maybe. Nothing's perfect."

"All right. One more time, I'll trust you. But if you're running a shuck here, Cole, I promise I'll put the cuffs on you myself.

"Sure," Springer said. "You feel better about things now?"

Nicco hung up the phone and said, "Okay, so the guy just called. Told me where he was going to meet me."

"Meet you? Where?"

Nicco looking perturbed, like he was tired of answering questions to this dumbshit cowboy. "Said he had a place, rented a meeting room off the Strip. Says he can tell me how to get the money."

"He's pulling a fast one. You can't see that?" Smiling big and rolling a toothpick around in his teeth. "Maybe you could get a shirt says 'Springer's Poke' on it."

The Jersey guy getting a dark look in his eyes now. All of 'em thinking they were hard men when they were just city boys in the wrong place, which was out here in the desert.

Nicco said, "Keep fucking with me." Nodding his head. "That's right. See what it gets you." The guy's lower teeth showing.

Powers chuckled to himself. This guy was funny. Didn't mean to be, but he was. "Why would we want to go there?"

"Because he's going to pay me off."

Cody Powers said, "So, what if he's setting you up?"

"It's forty thousand dollars," said Nicco, like the guy was thick about money but only telling him half the story. No use letting him in on the whole take. "Why miss a chance to make that kind of money. I'll split sixty-forty with you."

"Sixty for who?" said Powers, knowing the answer. He was thinking of that James Garner movie, the one with Jack Elam pretending to be a reputed gunslinger. Garner and Elam are getting $5,000 but Garner, being a con man, tells him they're getting a thousand and promising a fifty-fifty split. Then Garner tells Elam, "That's four hundred for you." But, in this deal, it was Springer who was playing Garner's part. Nicco was Elam. That part he was sure about.

Thing was, no matter Springer could be dry-gulching them, just like Jersey boy, Powers wanted to know what was at the end of this trail. Too much *dinero* to pass by.

"Who you think?" Nicco said. "You can be happy with that. Why should I give you anything?"

Powers struck a match with a thumbnail. "Didn't kill you, partner." He lit his cigarette and shook the match out. "Think about that."

The phone rang and Vince answered like he always did, saying, "It's your nickel, go."

"Vince?"

"Yeah."

"It's Don."

"You sound funny."

"It's the cigarettes. I'm smoking again and they're getting to me."

"What do you want?"

"I want to pay you what I owe."

"Good to hear. You're doing the right thing."

"But I'll only pay you if you haven't told anybody about our deal."

"*No problemo*. It's in the vault."

"That so? Then why were Nicco and some fat guy in my office asking where the money was?"

"Who's Nicco?"

"Keep playing it that way and I'll hang up."

"Okay. Okay. Don't do that. Nicco, he . . . See, Nicco's got ideas, a dude who's got wires crossed in his head, no shit, and all pissed off about Springer hitting us and then the bags being full of casino chips. He made the connection himself. Honest. I didn't tell him. He's a real mistrustful sort of guy. Felt like punching him out after it was done."

"All right. I believe you. But if you're lying, I'm going right to Cavanaugh."

"You're blackmailing me?"

"No, I'm taking out insurance. You on my side or not?"

"Yeah, Don, sure. I just want my money."

"All right, then. Here's what you do. Half of it is waiting for you at the airport terminal."

"Half?"

"Don't interrupt. You'll get the other half at a place you'll learn of when you pick up the money."

"This sounds like bullshit."

"Then forget it."

"What if I just take the money at the airport?"

Distrustful now. That was good. "That's fine with me. Do whatever you want. It won't break my heart to pay half. Then you can explain to the other guys why you only have half of it. Like you said, Nicco seems a suspicious man to me, too."

The line was quiet a moment. Then Vince said, "Okay. It's cool. Where do I go?"

"Locker 133 at the airport. I'll have the key sent over within the hour. That good for you?"

"Yeah, sure. Then what?"

"The instructions are with the money. They'll tell you where to meet me for the rest. See you then."

He put the phone down, looked up, and said, "So, what do you think?"

Jesse Robinson said, "That's pretty good. You sure can sound a lot like Don when you want. How you do that, Springs?"

Tara St. John was drinking a decaf mocha latte with two squirts of raspberry when the call came.

"He's got it," said the voice on the other end of the extension, a uniformed cop named Patterson. Tara thanked him and turned her cell phone off.

She couldn't believe it. This crazy thing might just work.

Cole Springer was a rogue and a con man, however.

She smiled. "I think I'm in love," she said to herself and left Starbucks to drive to the Sands.

Vince was feeling good. He pulled the sniffer from his pocket and took a blast. There. Wow. Right to his head. Stuff was like lightning in a bottle. He patted the duffel bag, not believing it. A headful of feeling higher and one hundred thousand smackers.

He hefted the computer card that would open room 312 at the Sands. Another hundred waiting. Life was good.

He was whistling "My Way" between his teeth as he walked out into the Vegas sunshine.

TWENTY-EIGHT

"You get it done?" Jesse Robinson asked.

"Yep, it's in the vehicle."

"You got a lot of funny skills. Shooting people, stealing cars. This gonna work?"

"Got as much chance as anything," said Springer.

Jesse looking perturbed, but Springer knowing he'd be all right when it came time. "I thought you knew what you were doing. I don't want to do this and find out your plan sucks, bro, because my ass is hanging way out there."

"Who said I had a plan?" Having fun with Jesse.

Jesse shaking his head now, knowing how the boy loved to play. "Man, Springs, being your friend is a lot of work."

Springer had decided to head back to Aspen when this was over, taking Jesse with him to see Nate. Nate would be glad to see Jesse, and Springer would be glad to be back home, funny him thinking of Aspen as home now. He loved the mountains, looking off his deck, watching the parasailers circling Ajax Mountain. He could never see himself getting the nerve to jump off a place that high with a rig that was little more than an oversized kite. He admired the faith it took to do that.

Springer said, "It'll work. It doesn't, then what the heck, right? We get killed or put in jail. You've been jailed before. Do it standing on your head."

"Yeah," said Jesse. "And I'll tell you something, it ain't worth a shit, either. Man, this could get ugly. These are heartless mother-fuckers. You think about that?"

"Some."

"You thinking you may have to shoot one of them?"

He shrugged.

"You ever kill anyone? I mean while you were over-seas?"

Springer nodded.

"What was that like?"

"It's kind of final," Springer said, "and it stays with you. You feel funny afterward. It's not like shooting tin cans. You think about it."

The phone rang and Springer picked it up, saying, "This is Springer." Then he nodded, said thanks, and hung the phone up.

It was the call he'd been waiting for.

Jesse said, "That it?"

Springer nodded.

Jesse said, "Too late to back out now, right?"

Springer said quietly, "Too late."

"Damn. Here we go."

When Vince opened the door of number 312, which turned out to be a suite, at the Sands Hotel, he found a room service table inside with a cart laid out with a meat and cheese tray, a fifth of Jim Beam, and a bucket of iced-down bottled beer.

He had been at a loss what to do with the money he'd got at the airport. Leave it in the car? But then he thought about Springer stealing his car and another car and decided to carry it with him. Maybe not a great idea, but he could keep an eye on it.

He looked at the table. There was also a note attached to the whiskey bottle. It said, "Enjoy. The money's in the adjoining suite. Have a drink, eat, or just go get the money and leave. D.J." Not knowing whether that mean Don or Diane or both, but he didn't care.

Vince opened the bottle of Beam, took a good swig, swallowed it, and chased it down with a beer, then carried the bottle into the adjoining suite.

Sitting there was Sonny Parker. The door closed behind him and Vince saw Checkers and the two men who'd rousted him out of his sleep last night. There was another guy there also. A black guy, in a business suit, looked like a cop. Also a woman, a good-looking one.

Everybody looked at ease. That is, except the chick, who was staring him down.

Parker said, "What's it going to be, Vince? I think you know everyone except Agent Johnson. You turn yourself over to him, or do I have the boys convince you? He's going to step out of the room, you turn this offer down. I don't care how tough you are, they're going to rearrange your perspective, you don't cooperate."

Vince looked around the room. He looked at the fed. "You in on this? You're a cop, you can't let them do this."

"If I leave the room it's out of my jurisdiction. Assault is a local concern and you'd have to make a complaint. But you don't have any choice, really. Right now, I've got a search warrant"—patting his jacket—"right here in my pocket. I search your car, will I find anything implicating you in the armored truck robbery? Or you could cooperate and maybe we can make a deal. We've wanted to turn the key on your friend, Nicco, for a lot of years."

Vince's shoulders sagged. Nodded his head.

"I hope you choose the guys," said the woman. Her eyes were blazing. Who was she?

"Oh," said Parker. "This is my wife. The guy you guys ditched at the robbery? Her brother. Now she's mad. Really mad. Look at her. It's the way she is. You think this is bad, you ought to be married to her."

Vince handed the bag over to Agent Johnson. Johnson read him his rights.

Sonny Parker was smiling big and saying now, "You know, Vince, I wouldn't've missed this even for a retroactive patent on aluminum foil."

TWENTY-NINE

A guy met them in the lobby and gave Powers a bag. What you want's inside, was what the guy said. Meaning to Nicco a gun. They got in Powers's truck and drove it over to the hotel where Springer said to meet them.

"The guy's setting us up," said Nicco.

"Where do you get this insight? You must be one of those geniuses I'm always reading about. I already said that."

"Well, I don't like it."

"Yeah. You said that. About ten times. Your idea. Remember?"

"Nobody's got a gun to your head. You're greedy's why you're here."

All the guy ever did was bitch and moan like a winter calf, that is, when he wasn't scowling like he thought he was Bob De fucking Niro. Powers was getting worn out with listening to him bellyache. This was an East Coast tough guy? Wouldn't last two days on the open prairie in West Texas.

"You know, you're right. I am greedy. And I'm not going to let that much money float around without riding out to see if I can get my hands on it."

"Part of it."

"Okay, part of it. Are you going to act like those guys with Bogart in *Treasure of Sierra Madre*."

"What?"

"Never mind. I wouldn't want you to do any heavy-association thinking right now. Let's just get this done."

They arrived at the hotel and whooshed up a few floors to the top of the building, Nicco slid the card key the desk people had given him into the door and the little lights danced and the door clicked. They walked into the room and, boy howdy, there the son of a bitch was.

"Hello, fellas," said Springer, sitting in a chair. He had a gun in his hand. Pointed right at them. "Come on in. You want to hear something funny?"

Nicco was not believing this shit. There was the guy again, sitting there with a shit-eating grin on his face, a gun in his hand. Springer. The guy just *showed up* places. First at Janzen's place and now here. Spooky as hell, just like Chewy said. He looked at the dumb-as-dirt cowboy and said, "What'd I tell you?"

"You told me? You didn't tell me shit." The cowboy looked at Springer and said, "Say, partner, why the gun?"

Springer picked up the remote and turned on the television. One of those big-screen ones. A college football game came on. "If you don't mind, I like to follow them. I went to school there."

Like anybody here give a rat-fuck where he went to college. Besides, the way it was with this guy, it could be where he went to school, or not. Couldn't trust a thing with him.

The wiseass said, "There's a bar over there," waving the gun in the direction of the bar. "Help yourself.

But before you do that," Springer said, "get rid of the guns."

"We're all friends here," said Powers.

The guy saying nothing, smiling to himself, like the two of them were stupid, something Nicco was getting tired of. Powers trying to be folksy and slick, starting toward the bar, but the guy swung the pistol up, an autoloader of some kind, saying, "The *guns*? Over there on the bed." Meaning it. Like he was tired of telling them. "Now."

"You're kidding."

"I look like I'm kidding?"

"I believe you," said Nicco, putting his gun on the bed. No use provoking this guy. "I came to get the money, not to argue. But you fuck me and I'll make sure you wish you hadn't."

Springer was looking at the cowboy. "Now that your girlfriend is through scaring me to death, you need to . . . aha . . . comply with my wishes."

"You're probably right. But what the hell?" Powers said, and headed for the bar. This cowboy not learning shit about the way Springer was. Springer standing up now and extending the gun at Powers, saying, "Take another step and I'll shoot you in the kneecap."

"You're serious."

Springer nodded his head slowly. "Why doubt it? Nothing to me, you want to find out. I don't much care about you anyway but knew you'd come along."

"How'd you know that?" Nicco asked him.

Without looking at Nicco, Springer said, "Because you're still alive."

Nicco not knowing what that meant but later figuring it had something to do with Lunchbox getting iced. There was a lot going on here, but he could take care of it after he got his money.

Springer told Powers, lift your arms and turn

around and place your hands on the wall. Powers did it and Nicco saw the wheel gun in the waistband at the guy's back.

Springer walked over and took the gun from Powers. Powers said, "I must've forgot about that." Being a wise guy, but Springer ignoring him, patting him down professional-like, and Nicco could see he'd done it before. Maybe he'd been a cop or something but didn't act like any cop Nicco'd ever been around. Not even like a fed. Like a cop but like a con man, too. This Springer guy knew what was up. Nicco didn't like him, but he wasn't going to take him lightly, making Nicco wonder who the guy had been in another life.

Springer patted Powers down and when he got to the cowboy boots, lifting the cuff of the jeans, Powers turned his head around and said, "Listen, buddy, why don't we just—," and got interrupted, Springer jamming the pistol up the cowboy's ass. Powers grunted and stood on his toes, the cowboy not knowing when to shut up.

Springer said, "I pull the trigger and not even Ex-Lax will help. You know, you should maybe consider another line of work. I keep waiting for you to do or say something smart, but you keep disappointing me." He continued lifting the cowboy's jeans cuff, and digging in the boot he pulled out a folding knife, stuck it in his pocket, backing away from the cowboy now, and saying, "Okay. So you'll know I'm a regular guy, you want a drink, help yourself."

Powers turned around, giving the guy a look, before cracking the seal on a bottle of whiskey and pouring a good amount in a glass. He drank half of it down, asked Nicco if he wanted any. Nicco said yeah, some of the same, only put some ice in the glass. Powers telling him he could walk over and fix his own,

Nicco wondering why the goat-roper asshole asked him in the first place if he was gonna act like a bitch, but this wasn't the time or place for it. Time enough for that when this was all done. Nicco was promising himself both of these guys.

Nicco fixed himself a drink and asked Springer, "The money. Where is it?"

Springer said, "I'm getting to that. It's not here, though."

"Where the hell is it?"

Springer opened a drawer under the hotel phone and pulled out two envelopes and held them up. "One for each of you."

Nicco said one what, and Springer said one envelope. Then he told them in each envelope was an address and time where he would give them the rest of the money.

"What's this? A fucking scavenger hunt?"

"Like one, maybe."

Powers said that was fine, Nicco asking what made him think he had a say in it. Springer smiling some more and sipping the Scotch he'd poured himself, Nicco once again concerned the guy was so cool about things. Getting the feeling *he was getting set up* but not wanting to take a chance it wasn't for real. This is what this guy did to you. You knew you shouldn't trust him, but he kept you thinking maybe you could.

"And to show you this isn't a joke," said Springer, "I've got something for you. Over there in the bureau. Top drawer. You'll find two bundles. A thousand in each bundle. One for each of you. Go ahead, it'll be all right. I'm not going to shoot you unless, you know, I sneeze or something."

Nicco walked over and opened the drawer and found two bundles of money. He opened the drawer and there they were. Two short stacks of C-notes. Nicco took them out and turned around.

"Don't be selfish," said the wiseass. "Give Tex his."

Nicco tossed one of the stacks to the cowboy.

"Now," said Springer. "I'm going to leave the room and you two can decide to meet me at the designated site or not. I hope you boys can trust each other."

"I don't like it," said Powers.

"Then take the grand and go home. I'll keep the rest of the money."

"Why're you doing this?"

"Paying you off? Well, both of you are bottom-feeders. An observation, not a criticism. This money is so you get lost and stay lost. I don't want to see you or hear from you again. Long as you think I have the money, then you'll entertain impure thoughts about getting it back. I'd rather just give it to you and live my life peacefully. Don't even consider coming back. Think about this. I've known where you were every minute since you got off the plane."

Nicco *was* thinking about that after Springer left.

Driving out to the meeting place, which was way in the hell out in the desert, some rich guy's place, the cowboy said, "You know, that ballsy bastard had the gall to give me forty-eight hours to get out of town like it was the Wild West and we were in Dodge City or something."

"Pay attention," said Nicco, watching the highway signs slip by, not believing he was riding in a pickup. "You *are* the fuck outta town."

"Didn't think of everything. He took my gun and then gave it back."

Nicco not believing this. Guy was as dumb as Lunchbox about people. "We gotta take him out after we get the money, you know that, right?"

"I thought of that, and I expect he's thinking about it, too. Which surprises me he didn't take steps to disarm us."

"You don't get it, do you? You gotta pay attention to the way things are. He didn't take it away and then invite us out in the middle of nowhere because he was afraid you'd use it. He was making a point." Nicco nodding his head at the guy. "Telling you he knows he *can* take it away from you and he's *not* afraid. He *wants* you to use it. He's got us doing whatever he wants. Haven't you caught on to the fact he's been fucking with us for the whole time? He's got this thought out."

"He don't scare me."

"Yeah?" Nicco took a good pull on his cigarette. "Well, that tells me about you."

"You got a long way to walk in my boots before you know about me."

"Man, just once, it'd be nice you didn't have some cracker-barrel bullshit to bore the hell out of me with. Is everybody in Texas as dumb as you or are you some sort of special case?"

THIRTY

Springer was waiting for them. For one or both of them. He knew they wouldn't be able to resist, either out of greed or revenge. They would be suspicious, and he knew it. Now, if they didn't find the bag he'd left behind the seat of the big truck, this could be a lot of fun, it wasn't so dangerous.

At 3:45 he got up and walked back out on the large patio that looked out across the desert. Sonny Parker had arranged the place for Springer. Some guy that owed Parker a favor. Didn't bother to even ask why they wanted it, but Sonny telling him he didn't want to know.

They'd be along in a few minutes.

Springer had almost decided who'd actually beaten Tangent to death, the killer mistaking Styles, poor bastard, for Jesse Robinson. It all came together finally, and it was funny how it came to him. The day he'd lifted the money off of Vince and the boys, Nicco didn't know who Jesse was, but Chewy knew Jesse. Springer's problem had been thinking it was Don Janzen was the killer for so long. All the jealousy and other crap that had been swirling around them in high school had perhaps kept Springer from looking at things objectively. He didn't make the connection until later, thinking about when Nicco and Lunchbox showed at Streamers. Lunchbox dead now and Nicco and Powers in cahoots were the keys. Nicco, being smart, had recruited Powers.

And Springer had more or less figured where the murder weapon had come from which implicated Vince, but didn't think Vince was the killer, just the supplier of the instrument. The weapon implicated a couple of other people, but that was Tara's responsibility.

He'd also figured out the coroner was in on the deal. Springer figured the coroner had been paid off to say it was Jesse. Then the killer could find Jesse and dispose of him and no one would be the wiser. Springer had proposed this theory to Tara, but she was already on it and would know something by the next time he saw her, she told him. "Maybe I'll even cuff him and lead him to the lockup."

Now it was just a matter of connecting the dots and figuring out what to do about it.

Off in the distance, the heat shimmers sent up waves and he saw the dust cloud like the vapor trail of a jet coming up the road. Springer chambered a round into the Walther.

Now, Powers was thinking, was the time that separated the squatters from the tall pissers. In his head he knew Springer had a hole card up his sleeve but couldn't resist the urge to call with all the money on the table.

"This fucking guy," said Nicco. "He's got us going all over the place like we're stupid."

New Jersey was a funny little dark guy. Powers was sure the guy was tough, had seen it when he had a hogleg pulled down on him and the guy didn't blink.

But he was thinking about something else, too. Springer had them boxed in. Maybe he gave them the money, maybe he didn't. But there was only one way to find out, and this was it.

Well, there was a third way, too. Be regrettable if a couple of people had to go that way. But it wasn't something he was thinking about. Half the money'd be a county fair . . . but the whole poke, now there was something to smile about.

Still, this Springer had done some thinking on this thing and Powers was sure there was more to this than met the eye. Guy twisted more than a Mexican bull.

"Sonuvabitch's a rascal. You can say it," said Powers. Nicco, for his part, thinking only some Texan with pig shit in his ears would call a guy who played them for fools and then sat around laughing about it a rascal. Nicco didn't know, right now, who he'd rather shoot—Springer or this cartoon from fucking Texas. Nicco thinking he was gonna bust a cap right up this Texan's ass, first time he got a chance. Leave his ass out here in the desert for the snakes and the Gila monsters, wondering if they had Gila monsters out there.

But first he had to go through with this.

Think about the money.

THIRTY-ONE

There he stood. Nicco watching the wiseass standing there looking out across the desert like he was a tourist, then looking at his watch when they got close, like they were late or something, letting them know he got there early and was waiting for them. First thing out of his mouth? "Good to see you guys." Like they were old friends or something. Almost it would be worth the whole nut to drive one in the guy's ear and forget the money.

"Well, ol' pard," said the shitkicker, as much a piece a shit as the wiseass, "we are here, so let's get this thing done so I can head back to the barn and throw some Jack D down my neck."

"You got the money?" said Nicco.

"It's coming."

"It's *coming*? The fuck's that mean?"

"Well, you heard every word I said. Should I say it again, maybe slower?"

Nicco took a couple of steps but the big Texan grabbed him. "Whoa, whoa. Hold on there, hoss. You gonna blow everything with your temper yet." Nicco jerked his head around but controlled himself, jerking his lapels to straighten out his jacket.

"So," said Powers, "when's this coming?"

"First, there's a couple of things we'll need to work out. I want to know which one of you killed Styles Tangent?"

"What the—," said Nicco. "What're you talking about?"

"One of you two geniuses, I think, killed Styles because you thought he was somebody else."

Powers shrugged. "I don't know what you're talking about."

Nicco said, "I never heard of nobody named Styles."

"Ever hear of Jesse Robinson?"

Powers shaking his head, Nicco did nothing, saying instead, "Let's just get the business done with the money without all the monkey shit you come up with every five minutes."

"Thing is," said Springer, "the killer made a couple of mistakes, not least being he was sent to kill Jesse Robinson and ended up killing the wrong guy."

"Aw, bullshit," said Nicco. "You're more fulla shit than anybody I ever knew. Just get the fucking money here and then you're outta my life."

"Well," Powers said, "it don't mean a thing to me. I don't know anybody named Styles or that other name. But I'm guessing you do." Meaning Nicco. He looked at Springer now. "But you bringing us out here and not giving me my money's the kinda thing might piss a fella off."

"You're going to get your money, and I'll admit I'm impressed you didn't shoot each other before you got here. How'd you resist? Although that's still a possibility, isn't it?"

Nicco and Powers looked at each other.

"Yeah," said Springer. "I don't think you like each other all that much, and I'd say about right now you're both thinking how you can get all the money and terminate your partnership. How close am I?"

"You're not going to give us the money, are you?" said Nicco. Getting mad now and madder by the minute.

"Sure I am. All one of you has to do is confess to killing Styles and I'll give you the money. I won't even turn you in to the police." He raised his right hand. "Promise."

Powers looked at Nicco. "I'm thinking this boy believes you killed this Styles fella, right?"

"Fuck you," said Nicco.

"You know," said Powers, "I'm getting real tired of hearing you talk that way to me."

"So what're you gonna do about it? I'm not sitting in a chair unarmed."

"Why don't you just be stupid all the time? Can't you see he wants us to throw down on each other? You killed the guy. Just say it so we can get the money and get the hell outta here."

"He's got a wire on or something. I ain't saying shit."

"No confession, no money," said Springer.

"Well, I had enough of this," said Nicco, reaching into his jacket. He almost had his weapon cleared when Springer shot him high up on his chest near his right shoulder. It spun Nicco a half turn and his weapon flew out of his hand.

The crack of the Walther echoed across the mountains. Powers stood there, motionless, arms extended, a little edgy. Nicco was on the ground kicking his feet and moaning. Springer walked over, the Walther pointed in Powers's direction, and picked up Nicco's weapon and pitched it out in the desert.

Jesse Robinson came out of the house through

the sliding glass door, weapon in hand. "Damn, Springs." There was another guy with him. Guy in a business suit.

Business suit said, "I thought we agreed there would be no shooting?"

Springer ignored the man and said to Nicco, "I figured out you killed Styles. You want to know how I know, or you just want to sit there and bleed?"

Nicco wasn't in the mood to talk. Springer could see the wound wasn't deadly but had to hurt.

"Keep an eye on Nicco here," said Springer to Jesse. Looking at Powers now. "You and I have business."

"Yeah?" said Powers. "What business?"

"You know, Nicco was right about one thing. For all of the western bravado, you're basically just a bully. A coward who can't take a man on, face to face."

"You calling me yellow."

"I don't know how you missed it."

"I'd think you'd have had enough the day in the parking lot."

Springer said, "You're starting to understand. Get rid of your gun."

"We gonna have us a scrap?" Big smile on his face.

"No. I'm going to beat you like a stray dog. That's what's going to happen."

Business suit was getting agitated. "Springer, let's just do what we have to do without—"

"No," Springer said, interrupting. "First things first."

"Who're you?" Powers asked business suit.

"Special agent Tompkins. Federal Bureau of Investigation. You're under arrest."

"For what?"

"Racketeering, murder, and for the Safeguard armored robbery."

"I didn't do that." Powers looking at Springer now. "So, it don't really matter, does it? You'n me got unfinished business, you say. Well, I'm available you want to find out about yourself. As for your boy here"—nodding at Jesse—"tell him to be careful with his gun."

"Man, Springs. He calls me a boy one more time I'm gonna shoot him myself."

Powers placed his hands on his chest and leaned his head back. "Why, I'm mighty sorry, Mr. Nigger. I won't call you boy again."

"That's it," said Jesse, handing Springer his gun. "This cracker's mine."

"Well, just bring it on, then, tar baby." Powers tossed his gun and hat aside and got in a crouch. "I love stomping shit outta skinny children like yourself."

Agent Tompkins said, "This is way beyond what we agreed to."

"Something I need to tell you before you start," said Springer to Powers.

"Later," said Powers. "First, I'm gonna open up a can of whupass on blackie, here. Then I'm going to do the same for you."

"You're not going to allow this, are you?" Tompkins said to Springer.

Springer saying, "Looks like it."

"What about the evidence? Where is it?"

"In a minute," said Springer. "Just watch. You'll enjoy this."

Jesse and Powers circled each other. Powers moved closer and took a big roundhouse swing that Jesse ducked before jabbing Powers twice over the bigger man's shoulder. Powers was staggered. It surprised him, so this time Powers stalked in slowly, more cautious now. Powers faked a left and threw the right again, the dust churning up in clouds around their ankles as they fought. Powers threw a right hand which Jesse blocked and hit Powers eight times in the space of about five seconds. Left jab, right cross, left jab, right cross, three uppercuts to the body, and a hard left that opened up Powers cheek like he'd been cut with a knife.

Powers staggered back again, his face bloody. He reached up and wiped the blood off his face and looked at it. He bellowed, then bull-rushed Jesse. Jesse feinted left, shuffled back to his right, and cracked Powers on the left side of his face as Powers flew by. Jesse waited for the big man to gather himself before feinting an uppercut to the body and looping a left hook when Powers tried to cover up. The left caught Powers full on the jaw and it crumpled his legs and he sat in the dirt, his breath wheezing from his mouth.

"Call me boy again, cracker," said Jesse. "I fucking dare you to say that shit again."

Springer kneeled down by Powers and said, "The thing I wanted to tell you before?"

"Go to hell, asshole," said Powers, through swollen lips.

"Well, here it is anyway. First, I sure hope when Agent Tompkins searches your truck he doesn't find any evidence, you know, like money from the armored truck robbery."

Realization showing in Powers's face now. "I wasn't," coughing now and spitting a little blood from his teeth, "in on that." Breathing hard. "That was Nicco's deal."

"Shut the fuck up, dumb ass," said Nicco, still hurting.

"And," said Springer, "I thought it would be fun to let you know that at one time Jesse was a middleweight Golden Glove finalist."

"Northern California," said Jesse.

Springer saying, "So, what I'm telling you is this. You never had a chance." He reached down and patted Powers on the cheek. "Not with Jesse. Not with me. Not from the first day I saw you."

THIRTY-TWO

"I was surprised to hear from you," Diane Janzen said, handing him the drink, Grey Goose Vodka on the rocks. She was drinking a Rum Collins with cherries floating among the ice.

Don Janzen accepted the drink and sat down, then moved his chair where it was under the umbrella, out of the bright desert sunlight. Brown bodies baked in it, the pool water shimmered with it.

"Why would you be surprised. This thing is in the toilet, Di. We're so fucked if we don't think this out. Maybe even if we do. Look, much as we hate each other," he said, "we've got to stick together now."

"What makes you think I hate you, Don? I don't have enough feelings about you to work up a hate." She stubbed out her cigarette. "But you're right this time. We need to help each other here. I'm willing, if you are."

"What did you tell the police?"

"Nothing. What could I have possibly told them? I don't know anything. Not a thing."

"Cavanaugh called. He's hot, and he's not what I would call a stable individual. You get that, right?"

"He'll be fine." She was leaned back in her chair, a

blue and beige two-piece thong suit. Waxed her legs all the way up to her money-maker. She probably liked the pain. "I can handle him."

"Yeah, I heard you were working him on the side. But listen, sweetheart, you're not on his list of favorites. Here's what he said to me, an hour ago. 'Don, you tell that cunt . . .' aw, hell, there he is again." He pointed in the direction of the pool. "Over there. Here he comes. Shit."

Springer saw the good-looking redhead, sitting by herself, reading a book. Light-complexioned, sprinkle of freckles, her hair pulled back in a ponytail. Light tan, but not the type worried about things like that. Probably on vacation. He was feeling pretty good. Good enough to wear the Hawaiian shirt Tara had picked out for him. It wasn't really his kind of thing, but it was comfortable.

"Hello," he said.

She raised her eyes from her book, ever so slightly, and said, "Hi."

"So, what're we drinking today?"

"We?"

"Sure, you and me."

She put the book down and lowered her sunglasses and looked over the top of them. She gave him a wry look, saying, "How do you know I'm not meeting someone?"

"Well, you are. And I'm sorry I'm late." He waved down a waiter and ordered her a frozen maragarita. "Put a touch of Grand Marnier in, too, please."

"I love margaritas," she said. "How'd you know."

"Got a knack," he said. "I'm Cole, and you are—"

"Kim."

"Well, Kim, I've got to go talk to a couple of people and I'll be right back."

She nodded, still with the half smile on her face. "Okay," she said. "I'll take a chance. I'm in Vegas, after all."

He said, "Good." Then he walked over to where Don and Diane Janzen sat, looking as if they'd swallowed ice chips.

"Don't sit down," said Don, when Springer pulled a chair out.

"Don't talk tough, Don. It just makes me laugh."

"Yes, Don, don't be such a hard-on," said Diane. "Please, Cole, join us. That's quite a shirt you have on. Was it difficult to find a shirt as obnoxious as you are?"

"Aw, c'mon, let's be nice."

"Where's your little chocolate bunny?"

"I think she's down at the courthouse preparing warrants. You'll probably recognize the names on some of them." He waved down a waiter and ordered a beer. "Bring me a Tecate, please." The waiter nodded. Springer saying now, "I love Tecate on a hot day. You like Tecate?"

"Get to it and then leave," said Don.

"Sure, nice to see you kids together again. I always thought you belonged together. Just wanted to touch base with you and get your reaction to a couple of things." He had to admit it, Diane was cool, always was. By now she would've heard about the arrests of Vince, Nicco, and Powers. Vince was rolling over on the others for a reduced sentence and the money from the robbery that Agent Tompkins found in the back of Powers's truck was enough to put Nicco and Powers on ice with or without Vince's testimony.

Tara had turned the two dirty cops, Madison and Sullivan, with some help from Internal Affairs. That left only Diane and Cavanaugh. And Don. It didn't appear they were going to be able to implicate Cavanaugh, but he had something in mind to give Red anxious thoughts.

Springer said, "I've pretty much figured everything out. There's just a couple of loose ends I was hoping you could clear up for me."

Diane gave him a look. "I'm getting vibrations. As if there is some disclosure that is supposed to shock or unnerve me. Am I close?"

"I doubt much unnerves you. As for shock, well, that's more than I could hope for."

"Well," she said, laughing to herself. "Go ahead. I know how much you enjoy playing games. Don't let me spoil it for you. It's what makes you both appealing and insufferable at the same time." A little venom on the word "insufferable," her teeth touching together as she said it.

He told them about the arrests and asked if they knew about them and Don said he read the papers and was glad that it was all cleared up. Springer saying, well, maybe it is and maybe it isn't and that none of these men were capable of the sort of creativity to pull off a scam of this magnitude.

"They were being paid. All of them. A couple of them mentioned your name. Both your names. It seems there really is no honor among thieves. Human nature, huh?"

She said, "Yes, the police have already inquired about it, and it was interesting, but I had nothing to tell them. Vince, of course, deluded imbecile that he is, had some notion that he and I, if you can believe I would have anything to do with a specimen like him, were some sort of item. He did make a play for me, which I rebuffed, and being miffed, he has tried to implicate me. Ridiculous. To sum up, he's an idiot."

"I'll go along with that. Seems to be lot of guys not thinking clearly. But I can think of only one thing besides money causes men to think sideways."

Diane sipped her Rum Collins. Swimming pool noises in the background. "So, Cole, tell me, what's that one thing?" She gave him the eyes, the smile, and another inch of thigh. She had the look, the feel, everything . . .

Springer said, "Of all the commodities in the world, all the temptations, the variables, the things that make men do crazy things, there is this one thing"—he smiled and cocked his head to one side—"it's women." He gestured with his index finger. "Women like you. You make guys do things, if they could think things through, they wouldn't do. It's like that Eagles song, you know, her smile opens doors. That kind of thing."

"What the hell is this about? You don't have shit, Springs, and you know it," said Don. He had his forearm on the table and his leg was working.

Springer looking at Diane, saying now, "You influenced Vince, no doubt about that. Also, you tried to bring Jesse into the mix, but someone got anxious and decided to kill him. Or try. Too bad you picked a guy who thinks all black guys look alike."

She was shaking her head slowly, side to side. "This just gets better and better."

Springer said, "I had someone check out Jesse Jr. It was Royal who found out what I needed to know. You remember my cousin Royal, don't you?"

She nodded. "Yes, looks somewhat like you and nearly as irritating, but a cute kid. So?"

"Well, seems Jesse Jr. borrowed money from you. A lot of money. Six months ago. Wanted a car, I believe. In exchange, he gave you power of attorney and signed a note saying you were the beneficiary of any windfall assets that might come his way that would pay you off. It's amazing you added that clause and would scam your own kid. You don't really care about him or anyone for that matter. And you kept Jesse away from him."

Her mouth was working a little. "Jesse doesn't give a damn about his son. He's never cared about him."

"Actually, he kind of does, and I haven't told him that part yet. He thinks his kid doesn't want to see him, and that's why he hasn't heard from him. Now where do you suppose Jesse got the idea his own son didn't wish to talk to him?"

"You're telling it."

"You told Jesse his son was angry with him and didn't want to talk to Jesse. You know, one of those times when you had Jesse at his weakest point."

"Weakest point?"

"You know, naked and under the covers."

"You're such a delusional ass. Am I bad because I like men?"

"You're bad just because you're bad. I don't know how you got this screwed-up, but you're something different. You're like a force of nature, Diane. You had Vince and Nicco do your dirty work. But you hadn't figured on Powers getting greedy. Neither did Cavanaugh. Gee, I wonder how you paid Nicco and Vince? Bet I can get close. You use your body like a gun."

"Besides being delusional, you're also a bastard," she said, her teeth showing. A little scary.

"Hey, that's pretty good. You can do anger. I've already seen the poor-little-girl routine, the woman-scorned routine, and the composed-businesswoman and now I get the pissed-off female show. I'm impressed."

"So," she said, letting her leg brush against his,

relying on past successes, her attitude changing as she did. "You going to turn me in, Cole? That what you have in mind? Like Bogart in *The Maltese Falcon*?"

"No, that was different. You see, Bogart *loved* Mary Astor and hated to turn her in, but his code wouldn't allow him to let her go free. Remember? He was an honest man before he was a man in love, so, he *had* to turn her in."

"And you?"

"Well, I don't live by his code." He took her drink from her hand and took a sip. Made a face. "Too sweet," he said. "And I'm going to enjoy watching you sweat in court. Like a dream come true. You ever see the inside of a prison? They don't have shopping malls." He made a face. "Depressing."

"And to think I loved you at one time. I was a fool. And you used to love me."

"Used to think I did. I know different now. I was a kid. Now I know you're just capped teeth and a pair of fast hips. Lot of those around."

"You're such a shit, Cole. You always were."

Don was looking around now.

"Like Bob Dylan says, I was so much older then; I'm younger than that now."

"You never meant anything to me. Just another little boy looking for love." She looked at him, like she'd looked at a dozen other men in her life knowing she had them, no, knowing she *owned* them. "And, darling, you may not love me, but you want me. And you have no evidence."

He shrugged. "I'm not going to flip you. Won't have to."

"Why's that, baby?"

"Because you're going to turn yourself in."

She made a dismissive sound. "You always were a dreamer," she said.

"Either that or I let Red Cavanaugh take care of you. No matter how highly you rank your vamping ability, I'm telling you Red is immune. He has no heart and no compunction about killing even a beauty like you. No, I'd say, Red was an equal-opportunity thug. When I let it be known your intent was to ace him out of the land deal"—looking at Don now—"not to mention you, too, Don . . . well, I wouldn't want to be you. I mean, here's a guy tried to kill me twice, and all I did was drive his car into a fountain. I can't imagine what he'll do about somebody trying to swindle him out of millions of dollars, but I know even if it's years later, he'll take care of it. He'll wait. And he has a long reach."

Springer placed his hands behind his head. Leaning back, now, having fun making the ice princess squirm. "Here's what I'm saying. You go to the police and tell them some things, maybe not everything, and maybe you get a short sentence at some country club women's facility where you won't be stabbed with a rat-tail comb. I don't think they can stick you with the murder of Styles Tangent although I know it was you that set it up. The alternative? Red won't leave you around to tell anybody anything. It's not his way. He's very meticulous. He hates witnesses. You should have thought of that early on."

Don saying now, "You're so full of shit. I don't think you're going to tell Red anything."

"You're right, I'm not. The police will put it together, but Red will insulate himself. While you two amateurs were playing each other, Red was playing you, and Sonny and I were playing you. We gave you a chance. I knew you two were in on the whole thing; it's the only way to explain it. First, Don, your resistance to calling Vince, like Sonny Parker and I requested. Then, Styles was beaten to death with a blunt instrument that made unusual marks. Like some of the marks from one of those practice swords I saw down at your club. That means the killer had access to your club, meaning you. Or"—nodding at Diane—"someone close to you. At least that's my guess, and pretty soon that'll be the way the police see it, too. They've already got Madison and Sullivan on a couple of IA concerns and it's just a matter of time before they start giving you up. They're not going to rat out Red, as they'll need his clout in the yard, so no one shivs them while they're out on the playground. Also, Red's a scary guy. The police kind of muddle around, but eventually they get it right."

"I oughta kill you."

"You won't, though."

"That what you think?"

Springer nodded his head. "Yeah. I've bet my life on it. You're sneaky and you're underhanded, but you're no killer. It's not that you don't have the balls for it, it's that despite all your shitty traits, you're basically a civilized man. Not your style. That's why I know it was your lovely ex-wife who pulled the strings on the killing. Thing I had trouble figuring out was why you two would be in this together but I have a theory. And, it's a good one."

"Hit him, Don," she said, spitting the words.

"Yeah, Don," said Springer. "Take a shot."

"I ought to," said Don, rubbing a hand over his fist.

"But you won't."

"Do it, Don. Please. Are you going to let him sit there and insult us like this?"

Don dropped his eyes.

"You coward."

"Shut up, Diane," said Don. "Nobody's interested in your cracked theories, Springs." But Springer could see the wind was out of him.

"You're wrong about that. It has to do with Diane's son, Jesse Jr."

"I knew about him."

"How old do you think he is?"

Don looked at Diane, then at Springer. "What's that got to do with anything?"

Diane said, "Don't listen to him, Don. You know what a liar he is."

"Yeah," said Springer. "Go ahead. You trust her, don't you? I mean, it's not like back in the old days, she wouldn't screw us both at the same time, would she?"

Don was hesitating.

Springer saying now, "Aren't you curious? Why doesn't she want you to answer that question?"

Diane standing, saying, "That's enough. Let's go, Don."

Don waved her off. "No. I want to see what he's getting at. I'm sure it's one of his little jokes. Okay, Cole, Jesse Jr. is probably about, I'd say, twenty years old."

"You ever see him?"

Don thought for a moment. Shook his head slowly.

"He's fifteen. Be sixteen in a couple of months now."

"Bullshit!" said Diane.

Springer smiling again, saying, "Let's see, you were engaged, what, about seventeen years years ago. That means, let's see, I never was good at math—"

Don was looking at Diane now. "What the fuck, Di? You were fucking that black bastard after we were—"

"Shut up, Don, and think. He's making this up. Can't you see what he's doing? Come on, baby, you know better than that."

"Right to the end," Springer said. "She still thinks she can turn you. You're no different than any other man in her life, Don. She's played all of us. She's good at it."

Diane picked up an ashtray and threw it at Springer. He sidestepped and the ashtray tumbled over and over on the concrete.

Springer said, "That's a little extreme, Diane."

Don Janzen got up, a sick look on his face. Diane said, "Where are you going?"

Don started to speak, changed his mind, picked up his cigarettes, and started walking away.

"Come back here," said Diane. "You can't walk out now."

"You know what?" said Springer. "I believe he can."

Don kept walking, walking . . .

"You're a shit, Cole," said Diane, looking at Don's back, clicking her nails. "You fucked everything up. It could've been you and me and more money than you can imagine." She leaned toward him. "It still could be. There's a way. Surely, there's a way. There always is."

Springer saying now, "Feeling better? Don't you want to know how I figured this all out?"

"You don't know anything," said Diane. "Just like when we were kids. You thought you were smart, but you're only clever."

"Well, clever may be enough this time. The thing that told me what was going on was the fact that Nicco didn't recognize Jesse, whom you"—pointing at Diane—"sent to kill Jesse."

"Now you really are fishing. Why would I want Jesse killed?"

"Because with Jesse dead you inherit the land Cabot was leaving to Jesse because the only heir, Jesse Jr., had signed everything over to you. He's a kid; he didn't know he was signing away a fortune. Why wouldn't he trust his mother? You and Don were both trying to get majority control of the project. You knew that but Don didn't. Don pretended to have you in on the deal and you knew it the whole time and let him believe he was getting away with something."

"Oh, fuck you."

"It was Vince that told you about Don's plan. You and Don trying to screw each other out on the deal. That's funny stuff. The whole land deal would've fallen right into your laps. Of course, you would've had to deal with Red Cavanaugh, but you know, knowing you, I think you could've handled him. Hard as it is to imagine, I really think you would've pulled it off. What a mind you have. I have to admit, I'm impressed you think so far ahead. You always were two jumps ahead of everyone."

"How—" She stopped herself.

Springer shrugged. "Magic? No, that's not it. Your mistake was underestimating Sonny. He really has gone straight, but not above playing hardball in the business world. He was using his percentage of Streamers to keep his hand in. Now there's a guy who is one sharp man. I kinda like him.

"Anyway, Nicco was in contact with you because he was the killer. Vince went along and may have thrown a couple of punches but I don't see him as having the stomach to beat someone to death with a wooden sword. Boy, that's a nasty way to die, don't you think? I'm going to be particularly interested in watching your trial unfold."

"Go away, Cole," said Diane. "You've wasted what's left of your brain cells thinking this thing up."

"Oh, I'm going. I'm going right now. And thanks for the way you and Don livened up this trip. One more thing." He looked down at his watch. "In about, oh, say fifteen minutes to a half hour, Detective Tara St. John will swing by for a visit. I'm just the setup guy. She knows you're here." Diane looked around. "No use leaving, she'll just find you. And everything I just told you I told her. I can do and say things she can't. And you ought to see her when she's mad. I've seen it, and it's something. She's going to get a commendation and a promotion out of this thing, so she'll be willing to offer you a deal before she reads you your rights."

Springer took another pull on his drink, sat it down, and stood to leave.

"And I've gotta tell you, she's *really* looking forward to this."

"Get the hell outta—"

Springer put up his hands. "No, don't ask me to stay. I gotta go. You know, Diane, you just got greedy. You've got the heart of a whore. You think everybody's a mark. Shouldn't have tried to kill Jesse. My friend. From that point on, it was just a matter of time. Anyway, I doubt I'll see you at our class reunions."

Springer left her, feeling good, and was walking toward the redhead when he heard Diane Janzen say, "Cole Springer. You're a prick. You know that?"

He turned, spreading his arms, and shrugged.

What could you do about it?

EPILOGUE

Red Cavanaugh's stomach was screaming at him. The syndicate land deal was totally fucked and now in the hands of that black guy—Robinson, and, worse, Sonny fucking Parker. The police had thrown a net over everybody—Vince, Nicco, Powers, even the two cops he had on the pad. They'd even picked up the Janzens, who were out on bail. Red was swamped trying to plug holes and cover himself, and it was eating his stomach up. He was chewing Tums like bubble gum. He had expended a lot of energy and favors to ensure none of those people turned him for a lighter jolt.

The legal bills were going to be like the national debt. But there was no way around it. He had to get these people off or at least assure them that he was working for them. All it took was one, just one to start talking . . .

The one gave him the most night sweats was Don Janzen. No way that guy could jail. Not even for a weekend. He'd have to have him popped somehow. The bitch, too. Fucking lightweights. Who would ever believe that Red Cavanaugh wasn't part of a con game. A land scheme. You try to do something legitimate and you get involved with amateurs who act like crooks. Send one of the guys to see them both. Nicco would know how things stood; Vince was scared and turning against the Janzens. There was a black guy involved he didn't even know about. Some low-level street pimp.

No, the Janzens could not be allowed to testify. Disappeared. It wasn't the way he wanted to handle things, but he didn't want to take any chances.

It would have to happen before the DA got a shot at them for a deal.

On top of everything else, the smart-ass, Springer, still had his car. But he couldn't go to the police, what with everything going on. Fuck, could you hear that conversation? He made himself a stiff drink and shuddered when the stuff hit his stomach. Damned ulcer was screaming at him and he was having trouble sleeping.

The phone rang, and when they said it was the police, he like to have puked. But cops didn't call you to say you were arrested. No, they showed up at your door with papers. It was that woman, Detective St. John, calling him, telling him they'd found his Mercedes. He hadn't reported it stolen.

"We found your name in the glove box."

"Where was it?"

"Well, it's quite a story."

Red didn't like the next part.

She said, "The circumstances were unusual. You see everything in this business." Red was getting a bad feeling in his stomach. "Someone, apparently not a fan of yours, has an extraordinary sense of humor."

More drama, just what he needed. "Just tell me what happened and how I can pick it up."

"Well, the person we have in the holding cell says some man, he didn't know his name, told him to drive it into the fountain at Caesars Palace and that's where we found it. Is that crazy or what? Apparently this is the second time—"

Red slammed down the phone, breaking the connection.

Could you believe it? Red closed his eyes and felt sick. Shit.

Fucking Springer.